MOONLIGHT FEELS RIGHT

OCEAN SHORES #3

BARBARA FREETHY

Fog City Publishing

PRAISE FOR BARBARA FREETHY

"A fabulous, page-turning combination of romance and intrigue. Fans of Nora Roberts and Elizabeth Lowell will love this book." — *NYT Bestselling Author Kristin Hannah on Golden Lies*

"Freethy has a gift for creating complex, appealing characters and emotionally involving, often suspenseful, sometimes magical stories." — *Library Journal on Suddenly One Summer*

"Barbara Freethy is a master storyteller with a gift for spinning tales about ordinary people in extraordinary situations and drawing readers into their lives." — *Romance Reviews Today*

"Freethy is at the top of her form. Fans of Nora Roberts will find a similar tone here, framed in Freethy's own spare, elegant style." — *Contra Costa Times on Summer Secrets*

"The story grabbed me immediately and made me fall in love with it. The characters were well-developed and multi-faceted, not only the two main characters but all the minor ones as well. The Ocean Shores community is where I would like to live!" *Bonnie – Goodreads on Hopelessly Romantic*

"Barbara Freethy is a master storyteller!" *Romance Reviews Today*

"Freethy hits the ground running as she kicks off another winning romantic suspense series...Freethy is at her prime with a superb combo of engaging characters and gripping plot." — *Publishers' Weekly on Silent Run*

ALSO BY BARBARA FREETHY

Ocean Shores Series

Hopelessly Romantic

Summer Loving

Moonlight Feels Right

Blame It On The Bikini

Whisper Lake Series

Always With Me

My Wildest Dream

Can't Fight The Moonlight

Just One Kiss

If We Never Met

Tangled Up In You

Next Time I Fall

For a complete list of books, visit my website!

CHAPTER ONE

The nightmare was back. Engines roaring. The fiery crash. Tremendous heat. Stunning pain. Screaming—was it him or someone else? And then the relentless hammer pounding inside his skull. Hunter fought his way back to consciousness, knowing it was the only way to escape. But the pounding didn't stop when he opened his eyes.

Disoriented by the sunlight spilling through his bedroom windows, he glanced at the clock. It was four o'clock Thursday afternoon. He'd only meant to take a quick nap after his grueling physical therapy session, but he'd slept for over two hours.

He groaned as the pounding started again, finally realizing that someone was at the door to his apartment, and they weren't going away. Rolling out of bed, he pulled on a T-shirt and a pair of sweats, then headed into the living room.

He opened the door with a scowl—and froze.

Bree Larrimer, a thirty-year-old brunette, stood on the threshold, wild-eyed and panicked. Bree was the wife of his best friend—widow, he mentally corrected. Clutching Bree's hand was Olivia, a freckle-faced little girl with the same dark-red hair as her father.

"What's going on?" he asked, stunned by their appearance.

After Gary had died, Bree had taken Olivia and moved back to Nashville, where her parents lived. "Is everything okay?"

"No. It's not okay. I need help," she replied, her voice fast as she shifted her weight from foot to foot.

"What can I do?"

"Watch Olivia for me."

"What about your parents?" he asked, alarmed by her request. "I thought you were staying with them."

"I was, but my father is an alcoholic, and my mother is an enabler. I can't trust them to take care of Olivia while I look for work. And I have to work because I need money, and I need a career. I have to make a life for my daughter now. It's all on me."

Her voice cracked with panic and fatigue. Hunter hadn't seen her in months. Actually, he hadn't seen her since Gary had died. His own recovery had consumed him. Reaching out to Bree had just...hurt too much. Seeing her now, terrified and trembling, pulled at something deep inside him. *Guilt.*

"Come inside," he said quietly. "We'll talk."

"I'm not coming in," Bree replied in a hard voice. "You won't talk me out of this, Hunter. You owe Gary. You owe *me.* You said you'd take care of him. That you'd bring him home."

Her voice broke. And so did his heart.

"It will only be for a few days," Bree continued, clearly ready to run before he had time to think.

"Hang on," he said quickly. "I'm not a babysitter, Bree. I don't know anything about kids. What about one of your friends? What about a nanny? I'll pay for one."

"That takes time. And I don't *have* time. All my friends are gone. The ones from the base don't even want to see me. I remind them of what they could lose. I haven't heard from anyone in months, including you."

"I know. I'm sorry. I've been...dealing."

"Well, at least you're still alive to deal," she retorted.

That cut deep. But he didn't flinch. He deserved every harsh word she had to say, because he'd been in charge of that fatal flight. He'd failed to bring his team home safely. He only wished he'd been the one to die, because there wouldn't have been anyone to suffer like Bree was suffering. He wasn't married. He didn't have a girlfriend. In fact, he'd avoided long-term relationships because he'd grown up watching his mom pace the house every time his dad, who was also in the Marines, was unreachable.

"I shouldn't have said that," Bree added, wiping at her tears with a rough swipe. Then she knelt down and pulled Olivia close. "I'll be back soon, Livvy. Hunter will take care of you."

Olivia gave her mother a doubtful look. "He looks grumpy and mad."

"Hunter is a good guy. Your daddy's best friend. He'll make sure you're okay. You be good for him, okay?"

"I want to go with you."

"I know. But Mommy needs to find a job and a place for us to live."

"Why can't we live with Nonna and Papa?"

"Because we can't. It's going to be fine. Everything will get better." Bree kissed Olivia again, then stood up, grabbed a pink suitcase, and rolled it inside his front door. "Hold out your hand," she told him.

"Bree. You need to rethink this." He felt desperate to get her to change her mind. "Why don't you both stay? We can work on things together."

"I need time to myself. Please, Hunter. Give me your hand."

He saw the determination in her eyes and held out his hand. Bree put Olivia's tiny hand in his. The little girl gave him an unhappy and suspicious look, but she didn't pull away.

"I love you, Livvy. I'll call you soon," Bree promised, then turned and practically ran toward the parking lot.

"Wait, Bree!" he called. "You can't just—"

But she was already gone.

"You don't like me, do you?" Olivia asked, drawing his attention as she burst into tears.

He flinched, feeling completely out of his depth. A crying female had always been his kryptonite. He had no idea how to handle all that emotion.

"Is everything all right?" a female voice asked.

He turned to see one of his upstairs neighbors, Emmalyn McGuire, a pretty woman with blonde hair and hazel eyes. She approached him with concern in her gaze.

"I couldn't help overhearing," she continued.

Of course, she couldn't. She was one of his too-friendly neighbors who kept inviting him to things when he just wanted space to be alone.

"Is this your daughter?" Emmalyn asked.

"God, no!"

At his vehement words, Olivia cried louder. He stared down at her in alarm, her sticky little fingers still clinging to his. "Sorry, I didn't mean to yell. Don't cry," he begged.

"I want my mom," Olivia said through her sobs.

He wanted her mom, too. He awkwardly patted at Olivia's shoulder as his gaze met Emmalyn's once more. "She's my friend's daughter. She just got dropped off. And I—uh—you don't know how to make her stop crying, do you?"

Emmalyn came forward and squatted in front of Olivia. "Hi. I'm Emmalyn. What's your name?"

"Livvy," she mumbled in between sobs. "My mommy says I have to stay with him." She pointed an accusatory finger in his direction. "But he's too grumpy."

"Sometimes people just look grumpy when they're thinking hard," Emmalyn said.

"That's right," he said quickly. "I'm just thinking, Liv."

Olivia gave him a skeptical look, but her sobs slowed down.

"Do you like chocolate chip oatmeal cookies, Livvy?" Emmalyn asked. "I just made some, and they are warm and gooey, just the way I like to eat my cookies. What about you?"

"I like gooey cookies," Livvy said. "Can I have one?"

Emmalyn gave him a questioning look. As far as he was

concerned, Livvy could have anything if it would make her stop crying. "Sounds good," he said.

"I live upstairs. If the two of you want to come up, I'm happy to share."

"Do you have milk?" Olivia asked.

"Of course," Emmalyn said. "You can't have cookies without milk."

The last thing he wanted to do was go to Emmalyn's apartment. Actually, that was the second to last thing he wanted to do; the first was taking care of Olivia for however long her mother would be gone.

What he really wanted to do was go back to bed, even if it meant reliving his nightmare. But Olivia had let go of his hand to take Emmalyn's. She already trusted his neighbor more than she trusted him. That stung. But he told himself it was a good thing. Maybe he could get Emmalyn to watch Olivia for a minute while he tried to get Bree on the phone so he could tell her he was not at all equipped to care for a six-year-old child.

"One second," he said. "Let me put some shoes on." He dashed into his bedroom to put on sneakers, wishing he had time for a shower and a change of clothes. But he needed to get Bree on the phone before she got too far away.

After slipping on his shoes, he grabbed his phone and followed Olivia and Emmalyn upstairs. He couldn't blame Olivia for being upset. He wouldn't want to be left with a stranger either, especially not one who looked like he'd been dragged backward through hell, which was basically how he would describe his life for the past seven months.

But Livvy had had a rough time, too. She'd lost her dad, and clearly, the rest of her family was falling apart. He needed to be there for her. He just hadn't expected to have to deal with this situation today after completing a challenging rehab session that had taken a lot out of him, both physically and emotionally. He'd been pressing hard because he would have to take the physical exams required to prove he was physically fit for duty within the next two weeks. Then he'd have to convince the board he was also mentally ready, which seemed just as challenging. His future as a military pilot would be decided in the next month. Focusing on that had been his only priority until now.

Olivia's sudden arrival was an obstacle, a challenge he hadn't expected. But she was here, and he was going to have to deal with her because she was six, and she definitely couldn't take care of herself.

As he followed Emmalyn up the stairs, he realized he'd finally had to say yes to someone in the building after months of rejecting every invitation. He'd moved into Ocean Shores because it was close to Camp Pendleton and the hospital where he'd spent the majority of his time the past seven months. But he hadn't anticipated the complex being so friendly. There were community events every other day, and because the two-story building was set around an outdoor courtyard and pool, with everyone's front door facing that yard, it was difficult to go anywhere without running into someone, without being invited to a pool party or a poker game or a taco night.

He'd always said no, which made him wonder why Emmalyn had offered him a lifeline. He'd never been friendly to her. His grief and trauma since the crash had sent him into a dark hole of depression that had made things like simple greetings almost impossible. He'd just wanted to be left alone.

But he wasn't alone now...

"Here we go," Emmalyn said, interrupting his thoughts as she opened her door and waved them into her apartment.

The contrast between their apartments was immediate and jarring. While his place was sparse and utilitarian—a reflection of his military background and his current state of mind—Emmalyn's was warm and inviting. Soft throw pillows adorned a comfortable couch and matching armchair. Potted plants thrived on every available surface. The walls featured cheerful water-color paintings, many of the sea and local landmarks. Everything about her apartment was warm and inviting, maybe even a little messy, but it felt like her. She was attractive in a sweet, girl-next-door kind of way, with long blonde hair that was often falling out of a ponytail or a braid.

As Emmalyn took Olivia into her small kitchen, he pulled out his phone and punched in Bree's number. It went straight to voicemail, and he felt a wave of frustration at his inability to fix the impossible situation she'd put him in.

"Bree, it's Hunter. Call me back. We need to talk about this." His voice came out harsher than he intended, and he glanced up to see Emmalyn watching him from the doorway to the kitchen with concern on her face.

"I take it she's not answering," Emmalyn said as he ended the call.

"No."

"I'm not trying to downplay whatever is going on, but maybe a cookie would help?"

Her smile loosened the tense knot in his gut. "Well, it couldn't hurt," he said as he followed her into the kitchen. Olivia sat on a high stool at the counter, already eating her cookie, with a glass of milk in front of her.

His glance moved around the kitchen, noting more colorful touches and whimsical items that were mostly shaped like apples, from the salt and pepper shakers to the napkin holder, and the apple-shaped vase on the adjacent kitchen table that was covered with kid drawings and children's books.

As Emmalyn handed him a cookie on a red plate that was also shaped like an apple, he couldn't help but raise an eyebrow.

"It was a gift from a parent," Emmalyn said. "I swear I don't have an obsession with apples, but a lot of the parents do. I'm a kindergarten teacher."

"An apple for the teacher," he muttered.

"Exactly. And they're kind to think of me at all, so I've decided to embrace the new apple décor I get every year."

"It looks like you bring your work home with you." He tipped his head to the table.

"We did those pictures today. I'm going to hang them tomorrow, but I wanted to look through them since it's a new year and a new group of kids. Do you want some milk to go with your cookie? I also have water or juice."

"No, thanks." He took a bite of the warm cookie, surprised by the chocolate perfection. "This is good." He couldn't remember when he'd last eaten anything sweet, anything just for the pure pleasure of eating. In fact, most days he only ate because he needed the strength to do his rehab.

"You can sit down if you want," Emmalyn said, pointing to the stool next to Olivia.

"Actually, it's good for me to stand."

"How is your leg? I noticed you haven't had your cane for a while."

"It's healed." He saw the questions brimming in Emmalyn's hazel eyes, and the last thing he wanted to do was answer them. Thankfully, Olivia interrupted.

"Can I have another cookie?" she asked.

"One is enough before dinner," Emmalyn answered, not bothering to check with him, although she did immediately give him an apologetic look. "Sorry. Habit. I should have let you respond to that."

"No. You're right. One is enough for a snack."

"But I'm hungry," Olivia protested.

"How about a banana?" Emmalyn suggested.

Olivia sighed. "I don't want a banana."

"Then it sounds like you're full." Emmalyn picked up her own glass of milk from the counter and took a sip.

He was somewhat fascinated by the sight of her drinking milk. He couldn't remember seeing a woman drink milk in a long time—maybe ever. But then, Emmalyn had a wholesomeness about her, an innocence he could probably crush very easily. She was exactly the kind of person he should stay away from because sometimes his dark mood could spill onto others, and she didn't deserve to have her light dimmed.

Olivia didn't deserve that, either. He frowned, wondering again what on earth he was going to do about her.

"When is my mommy coming back?" Olivia asked, looking directly at him for the first time since her mother had left.

"I'm not sure, but she'll let us know."

"Mommy is sad. She cries a lot. She says Daddy is in heaven and he watches over us from the clouds, but I think she wishes he wasn't in the sky."

His chest tightened at Olivia's words. He should have been the one in the clouds—not Gary. His friend had had so much to live for.

"Mommy says if I close my eyes, I can still see him whenever I want," Olivia continued. "I do that a lot."

His heart squeezed again. Olivia should not have to close her eyes to see her dad.

"Are you a mommy?" Olivia asked, turning to Emmalyn.

"No. I don't have any kids of my own, but I'm a teacher at Ravenswood Elementary, so I'm around children every day."

Olivia's eyes lit up. "That's where I'm supposed to go tomorrow. Will I be in your class?"

Emmalyn looked taken aback by Olivia's words. "Well, I don't know. How old are you?"

"Six."

"Then I'm guessing you already finished kindergarten. That's what I teach."

Olivia's eyes filled with disappointment. "I'm in first grade now."

"Well, we have two great first-grade teachers, so you will love whoever you have." Emmalyn's gaze swung from Olivia to him, a question in her eyes. "Did your friend tell you about school?"

"No." The pink suitcase Bree had pushed into his apartment now seemed ominous. *How long was she planning to be gone? And why would she have enrolled Olivia in a school nearby if she wasn't going to be away that long?*

"I wish I could be in your class," Olivia said with a worried sigh. "I don't know if anyone in first grade will like me."

"You'll make friends, and you're going to love your class, too," Emmalyn quickly reassured Olivia. "In fact, I could go with you both to school tomorrow if that would help."

He wanted to refuse. He preferred to handle problems on his own, to not owe anyone anything. But he owed Gary and Bree, and Emmalyn knew a hell of a lot more about kids than he did. Still, he hesitated, looking back at Olivia. "Did your mother tell you anything else about school or where she was going?" he asked.

Olivia shook her head, her bottom lip quivering once more.

"It's fine," he said quickly, sensing tears were not far away. "Everything will be okay."

"You don't like me, do you?" Olivia asked, giving him an accusatory look.

"Of course, I like you," he said quickly. "I'm your godfather. And your dad and I were best friends. I was at your fourth birthday. I saw you jump off the diving board for the first time, remember?"

Olivia's tension eased. "Mommy didn't think I could do it, but Daddy did."

"He was right." Gary had also believed in him, probably more than he should have. And he needed to take care of Olivia the way Gary would expect him to. Which meant... His gaze moved to Emmalyn. "It might be easier if we go to school with you tomorrow."

"Then let's do that." She paused. "It's possible Olivia might need some things for school."

"There was a suitcase that came with her. Maybe Bree packed whatever she needs."

"Hopefully. What about food for tonight, breakfast tomorrow, or her school lunch?"

He frowned at her very practical but also unsettling questions. "I don't have much food in my apartment," he admitted.

"Then you'll need to get groceries for both of you. That small suitcase didn't look big enough to hold a backpack or a lunchbox, so you might need to pick those up as well. I can help you make a list."

"Why would you want to?" he couldn't help asking. "I'm sure you have your own life, your own problems to worry about."

"At the moment, I'm problem-free, but there was a time when I was in Olivia's situation, and if there's something I can do to make her life easier, I'd like to do it."

Her words caught him off guard and the shadows that suddenly passed through her golden eyes made him wonder if there was more to her than the sunny smile she usually wore.

"It's up to you, of course," Emmalyn added. "You don't seem like someone who accepts help. But there aren't any strings. Whatever I do is for Olivia, not for you. Does that make it easier?"

Surprisingly, it did. "All right. I'll take the help. Thank you." He blew out a breath at the end of his statement.

"That was really hard for you to say, wasn't it?" she asked with a knowing gleam in her eyes.

He had a feeling he was going to regret taking her help because it would probably take him down a path he didn't want to go. But he had no choice. "Just don't make me say it again."

CHAPTER TWO

Emmalyn would have never offered Hunter Kane help if he wasn't with an adorable and terrified six-year-old girl, because she had never felt comfortable around him. The few times she'd tried to be friendly, he'd shut her down. She'd made excuses for his abrupt, intense nature because, clearly, he was in both physical and emotional pain. But even when he'd healed, he had still stayed away from everyone, which had made her wonder if that was just his personality, his preference.

She'd told herself it was none of her business if he wanted to be distant from his neighbors. She'd learned a long time ago that trying to change someone's mind was a futile task. No matter how much she wanted to make someone feel better or act differently, if they didn't want it, too, it wasn't going to happen.

But while she'd made peace with letting him struggle on his own, her heart had gone out to Olivia, who reminded her very much of herself once upon a time. She knew what it was like to be dropped abruptly into a strange situation with someone she barely knew, and if she could make things easier for this little girl, she would.

When they went downstairs to check the suitcase that had come with Olivia, she wasn't surprised to see that Hunter's apartment felt a lot like him: cold, dark, and sterile. While his apartment was the mirror image of hers in the layout, that was where the similarities ended. Her space was filled with color; his walls were a stark white, with not one photo or picture breaking up the blank space.

A single couch faced a TV mounted on the wall, and the coffee table held nothing but a remote control and a stack of exercise pamphlets. The kitchen counters were empty aside from a coffeemaker, and a quick glance toward the open bedroom door revealed an unmade bed and not much else. The only thing at all interesting was a model helicopter sitting on the table next to the couch. The personal item almost felt out of place, and she couldn't help wondering why he'd chosen this one thing to put on display.

"My dad has one of these," Olivia said, running toward the helicopter. She picked it up and ran her fingers along the blades, a sad expression on her face.

She glanced at Hunter, seeing his tight, somewhat angry scowl. To his credit, he didn't say anything, but if Olivia looked in his direction, she would have no problem seeing his discomfort.

Clearing her throat, she drew his attention to her. "Where do you want Olivia to sleep?"

"She can have my room. I'll sleep on the couch." He paused, giving Olivia a worried look. "Livvy..." He licked his lips. "Do you want to put that down?"

She looked up as she spun the helicopter blades. "Daddy let me play with his helicopter. He said when I grow up, I can be a pilot, too. I like to fly."

"Me, too," he muttered, his jaw still incredibly tight. "But let's put the helicopter down. I don't want you to accidentally drop it."

Olivia set the helicopter down on its side, then said, "Where's the bathroom?"

"It's there," Hunter said, pointing to the door off the short hallway between the living room and bedroom. Then he quickly moved across the room and set the helicopter right side up.

Watching the reverence with which he did that made Emmalyn more than a little curious, and she couldn't help the questioning glance she gave him when he moved away from the couch, his gaze meeting hers.

"Did you fly with Olivia's father?" she asked.

"Yes," he said shortly.

"Is that why you and her dad have the same model helicopter?"

He didn't answer right away, then said, "Gary, Olivia's father, and I made the model helicopters together. It was one of those weeks when a series of storms grounded us, and we were going crazy with the inaction. We found the kits at a nearby store, and we put them together." He shrugged. "It's stupid to care about a kid's toy."

"Not if it reminds you of your friend. You should probably put it away, though, because I suspect Olivia will want to play with it again."

"If it makes her feel more comfortable, then I'm fine with it."

"I didn't realize you were Olivia's godfather."

He shrugged, as if that fact baffled him, too. "I'm not sure why they asked me to do it, but I couldn't say no. Gary and I met ten years ago, when we were twenty-four years old. We spent the last ten years flying together." He paused. "I still remember the night Olivia was born. She came two weeks early, and Gary was stuck with me on the other side of the world. We stayed up all night, waiting for word. I'd never seen him so nervous in my life. Bree and Olivia were everything to him. He should be here now, but he died in the crash that injured me."

"I'm sorry." She knew her words were meaningless, but she still felt the need to say them.

"So am I. You probably want to ask about the crash, about why Olivia is here," he said with a resigned sigh.

"I don't want to pry."

"We were flying a humanitarian mission in northern Africa, in a remote area that had been cut off by relentless fighting for more than three months. They needed food and water. There weren't supposed to be any enemy combatants in the area. That turned out to be false. We were hit by fire and crashed. I was the captain on that flight. And my best friend died."

The heavy guilt in his eyes touched her heart. "That's awful."

"The point is I owe Gary, and I should have checked on Bree and Olivia months ago, but I wasn't in a good place, mentally or physically. So, I need to step up now and take care of Liv. I just don't really know what to do."

His humble candor was surprising, but she didn't comment. Sympathy wouldn't help, but action would. "Okay, this is what we're going to do. We need to figure out what Olivia brought with her and what she's going to need for school tomorrow." She'd no sooner made that statement when Olivia came out of the bathroom and ran to her pink suitcase. She sat on the floor and unzipped the bag, pulling out three small stuffed animals.

As Olivia played with her stuffies, Emmalyn couldn't help but notice the file folder sitting on a small pile of clothes. She pulled it out and handed it to Hunter.

Then she said to Livvy, "Let's see what else you brought." She found enough clothes for three to four days as well as a hygiene kit and several well-worn books. But no backpack, no lunchbox. "You need to go to the store," she said, glancing back at Hunter, who was staring at whatever was in that file folder.

Since Livvy was distracted by her animals, she walked back to Hunter. "Did her mother give you any more information?"

"Bree enrolled her in school. She left me her medical records." He shook his head in bemusement. "But nothing about where she is now and when she's coming back."

"She also didn't leave her with a backpack or a lunchbox, which she's going to need for school."

Hunter didn't act like he'd heard her. He was still staring at the note Bree had left for him.

"I'm going to check the bedroom," she said, sensing he needed a minute to regroup.

Olivia followed her into the bedroom.

"Do I have to sleep in here?" Livvy asked with concern. "It's cold."

She could see why Olivia was distressed by the room, which was as empty as the living room. There was a dresser to go with the bed and the nightstand, but no other personal items.

"I'm going to see if Hunter has some clean sheets for the bed, and then I'll make it up for you," she said as Olivia dumped her stuffies on the floor by the window, as if she was desperate to stay in the small beam of light streaming through the blinds.

She walked back into the living room. Hunter was still standing in the middle of the room, staring at the file folder, desperate to find some answer that wasn't there. "Do you have clean sheets I can put on the bed?"

He started, then frowned. "No. I'll have to wash the ones that are on the bed."

"Or you could buy sheets appropriate for a six-year-old when you pick up the lunchbox and backpack at the store."

"She needs special sheets?" he asked in bewilderment.

"Well, she doesn't need them, but anything we can do to make the bedroom feel warmer and more welcoming would be good." She paused. "Should we talk about food? If you want to go to the store, I can watch Olivia for you. Or we can all go together."

"I don't see how I'm going to do this," he mumbled.

"You're going to do it because you have to. Her mother must have thought you could handle it, or she wouldn't have left her with you," she said, although she had as many doubts about that choice as he did.

"Bree was desperate. I don't think she thought this through. She was living with her parents, but I guess that situation fell apart. She needs to find a job and a place to live. She's also still trying to come to terms with Gary being gone."

"Did she say when she's coming back?"

"No, and it doesn't feel like it will be soon. I can't believe she didn't have someone else she could leave Olivia with. Someone better than me. I don't know what she needs, and I don't want to hurt her."

His last statement made her realize that his fear was coming from a good place and not a selfish place. "You won't hurt her if you care about her."

"Of course, I care. But I don't know what she needs."

"Let's make a list," she suggested, moving into his kitchen. She opened the refrigerator and found beer, eggs, juice, and some take-out containers. She started rattling off some basic items while he took notes on his phone. Moving to the cupboards, she found them just as bare. "Do you eat at all?" she asked, giving him a questioning look.

"I haven't been that hungry."

He was lean, almost gaunt, she thought. Clearly, whatever injuries he'd been dealing with had left him with little appetite. She added more items to his list: cereal, bread, and snack items, as well as fruit and veggies to go into Olivia's lunch tomorrow. As the list grew longer, she said, "Let's go to the store now. I need to get back by six for taco night. In fact, you don't have to worry about dinner tonight because you and Olivia can join the taco party. Gabe and Madison are bringing the food, and it's going to be fantastic."

He immediately shook his head. "No, thanks."

"Why not?" she challenged.

"Because I don't need to be part of a group right now."

"That's exactly what you need. Coming to taco night will give you a break from entertaining Olivia. And Paige's son, Henry, will be there. He's the same age as Olivia. She'll have someone to play with besides you," she said pointedly. "When the taco party is over, it will be her bedtime. But if you want to do it your way and spend the evening alone together..."

He held up a hand in surrender. "No, you're right. Taco night sounds like a better way to go."

"It is, and you might even enjoy it." She paused, then asked a question that had been burning inside her for a long time. "What do you have against us, anyway? Did someone in the complex do you wrong? Did they say something that annoyed you? Or do you just hate people in general?"

"What I hate are questions and looks of pity. I'm very aware of the gossip surrounding me and my accident. And I don't want to talk about any of it."

"Okay, that's fair. But no one here is going to push you to talk. We respect each other's privacy."

"Do you?" he asked dryly.

She didn't miss his not-so-subtle reminder that she was inserting herself into his life at this very moment. "Like I said, I don't have to help."

"Sorry," he muttered.

"Look, people here are very friendly and supportive. We're like a family. But everyone has a private life, too. I have secrets I've never talked to anyone about because I don't want to. And people respect that."

Her words brought a curious and doubtful gleam to his eyes. "You have secrets? That's a little hard to believe."

"Why?"

"Because you're so wide-eyed and innocent. I can't imagine you have dark secrets."

"Well, you don't know everything. You don't want me to judge you; don't judge me."

Their gazes connected, and she felt a surprising spark between them, which was very unusual. It was probably just anger, she told herself. It couldn't possibly be anything else. She would never be interested in someone like him. "So, do you want to go to the store together or not?"

"Let's go together. And thank you, Emmalyn."

"You're welcome, Hunter."

It was the first time they'd addressed each other by name, and it felt like they'd broken down a barrier between them that had once felt impenetrable.

The mysterious, attractive, dark-eyed stranger with the persistent scowl and pain-filled, weary expression had just admitted he needed help. And hopefully, she wouldn't regret giving it to him.

———

He had misjudged Emmalyn, Hunter thought as they finished loading his car with groceries and other items. The sweet woman who had given him tentative but wary smiles over the past seven months was also smart, practical, and firm in dealing with both him and Olivia. He'd always thought she was a little scared of him, and he'd been fine with that. He'd wanted space to be alone, and keeping people at arm's length had given him the solitude he needed. But Emmalyn wasn't being timid now.

She'd taken charge of their shopping trip, forcing him to focus on what Olivia needed right now and not think about the bigger, overwhelming picture that made him wonder how he could possibly take care of a small child when he was in the final push to complete his rehabilitation and return to active duty. But Emmalyn was making him take things one step at a time. And every time he ran into a wall, she found a way out. Like when she'd realized he didn't have a car seat and had dug one out of her closet that she'd used for school field trips. He was beginning to think she was a bit of a magician, and he couldn't imagine how he would have gotten through this day without her help, which was shocking since he rarely needed help with anything. In fact, he prided himself on being self-sufficient. But taking care of a child was definitely outside his area of expertise.

When they got back to Ocean Shores, Emmalyn suggested he put the new sheets in the laundry while she and Olivia put the groceries away. Since Olivia seemed to feel more comfortable and happier with Emmalyn than with him, he was happy to follow that suggestion. He also wanted privacy to call Bree again.

Deciding he might as well wash more than just the sheets, he grabbed his hamper and headed across the courtyard to the laundry room. There was no one in the small room, so he set the hamper on the ground and pulled out his phone to call Bree. She didn't pick up, and he left another pleading message for her to call him back as soon as possible, assuring her that he wanted to help her.

He thought briefly about calling Bree's parents. He'd met them a few times at family events, but after what she'd told him about her mom and dad, he decided to leave them out of this situation. Clearly, she was at odds with them, and he didn't need to stir up more drama.

As he slipped his phone back into his pocket, Liam Nash entered the laundry room with a full basket of clothes. The laid-back, brown-haired former professional surfer was one of the few people he'd spoken to in the complex. There was something about Liam's easygoing nature that had reminded him of Gary, a man who had never met a stranger. Liam seemed much the same way.

While they hadn't talked much, he knew that Liam had recently taken over the ownership of a sporting goods store called the Beach Shack and that his girlfriend, Ava, was some kind of numbers whiz, who was building her own financial investments business. Ava's sister, Serena, and her husband, Brad, also lived in the building, and the foursome often spent time together by the pool. They'd been celebrating what sounded like an engagement a few evenings ago, although he wasn't quite sure. There were a lot of celebrations in the court-yard. He'd never lived with a happier and more celebratory group of people.

"Hey, Hunter, how's it going?" Liam asked with a friendly smile.

"It's going," he replied as he opened the door of the nearest machine and began to load his laundry.

Liam nodded as if that was the answer he'd been expecting since most of their conversations had gone this way. Hunter would have made his usual quick exit, but he wasn't in a hurry to get back to his apartment where he had a lot of other problems to deal with. So, he said, "Did I hear something about you getting engaged?"

Liam's smile spread rapidly across his tanned face. "Yes. Ava finally said yes."

"Finally? Didn't you just meet like six months ago?" he asked dryly.

"Yes, but it feels a lot longer than that," Liam answered with a laugh. "In a good way." He paused. "Did I see you and Emmalyn with a kid earlier?"

"You did. I'm watching my friend's child for a few days."

"That sounds...fun?" Liam asked, a question in his gaze.

He sighed. "I'm not sure I'd call it fun. I don't know much about kids, but my friend was desperate. Emmalyn has been nice enough to help me get set up to take care of Olivia."

"That explains the unicorn sheets," Liam said with a laugh, tipping his head at the brightly colored sheets he was about to put into the washer. "They don't seem your style."

"Definitely not. Emmalyn thought Livvy needed sheets suitable for a child to sleep on. I didn't know that was important."

"I wouldn't have known that, either, but Emmalyn is an expert, so you're lucky she's around to help."

"She's been very generous."

"That's Em," Liam said with a nod. "You're in good hands. She's the real deal."

"I'm grateful," he said as he finished loading the sheets and then turned on the machine. "How's your store doing?"

"Business is good. School is back in session, but with the warm weather, there's still a lot of action at the beach. The surf school I started has also grown in popularity. You ever surf?"

"A couple of times when I was a teenager, but that was a while ago."

"If you ever want to go out, let me know. I'll give you a refresher—on the house."

"That's a great offer, but I'm focused on getting back to work."

"You look like you're feeling better these days. When will you return to duty?"

"That's the big question," he admitted. "I have some hoops to jump through before that can happen, but I'll get there."

Liam nodded, a gleam of respect in his eyes. "The Marines are lucky to have you."

He was hoping the review board would feel the same way.

"Are you coming to taco night?" Liam asked, changing the subject. "Gabe's fish tacos are not to be missed."

"I am going to come tonight," he said.

Surprise ran through Liam's eyes. "Well, good," Liam said. "I figured you'd either move or stop fighting the current at some point."

"The current of..."

"Friendship, neighborly interest—the Ocean Shores family," Liam finished. "It's not for everybody, but most people eventually end up a part of things. It's hard to fight, but you've been doing a good job of it."

"I've had a lot to deal with. It's nothing against anyone."

"Sure. I get that," Liam said with an easy, agreeable nod. "I'll see you later then."

"Later," he echoed, following Liam out the door.

As he went back to his apartment, he passed by several people starting to set up for taco night. He usually avoided eye contact, but today he found himself responding to the manager's warm smile with one of his own. Josie, the quirky sixty-something manager, gave him a surprised look, telling him she hoped he'd join them for tacos. He said he would, which shocked her even more.

Maybe Liam was right about the futility of fighting the current. But it wasn't the current of friendship at Ocean Shores he was concerned about; it was Olivia's arrival and the uncertainty of his own future that made him feel like he was being carried farther away from where he wanted to be.

CHAPTER THREE

Olivia was sitting on the couch, watching cartoons on the television when Hunter returned to his apartment. She gave him a wary, distrustful look, and he realized she was probably feeling the same way he was—that her life, her situation, was completely out of her control. She had to rely on him for her happiness, and she barely knew him. That had to be scary. And he needed to make things right for her. He would do whatever he had to do, including eating tacos with a bunch of people who seemed determined to bring him into their so-called family, whether he wanted to be there or not.

After giving Olivia a reassuring smile, he walked into the kitchen where Emmalyn was putting away groceries.

"I've put sliced fruit, veggies, yogurt, and a string cheese in Olivia's new lunchbox, which is in the fridge," Emmalyn said. "All you need to do is make a sandwich in the morning. Turkey and cheese with a little mustard. Olivia said she doesn't like mayonnaise. Can you handle that?"

"I can," he said dryly, wondering just how much of an inept idiot she thought he was.

"Good. Her backpack is also ready to go. She told me she took a shower this morning, so you don't have to worry about that until tomorrow night, but I put her soap and shampoo in the shower."

"You've thought of everything. You've certainly organized her life more than her mother did," he said, irritated with Bree's lack of responsibility. He knew she was grieving, but still... How could she have left Olivia with him so completely unprepared?

"I don't want to judge her too harshly," Emmalyn said quietly. "She lost her husband, and obviously she's in distress."

"I agree, and I want to help her. But she could have stayed here and let me help them both."

"I wish she'd done that, too. I feel bad for Olivia. She hasn't said much, except that her mom cries a lot, which breaks my heart. It's like Olivia has to be the strong one. It's not fair to put that on a kid, especially a six-year-old."

The passion in Emmalyn's voice surprised him, and he wondered if she was only thinking about Olivia, because it felt like there was something else going on, perhaps something to do with the secrets she'd hinted at. But asking that personal question might invite personal questions in return, and that wasn't a road he needed to walk.

Emmalyn grabbed her buzzing phone from the counter. A frown tightened her lips as she looked at the screen. Then she sent the call to voicemail.

"You can take that if you need to," he said.

"I don't need to, and I don't want to."

"Boyfriend?" he couldn't help asking.

She quickly shook her head. "No." Her phone buzzed again, and she declined the call once more. "I should go back to my apartment. I need to grab my cookies for taco night. Shall I meet you in the courtyard in fifteen minutes?"

"That sounds good," he said, knowing that even fifteen minutes alone with Olivia would probably be a challenge, but he couldn't tell her that. "Do I need to pay someone for this taco dinner?"

"Dinner is on Gabe and Madison. Some of the other residents are bringing apps and desserts. There's always a donation jar on the table, so you can toss in some cash if you want to. It's very easy and informal."

She had no idea how difficult it actually was to join their party. He'd spent the last seven months in isolation, and he felt like he'd forgotten how to be social, how to talk to people.

As Emmalyn walked toward him, she suddenly paused and put a hand on his arm. He almost jumped at the unexpected and warm touch. It suddenly felt like forever since anyone had touched him in a way that wasn't related to his rehab.

"Sorry," she said, dropping her hand. "I was just going to say I'll introduce you around tonight. It won't be as awkward as you think."

"I appreciate that. When it comes to parties, I'm a little rusty."

"You don't have to do anything. Just be yourself."

"I'm not really sure who that is anymore."

Surprise flared in her eyes. "Maybe it's time you found out."

"Well, I don't really have a choice, so..."

"So, you'll come and see what happens. Olivia's arrival might turn out to be a gift, Hunter, a reason for you to get out of this dark apartment and experience some light."

He didn't bother to answer, because she was already headed into the living room to tell Olivia she'd see her soon. He was still thinking about her words when he heard the door close behind her. He was starting to miss the light, but there was a part of him that didn't believe he deserved anything but darkness.

Olivia got off the couch and came into the kitchen, carrying two small stuffed animals in her arms. She gave him a sorrowful look, and he tensed for whatever she was about to say—that she wanted her mom—or worse, that she wanted her dad.

"What's wrong?" he asked.

"My show is over. Can I have another one?"

He let out a breath of relief. "Of course." He was happy he

could actually solve one of her problems. It felt like a small but important victory.

————

Emmalyn let out a breath of relief as she left Hunter's apartment. She was happy to help Olivia, but being around Hunter was unsettling. While he hadn't completely changed her initial impression of him being dark, moody, and withdrawn, she was beginning to understand why he had isolated himself from not only the Ocean Shores group but also the world.

He'd had to heal from his injuries while grieving his friend and dealing with a tremendous amount of guilt, which seemed to be unwarranted, but that didn't diminish the fact that he was feeling responsible for what happened. It wasn't the best time for him to take on a six-year-old girl who had her own dark pain to deal with, but Olivia's mother had left him no choice.

To his credit, he had allowed himself to take the help she'd offered because he cared about Olivia, even if he didn't know what to do with her. He was trying, and she respected that. She also hoped the taco party would make them both feel more comfortable at Ocean Shores and give them a chance to escape the stress of their losses for a little while.

As she headed toward the stairs, she ran into Lexie Price and Kaia Mercer, two of her best friends in the building. Lexie, a pretty brunette with a friendly smile, was the niece of their manager, Josie Bell, and had quit her high-powered career as an attorney to become a photographer and also to help her aunt with the building management. Kaia was a sharp-edged, quick-witted, red-haired paramedic who was a fiercely loyal friend and had a heart of gold that she sometimes covered up with biting sarcasm.

Kaia raised a questioning brow. "Did I just see you come out of Hunter Kane's apartment?"

"You did," she said, steeling herself for what was coming.

"Why? How? What's going on? Is he dead? Because I can't imagine he'd voluntarily let you in."

"He's fine," she said dryly.

"And..." Lexie prodded. "There has to be more to this story."

"When I came downstairs earlier, I saw a woman dropping off her six-year-old with Hunter. It was a tense scene. He looked uncomfortable, and the little girl started crying, so I stepped in to help."

"He has a kid?" Kaia asked with a raise of her brow. "Interesting. I wouldn't have imagined he had a child."

"It's not his daughter. Olivia is his best friend's child. His friend was killed in the crash that injured him."

"That's sad," Lexie murmured.

"It is. Olivia's mother dropped her off because she was desperate for help, and Hunter is now in charge of her until the mother comes back."

"That sounds complicated," Lexie added. "I feel bad for all of them."

"So, what's Hunter like?" Kaia asked. "He's so unapproachable; I've stopped trying to get to know him."

She didn't really know how to answer that question. "I'm not sure. He's definitely not an open book. He only accepted my offer to help because Olivia was crying, and he has no experience with kids." She paused. "I talked him into coming to taco night, but he's concerned he'll get asked a lot of questions."

"We're not going to grill him," Lexie said.

"I don't know. I have a few questions," Kaia said with a smile.

"Well, don't ask them tonight. Hopefully, he'll see what a good group we are. I think he could use some friends around here, people who aren't tied to the military, to his past."

"That makes sense," Lexie said with an approving nod. "I'm glad he's coming. And you're very sweet to help him, Emmalyn, especially since he's not the friendliest guy."

"He's not, but I don't believe he's a mean person. Just someone in pain."

Her words brought new expressions to their faces, a mix of speculation and curiosity. She immediately shook her head. "Don't start making something out of nothing," she warned.

"He is very good-looking, even with the rough edges," Kaia said. "You must have noticed that."

She ignored that comment. "I have to go upstairs and grab my cookies." As she went up the steps, her phone buzzed again, and Linda McGuire's name ran across the screen, making her stomach tighten once more. She sent the call to voicemail, but as soon as she got into her apartment, it rang again. Annoyed with the relentless persistence, she picked up the call. "Hello?"

"Finally," her aunt said, a mix of irritation and relief in her voice. "I've been calling you for two days, Emmalyn."

"I've been busy, Aunt Linda. What's so important you need to call me every thirty seconds? Or should I even ask?"

"It's your mother."

"Of course it is. What is it this time? You think she might be finally ready to leave? Because I don't believe that will ever happen, and at some point, you have to give up." She didn't enjoy being so cynical, but she'd finally made peace with the fact that her mother would never change, and she needed her aunt to do the same.

"She's sick, Em."

Her stomach tightened. "How sick?"

"I'm not sure. She needs to go to a doctor, but they won't let her leave the compound. Jeremy tells her to rest and take more herbs."

Jeremy was the latest in a long line of men who had been coupled with her mother, none of whom had ever been good for her.

"How do you even know that?" she asked. Her mother had been living in a commune on a remote farm in the hills north of San Diego. The members of the group called Haven had limited contact with the outside world.

"I go to the farmers' market in Criton once a month. She

first showed up there three months ago, and we've met twice since then. We talk for a few minutes when she takes a break."

Her aunt had been haunting the local farmers markets for years, since it was the only place her mother had ever been allowed to go.

"I thought she looked bad the first time I saw her there," Linda continued. "But the last two times, she looked even worse. I told her she has to leave, and for the first time ever she didn't tell me to stop trying to get her to leave Haven. She's scared that she's really sick. I think she's finally ready to cut the ties. And this Sunday is my next and maybe my only chance to make that happen. If you go with me, she won't be able to say no."

"Of course she could say no. I begged her to come with us before, when I was twelve, and the last time I saw her seven years ago, when I was twenty-one. She refused both times, remember? My wishes didn't matter to her then; they won't matter now."

"She was different this last time, Emmalyn. It can't hurt to try, right?"

It could hurt her. She'd finally gotten her life together. She didn't want to go back to the past, to feel conflicted again, to hope that her mom might make a different choice now.

"Emmalyn, please," her aunt begged. "I know it's not fair to ask, but I'm really worried."

Her aunt had always worried about her mother. Sara was Linda's younger sister by three years, and Linda had been living in Europe when Sara had taken her to live at Haven when she was five years old. Her mother had been alone and desperately poor, and the commune had offered her a family and support. It was only later it became clear once you came to Haven, you could never leave. It had taken seven years for her aunt to track them down, and to eventually get her away from the group, but her mom had refused to leave with them. By then, her mother had been brainwashed into thinking the outside world was bad, and the only people who loved her were at Haven.

"Your mom has made a lot of mistakes," Linda continued. "And maybe I'm wrong to ask you to get involved again in her life. You're doing so well now, but I don't know what else to do. This could really be it; the last time I can save my sister. I can't give up on her."

Her aunt's fear was palpable, and Emmalyn drew in a deep breath, struggling with what she needed to do and what she wanted to do.

"Are you still there?" Linda asked, desperation lacing every word.

"I'm here." Her hand tightened on the phone. "All right. I'll come to the farmers' market on Sunday, but I wouldn't get your hopes up. My mother has never taken my feelings into consideration—nor yours, for that matter."

"I keep hoping, Em."

"I know. Hope is a hard thing to let go of, but sometimes you have to."

Her aunt ignored her comment. "I'll be there at ten thirty. She usually takes a break around eleven. I'll send you the address and directions. Unless you want to go with me? I can pick you up. Or you can come by here?"

Her aunt lived twenty minutes in the opposite direction. "I'll meet you at the market."

"Are you sure?"

"When I make a promise, I keep it," she said.

"Then I'll see you Sunday."

She ended the call and sat down on her kitchen stool, feeling a little dizzy, and not at all sure she should have agreed to go. She had so many deep and painful feelings about her mother that her aunt was asking her to put aside so they could save her. But her mother had never wanted to be saved. That was the real problem.

How could she help someone who didn't want to be helped? How could she allow herself to hope her mother might finally choose her when she had never done so before? As she remembered the night her aunt had taken her away, her mind moved to Olivia. She'd seen the same confusion and pain in Olivia's eyes that she had felt when she'd ended up living with a woman she barely knew.

Forcing thoughts about meeting her mother out of her mind, she focused on what she needed to do right now, and that was make Olivia feel more comfortable with Hunter. To do that, she would need to help Hunter feel more comfortable, too. But he seemed a bit intractable. Hopefully, taco night would change that.

CHAPTER FOUR

The courtyard was bustling with activity when Hunter walked Olivia into the courtyard. The pool lights were on and gleaming, the tables pushed together and covered with colorful tablecloths. Lexie, the manager's niece, was setting up a margarita machine with help from Kaia, who, despite her dark-red hair and fair skin, was one of the most devoted sunbathers in the group, often relaxing on a lounger by the pool when she wasn't working as a paramedic.

Both were beautiful women in their late twenties and good friends with Emmalyn, who was often with them. There had been a time in his life when he would have appreciated being surrounded by so many attractive, energetic people his age, but that was not now. When Gary had died, a part of him had died, too.

He drew in a breath at that thought. He couldn't start thinking about Gary; that wasn't going to help. He looked toward the barbecue area where Liam and his fiancée, Ava, were talking to Gabe and Madison, who were creating amazing smells with whatever spicy meat or fish they'd thrown on the grill.

He had bought food from Gabe's food truck before he'd ditched it to open a restaurant with Madison. He didn't know much about her, except that she and Gabe had competed against each other in a cooking competition that had been the buzz of the building for a week at the beginning of summer. Now, they were apparently in a relationship, and there was a familiarity and intimacy between them as they cooked and chatted with their friends.

Olivia yanked on his hand, drawing his attention to her.

"Where's Emmalyn?" she asked, her worried gaze scanning the courtyard, as if desperate to find someone she could count on.

"I'm sure she's coming soon. There's a kid over there who looks about your age." He tipped his head toward a little boy who was throwing a beach ball to an attractive dark-blonde woman who he thought was named Paige. It was amazing how much information he'd picked up just by having his windows open on warm days.

"There she is," Olivia said with relief, pointing to Emmalyn, who was coming down the stairs with a platter of cookies in her hand.

Olivia dragged him around the pool until they reached the dessert table where Emmalyn set down her cookies.

"You're here," Olivia said, giving Emmalyn a hug.

Emmalyn smiled as she patted Olivia's head. "Of course I'm here. Have you met everyone?"

Olivia shook her head.

Emmalyn glanced at him.

"We just got here," he said defensively. "And while I've picked up a few names over the last several months, I don't really know anyone."

"Well, we are going to change that, because I know everybody. Let's start with Henry and Paige."

They walked around the pool to where Paige and her six-year-old son, Henry, were batting a beach ball back and forth to each other. Within minutes, Olivia started playing with Henry while Paige and Emmalyn chatted about some book they were reading for a book club.

He felt awkward and very much on the outside, but at least Olivia was smiling and having a good time. That was why he was here, so mission accomplished.

After a few moments, Paige interrupted the kids' game to ask them if they wanted to help her choose some toys to bring out. That was met with excited agreement, and he gave a nod as Paige asked if it was okay for Olivia to come with them.

As they left, Emmalyn said, "Shall I introduce you around?"

"I'm sure I'll meet people as the night goes on. No need to force anything," he replied.

"Whatever makes you comfortable. I remember feeling out of place the first time I came to one of these events, but now it just feels like a family dinner. Not that I actually know what a real family dinner is supposed to feel like," she muttered, talking more to herself than to him.

He tilted his head to the right, giving her a thoughtful look. Every now and then, she said something a little odd, and then stopped abruptly, as if she was sorry she'd said anything, which was exactly what she did now.

"Did you grow up with regular family dinners?" she asked.

"My father was in the military. He didn't make a lot of family dinners."

"Was it just you and your mom then?"

"I have an older brother, too. My mom tried to put good meals on the table for my brother and me, but she also worked, so as we got older, we fended for ourselves. I do actually know how to cook, even though there is no evidence of that in my apartment."

She gave him a faint smile. "I'll have to take your word for it."

"What about you? Why weren't you having family dinners?" he asked, preferring to delve into her life rather than his.

A shadow passed over her face, quick but unmistakable. "My childhood was...unconventional."

He sensed there was more to that story, but before he could decide whether to probe deeper, Josie approached them, camera in hand.

"Hunter! You finally decided to join us." She beamed at him like he was a long-lost relative who'd finally made it home for Christmas. She held up her camera. "Mind if I snap a few pictures? I'm documenting our Ocean Shores family for the community board."

Family. There was that word again.

He'd had a family—two actually: one born of blood, the other born of service and duty. But neither one of those was intact anymore. And he really wasn't up for a third. But he also didn't want to make a big deal about a photo he never had to look at.

"Fine," he said shortly, forcing what he hoped was a smile on his face as Josie motioned for them to get closer together, then snapped a photo of him and Emmalyn.

As Josie moved on to capture other residents, he let out a breath, and Emmalyn laughed. He turned to see the amusement in her eyes. "What's so funny?"

"Your complete distaste with having your photo taken. It's not like it's going online. It will just be on the display board next to the laundry room."

"I'm not big on pictures."

"Dinner's ready!" Gabe called from the grill area, where he was transferring fish to a platter. "Come and get it before Liam eats it all!"

The group began to congregate around the tables, and Hunter observed the easy camaraderie as they jostled for seats and passed platters. It reminded him of mess hall meals with his unit, that sense of belonging, of shared history and inside jokes. He felt a sudden, sharp pang of longing. The military had given him more than a career—it had given him a family of choice.

These past seven months of isolation had been a self-imposed exile, a punishment he'd felt he deserved, but now he felt a yearning for all that he'd lost.

"Are you okay?" Emmalyn asked quietly as they sat down together

"Yeah," he said, clearing his throat. "I'm good."

Olivia had returned and sat next to Emmalyn, with Henry and Paige on her other side.

A man slid into the chair across from him and gave him a cheerful smile. "Hi. I'm Brad Morrison. I own Maverick's with my brother Tyler. I've seen you in there a few times. Hunter, right?"

"Yes. You have a great bar."

"We think so," Brad said with a grin. "Heard you're a Marine Corps pilot."

"I am," he said, although he wasn't sure that was true anymore.

"Helicopters, right?"

He nodded.

"Serena," Emmalyn interrupted as Brad's wife sat down next to him. "You're back from your trip. How was it?"

As Emmalyn deftly changed the conversation to Serena's recent trip to Cancun, he was saved from having to answer any more questions, and he was very appreciative of her intervention. He knew Brad wasn't being particularly nosy; he just didn't want to talk about himself.

Another guy slid into the chair next to him. "Ben Mercer," he said, introducing himself. "I moved in a few months ago. I'm Kaia's brother."

"Hunter Kane."

"The pilot," Ben said with a nod.

"That's me. Where did you move from?"

"LA. I'm a detective with the Oceanside PD now. I much prefer a beat by the beach. Did you catch the Padres' game?" Ben asked. "That was quite a win."

"I saw that," Brad interjected. "Manny with three K's in the eleventh inning. Amazing game."

As they started talking baseball, Hunter sat back in his chair, happy to be out of the spotlight. The conversation flowed easily around him and across the three tables set up in the courtyard. He found himself surprisingly drawn to the rhythm of their banter, the verbal shorthand developed among people who knew each other well. It reminded him of his unit again, and that immediately dimmed his spirit, because one of the most important people in that unit was no longer alive. But he couldn't go down that rabbit hole of pain and anger, not here, not in front of all these people.

"Do you want more food?" Emmalyn asked, tipping her head toward his empty plate.

"No, but that was excellent."

"Gabe and Madison are the best. I can't wait for their restaurant to officially open next month. It's going to be amazing."

"What kind of food are they serving?"

"I'm not exactly sure. They come from different backgrounds, but I think it's going to be a blend of their styles, their favorite dishes." She paused, glancing over at Olivia, then back at him. "Olivia is enjoying herself."

"She is. I don't know how long her good mood will last once we get back to it being just the two of us, and she remembers her mother is gone."

"She just needs to feel safe with you. That's all that matters right now."

"I'm trying, but I think she feels safer when you're around."

"I'll come with you to school in the morning. We can meet in the parking lot, and you can follow me to Ravenswood. We'll go early so I can introduce her to her teacher, and you can meet her as well before the rest of the kids get there."

He hated that he still needed her help, but he wasn't stupid enough to turn it down. "Thanks. I'm sure Olivia will feel better if you're there."

"I'm happy to do what I can to make this easier. I know what she's feeling."

"How do you know?" he asked curiously.

She hesitated. "It doesn't matter."

"That's not the first time you've mentioned being able to relate to Olivia's situation. Care to add a few more details?" He really had no business asking about her life when he didn't want to share anything about his. But he was curious.

Before Emmalyn could answer, Josie's raised voice caught everyone's attention.

"I hate to bring business to taco night," Josie said, "but I wanted to let everyone know that the building owner is coming to town next week. I've heard rumors he might be thinking about selling the building. I want him to see that we have more than just a building here; we have a community. So feel free to share your thoughts if you see him wandering around. His name is Grayson Holt. Let's make him feel as welcome as we can."

"Do you really think he'll sell?" Kaia asked with concern. "And if he does, will we be able to stay as tenants?"

"I'm not sure he's going to sell, but he asks a lot of questions that make me nervous," Josie said. "The Holt family has owned the building since I first moved in over thirty years ago, and it's been passed down twice. This is the third generation to take over but the first to mention an interest in selling the building. I don't want anyone to be blindsided, so I will let you know as soon as I know."

As small conversations broke out around the table after Josie's words, Emmalyn muttered, "That's worrisome."

"It doesn't sound like anything will happen soon."

"You're right, and maybe it won't happen at all. I can't imagine us all having to move."

As he looked around the group, he could see that Josie's words had definitely put a damper on the party. He wasn't that concerned, because he'd never intended for Ocean Shores to be his long-term home, but he could see how troubled the others were by the idea of having to move, having to split up their makeshift family.

"I'm going to help clean up," Emmalyn said, grabbing his plate as she got to her feet. He looked at Olivia and saw her stifle a yawn. Then he met Paige's knowing gaze.

"Time for bed," Paige said as her son also yawned.

"I agree," he said. Olivia was definitely tired. She'd had a big day, but he was dreading bedtime and getting her to sleep. He wanted to ask Emmalyn to help, but he really couldn't do that. Olivia was his responsibility, and he had to figure it out. Plus, Emmalyn was talking to some of the others by the grill now, and he didn't want to pull her away. He got to his feet and told Olivia it was time to go inside.

Livvy immediately looked concerned, and he was afraid she was about to break into tears, so he threw her a quick buoy. "But Emmalyn is going to meet us in the morning and come with us to school. She'll introduce you to your new teacher."

"Can she sleep at your house, too?" Olivia asked.

"No. She has her own place, but she's just upstairs. She's not that far away."

"I want her to stay with me." He could see her lower lip tremble.

Fortunately, Emmalyn appeared, coming to the rescue once more. "Is it time to say goodnight?" she asked.

"I want you to stay with us," Olivia said, grabbing Emmalyn's hand.

He felt like a complete failure when he saw how eager Olivia was to be with Emmalyn and how reluctant she was to be with him, although he couldn't blame her at all.

"Why don't I walk you back to your apartment?" Emmalyn suggested. "I can help you get ready for bed." She turned to him. "If that's okay with you."

"More than okay," he said with relief.

They said goodnight to those still around the table and then made their exit. Once they got into his apartment, Olivia started to cry. "I want my mom," she told Emmalyn.

Emmalyn knelt down and pulled Livvy into her arms, stroking her hair. "She'll be back soon."

"I don't want to stay here."

"You are going to have so much fun tomorrow. And you can't have that fun until you go to sleep."

"What kind of fun?" Olivia asked skeptically.

"You're going to meet new kids and play games at recess. You'll get to read and do art, and it's going to be great. You will love first grade."

"Will my mommy be back tomorrow?"

"I don't know, but I'm sure it will be soon. Why don't you go to the bathroom and brush your teeth? Then you can put on the new pajamas we bought. They're on the bed with all your stuffies."

Olivia hesitated, then did as Emmalyn suggested and went into the bathroom.

"I don't think she's going to sleep tonight," he murmured.

"It's a difficult situation, but she's tired, so hopefully she will sleep. She has some books you can read her."

"Me? You should read to her. She wants you."

"I think you need to do this part on your own, Hunter, so she starts to feel more comfortable with you," Emmalyn said.

"As soon as you leave, she'll cry again. I really hate when girls cry."

"Sometimes, crying is good. It's better than holding emotions inside. Although, I suspect you wouldn't agree with that philosophy."

"I wouldn't. Emotions are better on the inside than the outside."

"Well, you're not a six-year-old girl." Emmalyn paused. "Instead of reading a book to her, why don't you tell her a story about you and her dad?"

He didn't like that idea at all. "That won't make her feel better. It will just remind her that he's gone."

"I think it will make her feel closer to you and remind her that you were her father's good friend."

"Maybe." He paused, giving her a thoughtful look. "I asked you earlier why you understand Olivia so well, and we got interrupted before you could answer."

"That's a longer story than we have time for."

"Is there a short version?"

She hesitated, then said, "When I was twelve, I went to live with my aunt, someone I barely knew. I felt abandoned and scared, which is why I can relate to Olivia's situation. That's the short version."

He now had a lot more questions, but Olivia was coming out of the bathroom, and she wanted Emmalyn's help with her PJs.

He hovered in the doorway to the bedroom as Emmalyn helped Olivia change, then tucked her into bed with her stuffies all around her. When they both looked at him, he felt another wave of panic. He wanted to beg Emmalyn to stay until Olivia fell asleep. But she was already saying goodnight to Olivia, and he needed to step up and show Olivia she could count on him.

Emmalyn gave him an encouraging smile as she walked toward him, murmuring, "You can do this." Then she was gone. And he was on his own.

He walked over to the bed and sat down awkwardly on the side of it. "Uh, do you want me to read you one of your books?"

Olivia shook her head. "Emmalyn said you could tell me a story."

He silently cursed Emmalyn for putting that thought in Olivia's head, but her expectant gaze was better than a crying fit, so he said, "Okay. What kind of story?"

"Can you tell me a story about my daddy?"

He had a million stories about Gary, but he had no idea if any of them were appropriate for a six-year-old. He thought for a moment, his gaze moving across the stuffed animals, and then he smiled. "Did your dad ever tell you about making friends with a monkey?"

Her eyes widened. "A real monkey?"

"Oh, yeah, but it was a sneaky monkey. We were in the Philippines, sitting at a café, when your dad decided to share his banana with a wild monkey."

"Did the monkey like the banana?"

"He devoured it. And then your dad decided to give him a name. He called him Captain Banana."

She giggled at that.

"But then, Captain Banana decided he wanted more than a banana. He grabbed my sunglasses and took off down the street."

"What happened?"

"Well, your dad wasn't going to let that monkey get away with my glasses, so he took off down the street, jumping over the curb, shouting for Captain Banana to drop my glasses. But the monkey just scurried up a light pole and gazed down at your dad, twirling my sunglasses in his little monkey hands. I caught up to them and told your dad to forget about it. I wasn't getting those glasses back."

"What did my daddy say?"

"That he wasn't giving up that easily. It was his fault the monkey had gotten that close to my glasses. Your dad grabbed another banana from a street vendor and told the monkey he would trade the banana for his glasses. I didn't think it would work, because a monkey couldn't understand what your dad was saying, but your father kept talking to the monkey like he could understand. And then, finally, by some miracle, the monkey came down the pole, dropped the glasses and grabbed the banana. Your dad handed me my glasses, and the monkey got another banana."

"What did Daddy do then?"

"We walked back to the café and ordered a banana smoothie to celebrate."

"Daddy was silly," she said with a shy smile.

"Yeah, he was silly," he said. "But he always showed up for his friends...for me, especially. He was going to do whatever it took to get my glasses back. You know what they call that kind of person?"

She shook her head.

"A hero. Your dad was a true hero, the best man in the world."

Olivia grabbed the little monkey next to her, then turned onto her side, giving him a sleepy smile. "I wish I could have met that monkey. Do you think he looked like this one?"

"Exactly like that one."

"Can you tell me another story about Daddy?"

"Uh, sure." He was still thinking about what to say when he realized Olivia's eyes were closed, and she was already fast asleep.

He got up from the bed, careful not to disturb her. As he walked back into the living room, he found himself smiling about the story he'd just told. And he realized that this was the first time since Gary's death he'd been able to think about his friend without thinking about the explosion, the fire, the fear, the pain... Instead, he'd remembered a good moment. Maybe not every memory had to hurt.

CHAPTER FIVE

Hunter woke before his alarm on Friday morning, his body still on military time despite months of civilian life. He lay in the unfamiliar discomfort of his couch, staring at the ceiling as the dawn shadows slowly retreated. His thoughts were a jumble of concerns: Olivia's first day of school, his physical therapy session later that morning, and the subtle but unmistakable push-pull he was feeling toward Emmalyn.

He didn't want to say it was a spark. He didn't want to admit he was attracted to her, because that was a complication he didn't need. And honestly, it had been so long since he'd even thought about a woman in that way, he wasn't sure what he was feeling. Maybe it was just gratitude and appreciation for her support.

It would be better if that was all it was. Because this chapter of his life, this apartment, this building was temporary and, hopefully, almost over. He'd always thought of Ocean Shores as a stopover, a few rooms in which to heal, to sleep, to eat, but he had never thought of it as home. Clearly, everyone else in the complex felt much differently. They were building lives here, creating a family. But his family was his unit, and he needed to get back to them.

Being in the Marines was all he knew. He'd started ROTC in college and had started serving immediately after graduation. He was turning thirty-four this year, having already put in twelve years of service. But he hadn't expected it to end this soon. He'd planned on being a lifer. If his time in the Marines was over, he had no idea what else he could do.

A small sound from his bedroom pulled him back to the present. He got up quietly and walked down the hall, then peered through the partially open door to find Olivia sitting up in bed, the stuffed monkey clutched to her chest, her eyes wide in the dimness.

"You're awake early," he said as he entered the room.

"Monkey doesn't want to go to school," she told him.

He sat down on the edge of the bed. "Why is that?"

"Because the other kids might not like him."

He saw the serious concern in her eyes, and he could understand why she felt that way. "You know, I had to change schools a lot when I was a kid."

"How come?"

"My dad was in the Corps, too. And we moved all the time. I hated starting a new school, but it always turned out to be good."

"It did?" she asked doubtfully.

As he stared into her eyes, he felt like he was looking at Gary again. Gary had had a ton of confidence, but once in a while, he'd had a vulnerable moment, like the night that Olivia was born, and Gary was waiting for news that everyone he loved was okay. He'd been more scared than he'd ever seen him and had looked to him for reassurance, just as Olivia was looking at him now.

"Yes," he said. "Because the kids at school were bored with each other. I was new. I was fun and exciting. Everyone wanted to meet me."

She didn't look completely convinced.

"And," he continued, "you're a lot like your dad. He was the best at making friends. He loved meeting new people."

"Like Captain Banana?"

He smiled. "Exactly like that. Is your monkey feeling better now?"

She slowly nodded her head. "Emmalyn is going to take me to school, right?"

"We both will. But she'll introduce you to your teacher before the other kids get there. It's going to be a good day, Liv."

"Do you promise?"

He hated to promise anything because he knew just how uncertain the world could be, but this six-year-old needed something in her world to feel safe. "I promise. And after school, maybe we'll get some ice cream."

Her eyes lit up with the enticing bribe. "Can Emmalyn come too?"

"If she wants. Now, are you ready to get up and have breakfast?"

She nodded and scrambled out of bed. As she used the bathroom, he went into the kitchen and grabbed the box of cereal they'd gotten at the store. He put the cereal in a bowl with a lot of milk and cut up a banana to go with it.

Olivia seemed happy enough when she sat down at the table and started to eat. While she was doing that, he pulled out the bread and made her a turkey and cheese sandwich with mustard only.

An hour later, he had managed to get Olivia dressed, fed, and ready for school, though not without a debate about whether the unicorn socks matched her pink shirt. Since he didn't really care if they matched or not, he was fine when she decided she'd rather wear orange socks with turtles on them. She definitely had a lot of her father in her. Gary had often shown up in mismatched clothes when they were off duty, declaring he hated to be like everyone else when he didn't have to be in uniform.

They'd just finished getting ready when Emmalyn arrived

with two travel mugs of coffee in her hand. "I thought you might need this," she said.

"You have no idea," he said gratefully. "I didn't have time to make any."

"I figured." Their fingers brushed in the brief exchange, and he felt an odd tingle run down his spine. It happened again when she gave him a smile and her hazel eyes sparkled at him, a mix of gold, green, and brown, changing with the light, and he found himself somewhat captivated by her gaze. She wore a simple sundress with a light cardigan, her blonde hair pulled back in a ponytail. She looked both professional and approachable—exactly what a kindergarten teacher should be.

She suddenly seemed to realize they were staring at each other for far too long. She cleared her throat and moved past him to greet Olivia.

"Are you ready for the big day?" she asked.

"Monkey isn't sure he wants to go," Olivia said, still clutching the monkey, who he had a feeling was going to school with her.

"He'll have a great time, and so will you," Emmalyn said.

"Hunter said we could get ice cream after school. Can you come with us?"

"Sure. I love ice cream," she replied. "We should get going."

"Let's do this." He grabbed his keys and ushered them out of the apartment. Then he followed Emmalyn to the school, which was located in a quiet, tree-lined neighborhood about two miles from the complex. Because they were early, he found a spot on the street. Then he and Olivia met up with Emmalyn in the staff parking lot and headed into the school. They stopped briefly in the principal's office, where he met Allan Perkins, the principal, who assured him that Olivia's teacher, Teri Hunt, would make sure Olivia felt welcome.

Allan was right. When they entered the first-grade classroom, Teri Hunt, a smiling brunette in her forties, greeted Olivia with warmth and enthusiasm, even making sure to let her know that her monkey was welcome to sit at the table with her. He was surprised that the classroom just had three big round tables and not individual desks, but it went with the rest of the décor, which was colorful and kid-friendly with art supplies in one corner, and big blocks and games in another, the ABCs spelled out on the carpet where they apparently had reading time.

"I better get to my classroom," Emmalyn said.

"I should go, too," he added. He turned to Olivia. "I'll be here to pick you up after school, Liv. Then we'll get ice cream."

Olivia gave them both a somewhat uncertain wave, then went with her teacher to the back of the classroom to put away her lunchbox.

He followed Emmalyn into the hallway. "Thanks for every-thing," he said. "You have made this so much easier for her."

"You're doing good, too, Hunter. You know that, right?"

He shrugged. "I'm winging it."

"Your instincts are good."

"So are yours. I told Liv a story about her dad last night, and she went to sleep right after that."

"I'm so glad that helped."

"Surprisingly, it helped me, too."

Her gaze softened. "Even better. I'll see you after school."

"You don't have to do ice cream if you don't want to. I feel like we're taking up a lot of your time."

"It's going to be a warm day. I'll be ready for a double scoop of something," she said with a smile that warmed him all the way through. "My kids get out at noon, but I'll be working in the library until two thirty. I'll see you in the playground when the first graders are excused."

"See you then." At some point, he would need to cut ties with Emmalyn, because she was starting to get a little too close, but that point wasn't going to be today. He had other things to worry about.

———

After leaving the school, he headed to the medical center for a session with his physical therapist, Jessica Bennett, who had been with him since the beginning of his rehabilitation. She was a no-nonsense, pragmatic, somewhat ruthless woman in her forties, who had pushed him through a number of dark days when he'd surprised himself with how much he just wanted to give up.

He had never thought of himself as a quitter, but there had been several times when he just didn't think he could keep going. But Jessica hadn't let him give up, and now, he was almost done.

After a grueling ninety minutes, Jessica handed him a towel, and he patted down his sweaty face, then took several long swigs of water from his water bottle.

"I can't believe this is the second to last time I'm going to see your annoyed face," Jessica said. "Monday is our last session before your medical evaluation next Wednesday."

"Do you think I'm ready?"

"You know you are. Stop looking for compliments."

He smiled. "I just figured you'd give it to me straight."

"I always do. You did the work, Captain. I told you in the beginning I could only take you so far. You had to go the rest of the way on your own, and you did. I'll see you Monday. Try not to over-exercise before then. Remember what I've always said about pushing too hard, too fast?"

"It will only set me back," he said.

"Exactly."

As she walked away, he turned to see his commanding officer, Colonel Jim Sullivan, enter the room. The forty-nine-year-old was a stocky, fit man who had always set high expectations and demanded the best from those under his command. He was surprised to see him here now as they had a meeting scheduled for Monday after his final therapy session. He hoped Sullivan wasn't going to tell him his evaluation schedule was being changed or postponed.

"Kane," Sullivan said with a brief nod. "I thought I might find you here."

"I've been coming every Monday, Wednesday, and Friday for months, so that was a good bet. But aren't we meeting next week?"

"Unfortunately, I have to go out of town tonight. My sister fell and broke her leg and needs help with her kids. I'll be with her until next Wednesday."

"Sorry to hear that."

"She'll be fine. But since I won't be here Monday, I wanted to check in with you before I leave. How did your workout go?"

"Good. I'm ready to move forward with my tests."

"Excellent. I understand your physical is scheduled for next Wednesday, with a psych evaluation the following Monday. If all goes well, you'll move on to the fitness tests, then the simulator and final flight assessment. It's a lot to deal with, and I would caution you to take things one step at a time. In other words, don't get ahead of yourself, Kane," he said, with a knowing gleam in his eyes. "You like to make things happen quickly, but this is a process, and one you cannot rush through. The stakes are too high."

It was the second time in less than five minutes he'd been told to take things slow, which was not his normal way of operating, and both his physical therapist and his commander knew that. "I understand. I will take it one step at a time."

"That's what I wanted to hear. You have been one of my best pilots and team leaders. The Corps needs you at your best. A lot of people wouldn't be able to come back from what you went through, Kane. And I'm not just talking about your physical injuries. You lost a team member and a good friend."

"I did," he said tightly. "But I can't change that. I can only move forward. And I've never been like a lot of people, sir." The cocky words made him feel more like his old self.

Sullivan smiled. They'd worked together for the last three years, and they knew each other well. "That's true. You've always risen above the pack, and you're a hell of an aviator. I want you back on duty, but the next few weeks will be stressful. You're going to be pushed to your limits. Try to relax and trust the work you've put in."

"I won't let you down." He didn't think caring for Gary's six-year-old daughter fit into the rest and relaxation prescribed by his CO. On the other hand, having Olivia around would force him to think about something else besides possibly losing the only career he'd ever had.

CHAPTER SIX

Emmalyn felt more impatient than usual as the clock ticked toward two thirty on Friday afternoon. She usually enjoyed working in the library after her kindergarten class went home, but today she felt restless. Since she'd promised her aunt she'd go with her to the farmers' market on Sunday, she'd been swamped by second thoughts and also memories of the past.

She'd locked most of those memories away a long time ago. She'd compartmentalized her life into three different eras: the first five years of her life, which she barely remembered, the next seven years of living at the commune, which her mom had sold to her as fun times on a farm, and the last sixteen years of her life when she'd become her own person, when she'd tried to forget everything and everyone from her first two eras, including the one person who had hurt her the most—her mother.

While she'd always hoped to get her mom back, the biggest disappointment had come when she was twenty-one, when she'd thought she could talk her mother into breaking away, choosing her blood family over the cult, but her mother had hesitated, then bolted, opting once again to return to Haven. Since then, her mother had been dead to her. She honestly didn't know how her aunt had the energy or the will to keep trying to communicate with her mother, because she'd given up.

But now, she was being coerced into trying again. While she told herself it was for her aunt and not for her mother, she was still dreading the whole thing, and she was afraid her entire weekend would be consumed with worry and anxiety. She didn't want that. So, she needed to put everything back in its compartment and lock it away until Sunday morning. It wouldn't be easy, but maybe she could find some distractions to make the time pass.

Going out for ice cream with Hunter and Olivia would help... or maybe not.

Hunter Kane was a complicated man with a lot of baggage. He was also devastatingly attractive, especially when he forgot how angry he was at the world and smiled. Then it was like a brilliant ray of sun coming out after a terrible storm, and it was so wonderful to see that smile on his face that it made her want to do something to make him smile again. She was too empathetic for her own good. When she saw someone hurting, she wanted to help them. That desire had gotten her into trouble back at the commune. When a child was being punished for breaking the rules, she'd try to sneak them water or a piece of bread if they were forced to go without, and if she got caught, which she did far too often, she would get them both into more trouble.

She had a feeling that could happen with Hunter, that she could get caught up in trying to help him, and her efforts would come back to hurt her.

But she was probably being too dramatic. She was really just helping him take care of Olivia. That was all he needed her for, and she could do that. She could give some childcare assistance without getting emotionally involved with Hunter. She wasn't trying to fix him, just assist with a difficult situation. There were definite boundaries between them. He had his guard up, and she would do the same. She'd be friendly but cool.

Finally, the bell rang, and she grabbed her bag in relief, eager to get away from her thoughts. But as soon as she saw Hunter waiting for Olivia on the playground, looking ridiculously handsome in faded jeans that clung to his lean body, and a short-sleeve button-down shirt that showed off his broad shoulders, a shiver ran down her spine, making a mockery of her resolve to be cool. He might be intimidating and closed off, but there was no denying his attractive male features.

When Olivia ran up to him, and he squatted down to give her a hug and a smile, her gut clenched because she saw a hint of the man he could be, someone more open to caring and affection, someone who was less of a loner and more of a family man. He'd probably give her an incredulous look if she said anything like that to him. He was very determined in his pursuit of self-sufficiency and solitude.

After giving them a moment to connect, she made her way across the playground, seeing some of the moms giving Hunter a second or third look. And when she joined him, those same gazes turned even more curious, but she didn't care. She knew what was going on, and that was nothing, she told herself again.

She avoided Hunter's gaze and smiled at Olivia. "How was your day?"

"It was good," Olivia replied. "I made a friend. Her name is Zoe, and she has a puppy named Pickles."

"Pickles? Really? Is he green?"

Olivia giggled at that thought. "No, but he ate a bunch of pickles her mom left on the counter, so that's his name. Zoe has a baby brother named Cam, and she likes monkeys, too. We made friendship bracelets. She gave hers to me, and I gave mine to her. See?" She held out her arm to show off her bracelet as the torrent of information came to a close.

"That's very pretty," she said.

"Can we get ice cream now?" Olivia asked, her gaze swinging to Hunter.

"Absolutely," he said, a somewhat bemused look on his face.

She couldn't help smiling at that. Clearly, Hunter was not used to the ramblings of a six-year-old.

"Are you coming with us, Emmalyn?" Olivia asked.

She glanced at Hunter. "Unless you'd rather go on your own?"

"Not at all. I was thinking we could just park at Ocean Shores and then walk down to Sandy Scoops. It's not far."

"That's a great idea. I love their ice cream," she said, hoping some ice cream would actually help her get her cool back because she was feeling way too hot and bothered.

————

Hunter couldn't believe how much Olivia had to say on the way back to Ocean Shores. She'd been shy and withdrawn yesterday, but not today, reminding him once again of Gary, jumping from one subject to the next, just like her father used to do. Fortunately, he didn't have to contribute much to the conversation, because she was more interested in talking than in listening.

As she told him the story her teacher had read about a frog and a cat making friends, his mind drifted to the woman whose car he was following into the parking lot of Ocean Shores. Emmalyn was a very attractive woman and so nice to Olivia and him. He wasn't used to such selfless generosity, and he probably didn't deserve it. He hadn't been friendly to her until he'd needed her, and he felt guilty about that. But once again, he had to remind himself he couldn't change the past, a fact he was being confronted with every time he turned around these days.

When he brought the car to a stop, Olivia finally quieted down. He told her to leave her backpack and lunchbox in the car, and they'd get them when they returned.

Once Olivia was out of the car, she skipped to Emmalyn, and the three of them headed down the beach path, which led into town and provided spectacular ocean views every step of the way. It was a warm September day, topping out in the high seventies, and there were many people sunning on the sandy beach or playing in the water.

On their walk, Olivia repeated the same story to Emmalyn that she'd shared with him, and he was happy to let them chat while he walked alongside, feeling oddly more relaxed than he had felt in a while.

The ice cream parlor had a line, but Olivia continued to entertain them while they waited for their turn. He was glad she'd had a good day at school, but he still needed Bree to call him and come back and get her daughter. One good day at school and an ice cream cone wasn't going to make up for the loss of her mother.

Finally, they stepped up to the counter, each of them ordering a different flavor. He went with his standard mocha fudge, while Emmalyn opted for an Oreo cookie crunch and Olivia asked for chocolate. They took their cones to the patio, where Olivia excitedly greeted her new friend, Zoe, who was also there with her parents, her brother, and the puppy named Pickles.

After introducing themselves to Zoe's parents and exchanging pleasantries, he and Emmalyn sat down at a nearby table while Olivia sat on the ground with Zoe and Pickles.

He was happy to have Olivia's rambling conversation directed at Zoe for a few minutes. "She is Gary's child," he said to Emmalyn. "He would talk my ear off, too."

"I didn't realize she was so chatty. She's clearly feeling more comfortable now than she was yesterday."

"I'm happy to see it. How was your day?"

"It was a good end to the first week of school. The kids who were nervous and scared the first day finally relaxed and had fun. I have a lot of personalities in the class, but that only makes it more interesting."

"How long have you been a teacher?" he asked curiously.

"I'm in my fourth year, the second at Ravenswood. I was at

another school in San Diego before that. But I'm much happier where I am now."

"Did you always know you wanted to be a teacher?"

"I did. School was my savior. It was where I finally found myself."

He frowned at her intriguing comment. "Okay, I really need the longer version of your story. Why was school your savior? Why were you sent to live with someone else when you were a kid?"

"Why do you care?" she challenged. "You've never been interested in getting to know me or anyone else in the building."

"That's true," he admitted. "I know I've been rude to you and others in the building. I was caught up in my own problems for a long time, and I couldn't find the energy to be friendly. I apologize for that, and I'm sorry I asked for information. I like my privacy, and I should respect yours."

"You should. But why did you ask, Hunter? Are you just bored and looking for a conversation that isn't about you, or are you really interested in getting to know me?"

He hesitated, seeing the demand for truth in her eyes, so he decided to give it to her. "I'm interested in getting to know you," he said.

"Why? Because I've been helping you out?"

"Not entirely. I can't quite figure you out, Emmalyn. You have a very sunny exterior. You always look bright and light, but a few things you've said have made me wonder what that hopeful optimism is covering up."

"I choose to be optimistic and to look forward. It's a choice I make every day because I didn't feel that way for a lot of my early life." She took a breath, her gaze moving to Olivia, who was still talking to her friend, while Zoe's parents were occupied entertaining their son. Then she looked back at him. "It was just my mom and me for the first five years of my life. I don't remember much about that time."

"What happened when you were five?"

"My mom met a man named Elias Ray. He ran a commune called Haven in the hills north of San Diego. At first, it seemed fun. I was so little, and there were lots of people, kids, and animals. Everyone was nice. It felt like we were camping, but as I got older, I realized how isolated we were, how little food we had to eat, how hard we had to work on the farm, even as young kids." She paused. "Some of the leaders had TVs and computers, but the rest of us had no connection to the outside world. There was no music allowed, no dancing, not even any laughing during workdays."

"What about school?"

"There was no school. My mom taught me how to read, and one of the other moms helped all of the kids learn math so we could add up the cost of the produce we were growing and eventually selling. It was very rigid and austere. There were a lot of rules."

"Was it religious?"

"Not specifically. They didn't follow a particular religion; it was more about living off the grid, being in nature, one with the earth. They didn't believe in medicine or doctors or anything materialistic. We all wore the same thing—pajama-like clothes or oversized dresses that went to the ground. It felt like the women and the girls worked the hardest. We had to clean, cook, sew, and take care of all the boys and the men. I didn't like it, but when I complained, my mother told me to stop, that this was our family now, and we had nowhere else to go."

"That sounds awful."

"I'm lucky that I was young enough to not really understand how awful it was."

"How could your mother stay there?"

"She would tell you that she stayed because they gave her everything she needed. We were really poor when we were on our own. We were sleeping in a car for a while. She was being taken care of at the farm, and she was grateful for that."

"It sounds like she was brainwashed."

"Definitely."

"How did you end up leaving?"

"My aunt found us. She had been looking for us for seven years, ever since we'd basically disappeared off the face of the earth. She figured out that the commune set up booths at various farmers' markets, and sometimes the women and children would go there to run the booth. It was actually a privilege to be allowed to do that, and I was thrilled when I finally got to go with my mom. But that's when I really saw how different our life was from other people. The kids I saw at the market were happy. They got to play and eat cookies and run around."

She paused as she licked her dripping ice cream cone. Then she continued, "My aunt said she'd gone to hundreds of markets before she found us. She waited for us to take a break, and then she pulled us into the parking lot. She said she was going to save us."

"What happened?" he asked as she quickly licked up some dripping ice cream. He was completely caught up in her story.

"My mom told her we didn't need saving. They argued. As I listened to my mom say how great things were and how happy I was, I got angry. I told her none of that was true, that our life was hard, and I wanted to leave. My aunt was promising me school, food, and freedom, and I wanted it all."

She popped the rest of her cone into her mouth, taking a minute before she continued her story. "I begged my mom to let us go. I said I didn't want to have to marry an old man like one of the girls a few years older than me had just done. And that's when something changed in her expression. I saw fear and worry. Finally, she said I could go with my aunt, but she had to return to Haven. She couldn't leave her family. She couldn't leave the man she loved. She'd never find anyone else to take care of her." Emmalyn's voice broke, and she cleared her throat, giving him a tight smile. "Sorry, I didn't mean to say all that. I'm as bad as Olivia."

He shook his head. "The last thing you have to do is apologize. How could your mother let you go? You were her daughter, her blood." He felt a fiery rage toward her supremely selfish mother.

Emmalyn shrugged as if she didn't care, but he knew she did.

"My aunt and I both made the same argument," she said. "But my mom walked away, and my aunt told me to get into the car. She said one day she'd get my mom to leave, and we'd be together again. I was terrified I'd made the wrong choice. I cried for weeks."

"That's understandable."

"My aunt was very kind to me, but I didn't even know her, and her life seemed so foreign. When she signed me up for school, I felt completely out of touch with the other kids. I was like an alien from Mars. I didn't know anything. I was lost." She paused. "I think that's why seeing Olivia's face when her mother left her with you hit me so hard. I could see myself in her. It's not the same, of course, and I'm sure her mom will come back, but her pain touched me."

He shook his head in bemusement. "I never would have guessed you had a story like that to tell."

"It's not one I like to share, so I don't. It's too embarrassing."

"You're a survivor, Emmalyn. You should be proud of that, not embarrassed."

"My aunt was the one who rescued me. I didn't escape on my own. There's not really anything to be proud of," she said pragmatically.

"That's not true. You had the courage to leave with your aunt. And look at you now. You're a beloved teacher, and you have great friends. Your past is way behind you. I'm sorry I asked you to go back to that painful place. I shouldn't have done that."

"You didn't know. And I didn't have to tell you. To be honest, I'm not completely sure why I did. But it's probably because my mom has recently resurfaced, so she's been on my mind."

"What do you mean?"

"The call I was trying to avoid yesterday was from my aunt. She has tried to stay in somewhat sporadic touch with my mother over the years. She said my mom is sick, and that she's going to attempt another rescue on Sunday. She wants me to go with her, to talk my mom into leaving so she can get medical care."

"That's..." He didn't even know how to finish that statement. Finally, he said, "That's a lot to ask of you."

"I said no at first."

"At first?" he echoed.

"I don't owe my mom anything, but I do owe my aunt, and her desperation made me agree to give it a shot."

"Have you seen your mom since you were twelve?"

"Once, seven years ago, on my twenty-first birthday. That was another surprise meeting arranged by my aunt. Another opportunity for my mother to leave, but she didn't. After that, I told my aunt I was done. She said she would respect my wishes, and she didn't ask me to see her again until yesterday."

"Where are you going to meet her?"

"My mom still works at farmers' markets on Sundays. They rotate around to different locations, and there's a chance she might not even be there. But if she is, we'll try to get her to leave."

"Are you ready to see her again?"

"No," she said candidly. "I have very mixed feelings about it."

"I'll bet."

"Anyway, that's my story." She paused, giving him a pointed look. "You owe me now, Hunter."

"Owe you what?" he asked warily.

"Your story," she said, meeting his gaze. "Or at least part of it. Not right now," she added hastily. "But one day, I would like to know more about you."

He'd known there would be consequences to asking her personal questions, but hopefully, *one day* wouldn't come for a long time.

"I'm going to get a water," she said, getting to her feet. "Do you want one?"

"No, thanks."

As she left, he sat back in his seat, mindlessly watching Olivia and Zoe playing with the puppy as he thought about the incredible story he'd just heard. He could not believe everything Emmalyn had gone through, and he was incredibly happy her aunt had saved her from that life. She'd gone above and beyond for her niece, making him think that might be where Emmalyn got some of her selfless generosity from, because she, too, was willing to step up and help someone, even someone like him, who hadn't been very nice to her in the past.

She returned a moment later with a cup of water and gave him a nervous smile. "By the way, I'd appreciate it if you kept that story to yourself."

"Of course. You know I don't talk to many people anyway, so you really shouldn't worry about that."

She gave him a small smile. "I have a feeling that's going to change because your little chatterbox over there will drag you right into the middle of things, and maybe that's not bad."

"Well, I'm hoping her mother will be back before that happens." He paused as Zoe and her family got up to leave and Olivia rejoined them.

As Olivia launched into a new story about Zoe and her puppy, he saw Liam walking down the path. When Liam saw them, he came over.

"It's a perfect day for ice cream," he said. "How was it?"

"It was great," Olivia answered for all of them.

Liam laughed. "Good to know. I might have to get some later." He paused. "By the way...I have a five- to seven-year-old body surfing class tomorrow morning at ten, if Olivia has any interest. Paige is bringing Henry. It will be gentle and fun, just to get the kids used to the water. Parents and guardians are welcome to participate as well."

He hadn't been thinking of himself as a parent or a guardian, more like a temporary babysitter.

"I want to do that," Olivia piped up. "I want to go in the ocean. I know how to swim, and I swam in the pool without my floaties this summer."

"That's good, but we have all the kids wear a life vest," Liam put in. "No pressure, but you're welcome to come."

"I don't know. I don't want to take any risks with someone else's kid," he said.

"Daddy would let me do it," Olivia said, giving him an irritated glare.

"Sorry, I should have asked you when you were on your own," Liam said, giving him an apologetic smile.

"I'll think about it," he said.

"Sounds good. See you later."

As Liam walked away, Olivia said, "I want to go surfing with Henry. He's my age. If he can do it, I can do it."

He looked to Emmalyn for guidance.

She shrugged. "It's your call, Hunter."

"What would you do?" he asked her.

"I honestly don't know. Maybe you can talk to her mother before then?"

"I've been trying all day to get a hold of her. I'll think about it, Liv," he added, seeing the stubborn glint in her eyes that once again reminded him of Gary. He didn't know what call Bree would make about this body surfing class, but he knew that Gary would have been the first to sign up with his daughter. He'd believed in trying new things and having adventures. He'd want the same for Olivia.

"I really want to go," Olivia whined.

"All right," he said, giving in, because he also didn't want to spend the night with an angry little girl. He would keep her safe. Everything would be okay.

"I didn't take you for a pushover," Emmalyn said with a smile as they stood up to leave.

"I weighed my options, and this seemed like the best one if I want to make it through tonight."

"You're probably right."

"What are we going to eat for dinner?" Olivia asked, moving on to the next subject. "Can we go out somewhere?"

"I can make us something at home," he said.

"Can you eat with us?" Olivia asked Emmalyn.

As she hesitated, he said, "You're welcome to join us. Even though I don't know what dinner looks like yet."

"I'm sorry, I can't."

He shouldn't have been surprised by her refusal. He'd been taking up a lot of her time, but he was disappointed by her answer, and so was Olivia.

"Are you sure you can't come?" Olivia asked her.

"I wish I could, but I have other plans tonight."

"It's fine," he reassured her. "Are you going out with your friends?"

"It's actually a date."

"Oh, sure. It's Friday night." Of course she'd have a date. She was an attractive single woman. He shouldn't be surprised.

But *surprise* wasn't the only emotion he was feeling. It was something else, something he didn't want to define, so he just said, "I hope you have fun." But he didn't mean one word of that statement, and he was not going to define that, either.

CHAPTER SEVEN

Emmalyn had been staring at the menu for at least two minutes, not really seeing it, and not all that interested in eating or even being on this date. She didn't know why she couldn't get more excited about it. She'd been looking forward to getting to know Steven. He'd invited her to dinner at a popular restaurant with a great view of the water. He'd been on time and eager to see her, but she felt oddly disconnected.

"What looks good to you?" Steven asked, his voice bringing her gaze to his.

She forced a smile onto her face. Steven Matthews was exactly the kind of guy she should be interested in. Friendly, open, with an easy smile that reached his eyes. A middle school history teacher who also coached baseball, he had sandy blond hair that fell across his forehead in a boyish way, and when he laughed, which was often, it was infectious.

"I'm leaning towards salmon," she said. "How about you?"

"Steak. The pasta looks amazing too." He smiled at her over his menu. "I'm really glad we're doing this. I don't usually like setups, but ever since I heard about you from Erica, I've been excited to meet you."

"I'm happy we're doing this, too." She had agreed to the

date because Erica, another teacher at Ravenswood had said Steven was a great guy, and he did seem to be very nice. It certainly wasn't his fault that her mind kept drifting to Hunter's dark eyes, to the way they'd gotten angry when she'd told him about her mother's choices, and the way they'd softened when he'd looked at Olivia eating her ice cream. There had also been an odd note in his voice when he'd asked about her date, as if he didn't really like that she had one. But that was ridiculous.

Hunter didn't care that she had a date, at least not for any personal reason. If he cared at all, it was only because he had to deal with Olivia on his own. That was probably why he'd looked a little disappointed when she'd turned down his invitation for dinner.

Hearing Steven laugh, she realized she needed to pay attention. Steven was sharing a story about his day at school, something about a student's hilarious misinterpretation of the Civil War, and she forced herself to focus.

"So then," Steven said, "this kid asks, in complete seriousness, 'But Mr. Matthews, why didn't they just text each other instead of fighting?'" Steven laughed, shaking his head. "Seventh graders, I swear."

Emmalyn smiled. "One of my students asked me yesterday if the sun turns off at night like a light bulb."

"It's fun to watch their brains develop." Steven reached across the table to touch her hand. "That's what I love about teaching. Every day is unpredictable."

His touch should have sent a little thrill through her, but instead, she found herself comparing his easy gesture to the brief moment when Hunter's fingers had brushed against hers as she'd handed him coffee that morning. Hunter's touch had been accidental, fleeting, and yet, somehow, it had lingered on her skin for hours.

"You seem a little distracted," Steven said gently. "Long week?"

"I'm sorry," she said, genuinely apologetic. "It was a busy first week back."

"No need to apologize. We could have done it another night."

"No, no," she said quickly. "I'm fine. Let's order. I'm starving."

Two hours later, she'd eaten a good meal and enjoyed getting to know Steven, though they'd spent most of the evening exchanging stories about teaching. Still, by all objective standards, it was a good date with a good guy. She just didn't feel anything special. There wasn't any heat. No nervous tingles.

As Steven insisted on paying the check, he said, "Would you be up for doing this again sometime? Maybe next weekend?"

She hesitated. The right thing would be to say no. It wasn't fair to waste his time. But she couldn't let her mixed-up feelings about Hunter send her down the wrong path. "I'd like that," she said finally, deciding to give it another chance.

"Good. I'll text you."

After paying the bill, they walked out to her car. Steven gave her a kiss that was warm and perfectly nice but did absolutely nothing for her.

"Night, Emmalyn," he said with a smile.

"Thanks for dinner." As she got into her car, she wished she hadn't agreed to another date, because there was no way Steven was going to drive Hunter out of her head.

She didn't even know why she was thinking about Hunter. They were barely friends. Although, she had shared her deepest secrets with him for some crazy reason, and she didn't know what to think about that. She could have easily told him nothing or the made-up story she'd spent most of her life sharing.

But instead, she'd gone deep into her past, saying things she hadn't said out loud in years. In some ways, it had felt cathartic to see his reaction to what she had gone through and to hear his compliments about her survival skills. But she also felt vulnerable now. He knew more about her than everyone at Ocean

Shores. Not that she thought he was going to shout her story from the rooftops, but she'd put her trust in a person she didn't even know, and she had no good reason for doing it, except that he'd asked, and somehow, she'd wanted to tell him.

It was probably because her mother was on her mind, but that still didn't completely explain her sudden desire to tell all her secrets.

And he'd told her next to nothing about his own life. That was definitely a debt she was going to collect on, not just because he owed her, but because she was interested in learning more about him. He'd seemed so one-dimensional before Olivia arrived, but now it felt like he was shedding his protective layers one by one, and she was intrigued to see what else he would reveal.

———

Saturday morning, after too much wine the night before and too little sleep, Emmalyn woke up with a headache and a grumpy attitude. She took a shower, threw on a pair of shorts and a tank top, then made coffee. She was feeling marginally better when a knock came at her door just before nine. She opened it to find Hunter and Olivia on her doorstep and her mood lifted when her gaze met Hunter's. He was also in shorts and a T-shirt and looked more relaxed than she'd ever seen him, his smile warm and inviting, sending a tingle down her spine.

"Good morning," he said.

"You two look like you're ready for the day."

"And we're hoping you'll join us."

"We're going surfing," Olivia put in with excitement. "And we want you to come."

"I'm not a good swimmer."

"We're going to be wading more than swimming," Hunter said.

"Please come," Olivia begged.

She hesitated for another minute, then said, "Okay, I'll come to the beach. But I'll leave the surfing to the two of you."

"It's going to be easy," Olivia said. "Hunter showed me a video, and we practiced on the floor last night."

"Really?" Emmalyn said, the image of Hunter and Olivia practicing together making her heart do a little flip. He was really trying hard to connect with Olivia, and that was impressive. "That was a good idea to practice beforehand."

"I've been known to have a few," Hunter said dryly. "We're going to leave in about twenty minutes."

"I'll put on my suit, and I'll meet you at your place." She was probably making a mistake to spend more time with them, but Olivia would be there, so nothing would happen between Hunter and herself. It was just a day at the beach with friends, she told herself, but she couldn't stop the smile from spreading across her face as she went to put on her bikini.

———

Twenty minutes later, they walked down to the beach together. The sandy area near the surf school was already alive with movement—five kids, their parents, and a scattering of beach bags creating a little semicircle around Liam and a tanned, teenaged instructor named Jack.

"Hey, you made it!" Liam called when he spotted them. "And Emmalyn—finally. I've been trying to get you on a board for *years*."

She shook her head with a smile. "I'm just here to watch, Liam."

"We'll see about that," he replied with a wink. "We start in ten."

They set their things on the sand, and Emmalyn slipped off her cover-up, revealing a modest teal bikini that felt more daring than it looked. She was a teacher, after all, and she was acutely aware of the possibility of running into parents and students on the beach. Still, she felt Hunter's gaze brush across her, lingering.

She flushed, thinking he looked unfairly good in his shorts and T-shirt, the sleeves clinging to his biceps in ways that made her thoughts go in a dangerous direction.

Hunter knelt to spray sunscreen over Olivia's wiggling limbs, coaxing her to hold still long enough to protect her nose and cheeks. Emmalyn watched, a quiet warmth stirring as he gently dabbed her face with careful attention. Whatever Hunter did, he did with a lot of focus to detail.

"Nice to see you both here," Paige said, dropping her bag next to Emmalyn's. "Henry had a great time with Olivia the other night."

"She had fun too," Hunter said, standing up as Olivia dashed toward Henry and the stack of boogie boards.

"She's a sweet kid. I'm sorry about her dad, Hunter."

Hunter gave a quick nod. "Thanks."

Paige turned her gaze to Emmalyn, a little smirk forming. "So...how was your hot date last night?"

Steven paled in comparison to the man standing beside her now, and she really didn't want to answer that question, especially in front of Hunter.

Hunter apparently wasn't interested in her answer. "I'm gonna help the kids," he said, walking off without a glance.

Her stomach dipped.

Of course he didn't care. Why would he?

"Emmalyn?" Paige prompted.

"It was fine."

"Fine doesn't sound hot."

"He was nice. Maybe my expectations are too high."

"They should be high, especially on a first date. No sparks at all?"

"Not really."

Paige gave her a sympathetic look. "Too bad. Hopefully, you at least got a good dinner out of it."

"I did. What about you? Are you seeing anyone?"

"I've been on a few dates, but it's tough to find time as a single mom. And I'm not introducing anyone to Henry unless I know it's serious."

"I'm happy to babysit whenever."

"Thanks. But I might take a break from dating unless someone amazing pops up."

Liam called the group together, and they moved over to join the rest of the class.

Liam planted his surfboard in the sand like a flag. At thirty-two, he had the sun-lined skin and easy confidence of someone who'd spent more time in water than on land. "Welcome to Little Wave Riders!" he said. "Rule one: Respect the ocean. Rule two: Look out for each other. Rule three: Have fun!"

The kids giggled. Liam grinned.

"We're starting with boogie boards," he continued. "These little beauties will catch your first waves. Who's been in the ocean before?"

Olivia raised her hand proudly. "I went with my daddy. He held me real high!"

Hunter's jaw tightened almost imperceptibly. But when Olivia looked at him, he smiled and nodded.

"That's brilliant," Liam said. "You're already mates with the ocean."

Henry flailed beside Olivia. "I know how to splash!"

"Love that energy!" Liam said with a laugh. Then he demonstrated how to lie on the board and paddle.

As the kids and parents followed his directions, Hunter knelt to adjust Olivia's position. "Just like we practiced, Liv."

Emmalyn's heart squeezed at how gentle and enthusiastic he was. Hunter was definitely putting his heart into this surf lesson, which surprised her, since one, she hadn't known he had a heart, and two, she couldn't have imagined he'd be so interested in a kid's lesson.

"Adults too," Liam called, catching her eye. "No spectators!"

Hunter appeared moments later with two boards, holding one out to her.

"Don't be scared," Olivia told her. "It's fun."

Hunter smiled. "What she said."

She took the board because, apparently, she was weak in the face of encouragement from six-year-olds and men with devastating smiles.

They practiced on land, then moved into the water. Foam lapped at their ankles. Liam explained how to read the ocean. Then they waded in. Everyone but her.

She sat on her board just above the water line, content to watch.

Hunter positioned Olivia on her board and then gave her a gentle push with the first gentle swell. Olivia rode the wave all the way to shore, beaming.

"Did you see me, Emmalyn?"

"I did," she said. "That was amazing."

"Let's do it again," Olivia said to Hunter as she ran back into the water where he was waiting.

Emmalyn smiled at Olivia's excitement, but it wasn't just Olivia who was having fun; it was Hunter, too. He looked younger, lighter, the weight of his grief momentarily lifted. It was like he was a different person. He and Olivia were paddling side by side now, and when they finally came in together, she caught her breath at the look of pure joy on both their faces. The grief was still there, just underneath—but so was life. And it was beautiful.

Fifteen minutes later, the class wound down. Olivia and Henry began building a sandcastle under Paige's watchful gaze.

Hunter walked over. "Your turn."

"I'm good. Watching was fun."

"Come on. Body surfing's better."

She hesitated. "I didn't learn to swim until I was a teenager. The ocean... scares me."

"It should," he said. "But it can also make you feel invincible. I promise I'll keep you safe."

She raised a brow. "Stronger than the ocean, are you?"

He grinned. "This shallow and calm part of the ocean—I'm going to say yes." He held out his hand.

She reluctantly took it, and they waded into the water. When they got waist-deep, Hunter said, "Lie down on the board."

"What about you?" she asked, realizing he'd left his board on the sand.

"This is your ride," He kept a hand on the board as she stretched out. Then he pushed her board a little deeper into the water, and her nerves tightened.

"I think this is good," she said, looking over her shoulder at the waves gathering behind her.

"I've got you, Emmalyn," he said. "Are you ready?"

She looked into his dark eyes and saw the promise there. "I'm ready."

"We're going to wait for the right wave."

She tried to focus on the ocean, but her awareness kept shifting to Hunter—to the droplets of water clinging to his shoulders, the way the sunlight caught in his dark hair, and the unexpected gentleness in his eyes when he looked at her.

"This one," he said, nodding toward an approaching swell. "Get ready to paddle when I tell you."

She turned to face the shore, arms extended as Liam had demonstrated. She could feel the swell building behind her, water drawing back slightly in that telltale sign of a wave gathering force.

"Now!" Hunter called, and she pushed off with all her strength, kicking her legs as the wave caught her.

The sensation was indescribable. She was probably barely moving, but she felt like she was flying, carried by a force so much greater than herself, momentarily part of something powerful. She could hear Hunter shouting encouragement, then his deep laugh carrying over the rush of water as her board hit the sand. She rolled off into the water, breathless and smiling, and then got to her feet.

"That was amazing!" she gasped as Hunter waded out of the ocean. "I know I wasn't very deep, but it was more fun than I thought."

"Told you," he said with a smug smile. "Want to do it again?"

"So much," she said with a laugh. "But you should get your board, too."

He looked over at Olivia, who was content working on the sandcastle. "Let's do it."

For the next fifteen minutes, they rode the small waves, and she loved every minute. When they finally called a halt and sprawled on the sand next to the sandcastle under construction, Paige gave her a speculative smile, but didn't say anything until Hunter took the kids down to the water's edge to fill their buckets with wet sand.

Then Paige said, "So you know what you told me about no sparks last night with your date..."

She gave her a warning look. "Don't say it."

"You and Hunter are throwing off some serious electricity. You like him, don't you?"

"I'm just helping him with Olivia," she said, desperate to hang on to that narrative.

"That's not what I asked you."

"I barely know him, Paige."

"Seems like you're getting to know him."

"I am, but to be honest, I'm not sure it's worth it. He'll be going back to active duty soon."

"Soon isn't now. You still have time for fun. Not everything has to go somewhere."

She knew that, but every minute of fun with Hunter seemed to make her want another minute, which meant the end of the fun could be brutal. And she didn't really want to deal with that kind of emotional fallout. After today, she should put some distance between them.

But fifteen minutes later when Olivia declared she was starving, and Hunter asked if she wanted to grab a burger, she couldn't find the will to say no. However, she did have the good sense not to meet Paige's amused smirk.

They asked Paige and Henry to join them, but Paige said Henry had a birthday party, so they'd see them later. Then they gathered their things and headed down the path to find lunch.

CHAPTER EIGHT

After leaving the beach, they walked a few blocks to a beachside grill, grabbing a table on the outdoor patio. They ordered burgers, fries, and shakes, and Hunter couldn't remember when he'd gone all-in on the favorite foods of his childhood. But he felt hungrier than he had in months.

While they waited for their food to arrive, Olivia colored on the kids' menu and Emmalyn checked her phone for messages. He sat back in his chair, glancing out at the water that was shimmering in the sunlight. It had been a successful morning, and he could almost feel the warmth of Gary's smile watching over them, hearing his voice telling him he'd done good getting his daughter in the water and teaching her something new. Gary had always had an appetite for life, which made it all the more cruel he was gone so young.

But his daughter was here, and Olivia was Gary's legacy. And Hunter would do everything he could to ensure that Olivia had the life her father would want her to have.

The distant *whump-whump-whump* drew his attention skyward. Two CH-53E Super Stallions from Pendleton were moving in tight formation across the cloudless blue sky. Another formation followed, this one lower—a pair of sleek AH-1Z

Vipers on a training exercise, the thunder of their engines vibrating in his chest. The attack helicopters banked sharply, executing a textbook tactical maneuver he'd done himself many, many times, and he felt a wave of longing for the life he'd once led.

"You miss it," Emmalyn said, drawing his gaze to hers. She tipped her head to the helicopters fading in the distance.

"Yeah," he admitted. "I do."

"When will you go back?"

"When someone tells me I can. I have to pass a lot of tests before that can happen."

"What kinds of tests?"

"I have a basic physical next Wednesday. If I pass that, I move on to the psych evaluation, followed by combat fitness tests. If I clear those, I'll get into a simulator to test my aviation skills. After that, there will be a flight evaluation where I'll have to run through a lot of maneuvers and various training scenarios."

"The Marines really want to make sure you're in perfect shape, don't they?"

"They do. And even if all those tests go well, I'll still have to go before a review board."

"It almost feels like they're punishing you for getting hurt on the job."

"Sometimes, it feels that way to me, too. But logically, I know the tests are necessary. They want to be certain I'm fit for duty. They don't want to put me back in the sky and jeopardize someone else's life if I can't do the job."

She met his gaze with a curious gleam in her golden eyes. "Do you feel ready to do the job?"

"Physically, I've completely recovered from my injuries, and I'm working on getting even stronger than I was before."

"And mentally and emotionally?"

"That's a little trickier, but I'm getting there."

"It can't be easy getting past everything you've been through."

"It doesn't matter if it's easy or difficult. I'm a pilot. I'm a Marine. It's my life. I don't know how to do anything else. I have to get back to my job."

"I'm sure you could fly outside the Corps."

He tipped his head in acknowledgment. "I probably could, but I don't want to. I want to get back to my unit, do what I'm good at. I know it won't be the same because..." His voice drifted away as his gaze moved to Olivia. "It just won't be the same," he finished. "But life goes on."

She gave him an empathetic nod. "Yes, it does. And staying in the present is the best thing you can do. Today has been a good day."

"It has been good," he agreed.

"Thanks for pushing me to get in the water, Hunter. Liam has been trying for weeks, but I've always refused."

"Why did you say yes to me?"

"I guess I didn't want to look like a coward."

"I wouldn't have thought you were a coward even if you said no. Fears are fears, and I respect them."

"I have too many fears, too much anxiety, but I'm working on it. Staying in the present helps me with that, but my aunt is pulling me back into the past."

"Are you worried about your meeting tomorrow?"

"I'm trying not to think about it." She paused as two servers delivered their meals. "And this is perfect timing."

He was happy to eat but not as happy for their conversation to end. He'd been so isolated the last seven months, he'd almost forgotten what it was like to talk to someone besides his physical therapist or his doctor. And Emmalyn was an interesting woman. She was smart and thoughtful, and she spoke with a candor he found charming. She also seemed to understand and appreciate the complexities of his life over last several months, which had made it easier to share his thoughts with her than anyone else.

She could listen without making suggestions or judgments, which was something the very few other people he'd spoken to had been able to do, but that was probably because they were all military men: his father, his brother, one of his team members. They'd looked at his situation from the perspective of how fast he could get back.

Pushing that thought aside, he encouraged Olivia to stop coloring and start eating. Of course, she couldn't do anything without talking, and as they ate, Olivia asked them random questions about things he had no answer for, like why the ocean was salty, if the fish slept at night, and where the sun went when the moon came out. He tried to come up with answers, but he was often stumped. Thank goodness, Emmalyn was there. She either answered the question or turned it around so that Olivia had to think of an answer herself. She must be a hell of a teacher, he thought, and he wasn't surprised the kids loved her. *What was there not to love?*

Em was a sweetheart, someone who truly did have a heart of gold, and he hated to think about what she'd gone through in her life. He couldn't imagine how her mother could have let her go when she was twelve years old. It seemed insane. But then, he also had trouble understanding why Bree had dropped Olivia off with him, a man Olivia had only met a few times in her life. He hadn't even had much contact with Bree the last few years. When Gary had gone on leave, he'd gone home and Hunter had gone elsewhere, because he didn't have a home to go to.

He'd always thought it was easier not to have anyone waiting at home for him. He'd seen the guys in his unit worry about their loved ones, stressed about not being around for important personal events: birthdays, weddings, and graduations. Not that anyone had been unwilling to serve to the best of their ability, but it had put a burden on them he didn't have. The flip side was that they had spouses who cared about them, kids who welcomed them home, and lives that existed outside the military.

He would have never had a day like this, playing in the ocean with a six-year-old, teaching Emmalyn how to body surf, or having lunch with what felt like a family if he was still living his former life. It was a strange feeling, both good and bad. This wasn't a life he'd ever thought he wanted, but it wasn't really his life now, he reminded himself. They were just taking care of Olivia until Bree got back. The three of them weren't an actual family, but he had to admit this picture, this moment was more enjoyable than he would have imagined.

As Emmalyn laughed at something Olivia said, her whole face lit up, and he found himself fascinated by her sparkling eyes, her pretty features...especially her soft parted lips. His chest tightened as the urge to lean across the table and kiss that sweet mouth was suddenly overwhelming. But he couldn't do that. This wasn't a date, and they weren't alone. He couldn't confuse everyone, including himself.

Emmalyn gave him a questioning look. "Everything okay, Hunter?"

"Fine," he muttered as he averted his gaze, then picked up his glass of water and took a long sip.

"Can I be done?" Olivia asked.

He glanced at her plate. She'd eaten half her kids' burger, all of her fruit, and some of her carrots. He had no idea how much she was supposed to eat, but he'd always hated it when his father had insisted he clean his plate, so he said, "Sure." Then he turned to Emmalyn. "Do you want anything else?"

She smiled as she finished her milkshake. "Nope, I'm stuffed. I can't remember the last time I had a milkshake. It was so good."

"I can't remember the last time, either. I don't eat a lot of sweets."

"Do you eat much at all?" she asked dryly. "I've seen your refrigerator and your cupboards."

"Haven't had much of an appetite until very recently, like yesterday," he said with a grin, feeling like he also hadn't had much of an appetite for smiling until recently, either.

When the check came, he pulled out his wallet, waving away Emmalyn's request to split the bill. "You've been helping me a lot," he said pointedly. "This is on me."

"Well, thank you, but next time, I pick it up. I mean, if there is a next time," she added hastily as if she were getting ahead of herself.

"Deal." He definitely wanted a next time. Although, he shouldn't want that at all because he was heading back to a life that could take him away from Oceanside, and the last thing he needed was to get involved with anyone.

But as she'd suggested, he was going to stay in the present, because he had no idea what the future held for him. He was going to worry about that later.

After paying the check, they headed back to Ocean Shores. As they neared the entrance, he said, "What are you up to the rest of the day?"

"I need to put together my lesson plan for next week. I'll probably work on that. I need to distract myself from tomorrow."

When they entered the courtyard, he saw an excited puppy jumping up between Lexie and Josie that immediately drew Olivia's attention.

"Can I go see the dog?" Olivia asked eagerly.

"He's friendly," Lexie said, overhearing Olivia's question. "We're just watching him until Frank gets back from having lunch with his daughter."

As they moved closer to the table, Olivia dropped to her knees to pet the puppy, who started licking her. She laughed in delight, and he smiled at the happiness on her face.

He looked over at Emmalyn, who gave him a soft smile. "It's the little things, isn't it?" she said. "That bring us the most pleasure."

"It is," he admitted.

"Where are you three coming from?" Lexie asked.

"Just got lunch," Emmalyn said vaguely. "I have to get some work done. I'll see you all later."

As she moved a few steps away, he quickly followed. "Wait, Emmalyn."

She paused, giving him a questioning look. "What?"

He looked back to make sure they were out of earshot, then said, "You're meeting your mom and aunt tomorrow at a farmers' market?"

"Yes. Why?" she asked, stiffening at his question.

"Do you want company? Not for the actual meeting," he added quickly. "But for the drive, for moral support? Olivia and I could come with you. We can check out the market while you're having your meeting."

She stared at him, genuinely surprised. "Why would you want to do that?"

"Because it seems like a difficult situation and maybe you'd want some company?"

She hesitated for a long minute. "I feel like I should say no. I don't know what's going to happen. And Olivia..." She shook her head. "It's too complicated."

"Olivia will be fine. She'll love going to a farmers' market. You can have your meeting and we'll be there when you're done. I assume if your mother agrees to go, she will leave with your aunt. Or were you planning to go with your aunt to the market?"

"No. We're coming from opposite directions, so we're meeting there."

He nodded, not sure why he was pushing so hard, but he hated the idea of her facing a potentially painful situation on her own. Since she hadn't told any of her friends about this, he was the only one who could offer to support her, and she'd been helping him so much, it seemed the right thing to do. "Why don't you come with Olivia and me? I promise we won't get in the way."

"You're very persistent." She gave him a puzzled look. "I

don't get it, Hunter. You've tried to stay out of everything. Now you want to get into the middle of my crazy situation?"

"I don't want you to do it alone."

"Says the man who has been recovering alone for months. It worked for you."

"Maybe not as much as I would like to think it did," he said candidly. "I've actually felt a lot better since I started talking to people, since I started talking to you, in particular."

She met his gaze with surprise. "Really?"

"I'm as shocked as you are," he said with a shrug. "But apparently being forced to parent a six-year-old has been good for me."

A smile slowly curved her lips. "I think it has been, Hunter."

"You've played a big part in helping me be a good temporary guardian. Let me help you."

She let out a sigh. "I don't know. When it comes to my past, I don't like to involve anyone else in it."

"I'm already involved."

"I shouldn't have told you the story."

"But you did. So, what do you say?"

"All right," she said with a helpless shrug. "I'll need to leave by 9:45."

"Not a problem."

"Okay. Thank you."

"You're more than welcome." As she headed up the stairs, his gaze followed her all the way to the landing. He finally turned around and moved back to the table. When he rejoined the group, he caught Lexie watching him with a curious gleam in her eyes, and he had a feeling he'd just given far too much away. But to her credit, Lexie didn't say a word, and for that, he was grateful. Because if she asked him how he felt about Emmalyn, he really wasn't sure what he would say.

CHAPTER NINE

Sunday morning, Emmalyn awoke with a knot of anxiety in her stomach. She'd barely slept, her dreams filled with fragments of memories—her mother's face, the commune, the night her aunt had taken her away. She'd woken several times, heart racing, before finally giving up on sleep around six.

By the time Hunter knocked on her door at nine forty-five, she'd been through three outfit changes and two cups of coffee. She also felt sick to her stomach.

"Morning," he said when she opened the door. "Are you ready?"

"Not really," she said, wondering why he was alone. "Where's Olivia?"

"She's with Paige and Henry. We ran into them last night, and Paige invited her to play with Henry this morning and then go to a movie with them at noon. She'll be tied up with them until about three. So, we have plenty of time."

"That will be fun for her, more fun than this farmers' market run. Are you sure you wouldn't rather take your sudden alone time for yourself?"

"I'm sure. And I can pick up some fresh fruits and vegetables for next week. Now that I'm feeding a six-year-old, I need to get on top of my grocery game."

"That's true. All right, let's go," she said as she stepped outside and locked the door behind her.

It wasn't as warm as yesterday, so she'd put on jeans and a short-sleeved T-shirt. She hadn't seen anyone from the commune since she was twelve years old, and she doubted anyone would recognize her. As a child, she'd never worn anything but loose-fitting pants and shirts, and her hair, while shoulder length now, was much shorter than it had been when she hadn't had a haircut for seven years. She'd been able to sit on her long blonde braid.

As the memories ran through her, she forced herself to take a calming breath. Hunter gave her a speculative look as they walked down the stairs. "You're nervous, aren't you?" he asked. "Are you afraid there will be some kind of confrontation? Not necessarily with your mom, but others who might be there with her?"

"I hope not, but I don't know. As I mentioned, my aunt has had a few covert meetings with my mother over the years and nothing has happened, so hopefully that will be the case today," she said as they walked out to the parking lot and got in his car. She still couldn't quite believe he was going with her, that she was allowing someone to see that part of her life.

Hunter gave her a reassuring smile as she fastened her seat belt, and the warmth of his gaze sent a different kind of butterfly through her stomach. "Why are you being so nice?" she couldn't help asking. "For months, you barely acknowledged me."

His smile faded. "I regret that, Em. I was lost in a world of pain and anger. I couldn't get myself out of it. And I didn't want to bring anyone else into it."

"So, you suffered alone."

"It seemed like the best option. But the last few days have proved otherwise. Maybe if I had started talking to other people sooner, I would have gotten out of my funk faster," he said as he started the car. "But I feel better now, so that's what matters."

"I do kind of understand why you wanted to be alone to deal with your injuries and your grief. There's a part of me that still thinks I should be doing this alone, that I'm crazy to involve you."

"Too late now. And as I promised yesterday, I won't get in your way. Think of me as your driver."

"You're definitely not just my driver," she said. "You kind of seem like my friend, which is also weird since we've only been speaking to each other since Thursday, which was only a few days ago."

"Friendships can happen fast."

She nodded. It wasn't just friendships that could start fast—relationships could, too. But she couldn't let herself think of this as anything more than a friendship. Hunter had a life to get back to. He was just offering his support as a thank-you for what she'd done for him. She couldn't let herself believe it was anything more.

"There is something I'm curious about," Hunter said a few moments later.

"What's that?" she asked warily.

"You seem very close to your friends at the complex: Lexie, Kaia, Paige...everyone. Why didn't you tell anyone about your past?"

"Habit," she said with a shrug. "When I went to live with my aunt, I was ashamed of my past, the way I'd been living. I was such an awkward twelve-year-old, stunted in every way. I'd eaten so poorly that I was very thin. My emotional and mental growth was probably closer to a ten-year-old than a twelve-year-old. I started school in the seventh grade, and within a day, they dropped me down to sixth grade, which was embarrassing. My aunt got me a tutor to help me catch up, but the first few years were so difficult. I felt out of touch and out of sync with other kids. But my teachers were great, and eventually, school became my salvation. I would spend hours in the library after my classes were over, and I would read everything I could get my hands on. I was a sponge for new information. I started to catch up, but it probably took at least three to four years before I didn't feel like an alien."

"I can understand that feeling a little," he said. "Not to compare our situations. But I was a military brat, so I had to start over at new schools fairly frequently, and sometimes I felt like an alien, too, especially when we moved overseas, and I couldn't speak the language. But even when we went from the Pacific Northwest to the Deep South, I felt out of step."

"I can see that. Very different cultures."

"But not even close to what you went through. What did you tell the other kids about your past?"

"I made up a story that my mom was a nurse, and she had taken me to Africa with her while she worked. When some wars broke out there, she sent me back to the US to live with my aunt."

"You turned her into a hero. That's interesting."

"The psychologist I saw said the same thing," she remarked. "At times, I thought about killing my mother off in my story, but I never did. I guess I still hoped that one day she'd show up and we could start over. That never happened."

"Maybe it's happening now."

"I can't believe she'll leave, but I guess we'll find out."

Hunter reached across the console and took her hand, squeezing it gently. "You got out, Emmalyn. That's what matters most."

His touch anchored her, pulling her back from the swirl of old fears and memories. "I know. I have made peace with what happened. Most days, I don't even think about it. I'm okay, Hunter. I don't want you to think I'm an emotional mess."

"I don't think you're a mess, but if you were, it would be understandable and okay."

"Do you ever tell yourself that?" she asked, sending him a pointed look as he moved his hand back to the wheel. "That it's all right if you're not completely together?"

He shook his head. "No. I never tell myself it's okay not to be all right because I can't do what I do if I'm not together."

"That's true. You have a high-risk, high-stakes job. How are you feeling about going back to active duty?" she asked, eager to get the conversation on a different track.

"I'm looking forward to getting back to my life, but it won't be the same without my copilot."

"Do you blame yourself for the crash?" she asked, knowing she was treading into dangerous territory, but she'd been open with him. Maybe he would want to be open with her.

After a moment, he said, "My best friend is dead, and I promised his wife I'd always have his back, so, yes, I wish I'd found a way to save him."

"What if it had gone the other way—if you had died, and he had survived? Would you blame him?"

"No, but he wasn't in charge."

She frowned. "Wasn't your helicopter hit by some kind of missile? Did it really matter who was in charge?"

His jaw tightened making his profile hard and unforgiving, but she knew that lack of forgiveness was directed at himself and not at her. "Yes, we were hit by enemy fire. According to the intel I had, there were not supposed to be combatants in the area, but that information was clearly incorrect."

"So, whoever compiled that information made a mistake. Not you. You were operating off what you believed to be true."

"Logically, I understand that the blame belongs on the enemy that shot us down."

"But emotionally..."

"I think I could have done better," he admitted.

Hunter was a guy who probably always thought he could do better. He held himself to a very high standard. It must be difficult for him to live up to his own expectations, but it was admirable he had set the bar high. Most people seemed more than willing to lower the bar, not raise it.

"So, it looks like we're about fifteen minutes away," Hunter said, clearly done with the subject.

She was happy to have gotten as much information as she had, so she was okay with that, especially since the road they were on was taking her back in time, and she needed to focus on what was ahead. She felt anxious and worried about so many things, whether they would even see her mother, if she'd be alone, if someone else from the cult would be there, even the ridiculous notion that she might somehow end up being sucked back into that world. That definitely was not going to happen, and she reminded herself that at the end of whatever conversation she would have with her mother and her aunt she was going to leave. Whether her mother would be with her or not was anyone's guess.

CHAPTER TEN

When they reached the parking lot, a dirt field next to the farmers' market, Emmalyn's hands were sweating, and her heart was pounding hard against her chest. Her anxiety was moving into panic, and if she'd been driving, she might have turned around and left.

Hunter gave her a questioning look as he turned off the engine, and she made no effort to get out of the car.

"I don't know if I can do this," she muttered, meeting his concerned gaze.

"You don't have to," he returned. "We can leave right now."

The fact that he didn't say she should suck it up and do what she'd come to do made her like him even more. "I don't have to," she agreed. "I don't owe my mother anything. But I do owe my aunt. She saved me, Hunter. And she's the one who asked for my help. She's the reason I came. I can't let her down."

"Okay."

"I also don't want my mother to be sick or unhappy. And I do want her to leave Haven. I just don't know if I can face hearing her say no again. I'll be angry and also incredibly sad. Why do I need to put myself through that?"

"You don't."

"But my aunt is trying so hard to save her. She has never given up on my mom. She's a better person than me."

"They have a different relationship. It's not the same."

"But her determination and courage are why I'm free. Why I've been able to live a normal life."

Hunter didn't say anything, and as the quiet of the car swirled around them, she knew she couldn't leave. She also couldn't sit here all day. "I'm going to do it."

He gave her a faint smile. "I figured."

"Really? You didn't think I was going to run? Because I did."

"You're a strong woman, Emmalyn, and surprisingly more complex than I imagined you'd be when we first met."

"Most people are complex. I used to think when they made us all wear the same clothes at the compound that they wanted us to believe we were all exactly the same, but we weren't." She shook her head and let out a breath. "None of that matters now. I'm going to get out of this car, meet my aunt, and hopefully have a conversation with my mother. I doubt whatever we will say to her will work. But at least, I will have tried. And I can live with that."

"Then let's go."

Hunter swung open his car door and stepped out. Emmalyn followed suit, her heart hammering against her ribs as they walked through the entrance. The farmers' market contained at least fifty booths arranged in meandering rows, each one a small universe unto itself. Fresh produce gleamed under the morning sun: pyramids of bright red tomatoes, bundles of kale and arugula, and crates of ripe peaches and strawberries. Artisanal bakers arranged displays of sourdough loaves alongside pastries that sent delicious scents of cinnamon and butter into the air.

Beyond the essential provisions, the market boasted a gallery of local craftsmanship. Silver jewelry caught the light, hand-woven textiles draped from rustic displays, and watercolor landscapes captured the hills visible in the distance.

Children's laughter spilled from a cordoned play area where

face-painted toddlers chased bubbles, their parents watching from shaded tables near a retrofitted Airstream trailer that dispensed everything from espresso to botanical teas.

The market pulsed with weekend joy, everyone reveling in the simple pleasure of buying fresh food. *Everyone except her.* The weight of her impending reunion pressed against her chest, making each breath shallow.

Hunter suddenly reached out and took her hand. His touch was warm and shockingly welcome as she sought stability in a swirling sea of uncertainty.

"Do you see your aunt?" he asked.

"Not yet," she said, but then she turned her head and there she was—Linda McGuire, a tall woman with brown hair and brown eyes and an energy that never seemed to flag. When Linda wasn't trying to save her sister or raise her niece, she'd been running an interior design business that had supported both of them. She was the kind of woman who could juggle a million balls and never drop one.

She let go of Hunter's hand as Linda looked up from her phone and saw her. Relief ran across her features, and she quickly moved forward, as if she were afraid Emmalyn might disappear.

"You made it," Linda said, giving her a hug. "Thank you."

"I don't know if I'm going to be able to help you get the result you want."

"You're here. That's all I wanted." Her aunt's gaze moved to Hunter, then back to her, with a questioning gleam in her eyes.

"This is Hunter Kane. He lives in my building," she said. Hunter was quickly becoming more than just a guy who lived at Ocean Shores, but she was too stressed out to even try to explain who he was to her.

"Nice to meet you, Hunter. I'm Linda McGuire."

He gave her a nod. "I'm going to let you both do what you need to do. But I'll keep an eye on you, if that's okay. I won't be too far away"

"It would be better if you kept your distance," her aunt said. "I don't want to spook Sara. She's going to be very nervous just seeing Emmalyn."

"What about the people she's working with?" she asked. "Will they let her leave?"

"It's usually a group of three women, and they each take breaks. Sara has told me in the past that they have a driver who drops them off and comes back at two when the market closes, so hopefully, this will go smoothly."

"Where are we meeting her?" she asked.

"I'll hang back," he assured Linda.

"Behind the last jewelry booth in the second row," her aunt said, checking her watch. "It's almost eleven. We should go now."

"Does Mom know I'm coming?" she asked as they started walking, Hunter lagging behind them.

"Last time I saw her, I told her I would try to get you here," Linda replied. "But she seemed doubtful you'd come."

"I almost didn't. It feels so hopeless, Aunt Linda. Mom will never leave Haven."

"She was different the last time I saw her, Emmalyn. She knows she's sick, and she's afraid she's getting worse. But it's not just her illness that's weakening her tie to them. Jeremy has moved on to someone else, someone younger. She said she got moved into a room with three other women. She's sleeping on a bunk bed and working from dawn to dusk."

"I'm sure she'll find another man to take her into his room and pretend to care for her. She's always been so needy for male attention."

"I know," Linda agreed. "She never got love from our father, and she kept trying to find it somewhere else. I'm just praying that if she's not so tightly tied to Jeremy, she'll be able to walk away."

She looked at her aunt in admiration. "You never give up, do you?"

"I can't give up. Sara is my sister. I'll fight forever to get her back."

She felt guilty for not feeling the same, but the only way she'd been able to move on with her life was to let go of her mother and stop praying for the impossible.

When they reached the jewelry booth, they walked around the side of it, and there was no one there. She exchanged a worried look with her aunt.

"We're a little early. She'll show up," Linda said confidently.

She saw Hunter meandering around the booth across from them, which featured leather belts and wallets. At least he wasn't stuck pretending to look at earrings.

Tapping her foot and crossing her arms, she tried to take some deep breaths, because she had a lot of anxiety coursing through her body, and it had nowhere to go.

Finally, a woman came through the crowd. She was short and thin, wearing a long blue skirt and a long-sleeve white blouse, which was the travel uniform.

Emmalyn's breath caught in her throat as she realized how much weight her mother had lost. While the clothes masked her body, her mom's face was very thin, and her hair had turned gray.

When her mom saw them both, her step faltered, and for a moment, Emmalyn thought she might run in the opposite direction. Then she took a breath and moved forward, coming around the side of the booth. They moved farther toward the woods behind them, putting some distance between themselves and the crowded market.

Her mother's gaze ran across her face and down her body. "You're so pretty, Emmy," she said, her old nickname slipping through her lips.

Her heart squeezed despite her resolve to not get emotional. "Hello, Mom."

"You look well," her mother continued. "Are you happy?"

"I am. I'm a teacher now."

"That's what Linda told me. Kindergarten, right? You were always so good with the younger children, so kindhearted."

"I didn't come here to talk about me. You don't look good, Mom. Aunt Linda says you're ill. You need medical care, and I want to help you."

"I'm feeling better," her mother said, which was clearly not true. There was not one part of her that looked healthy—not her hair, her skin, or her body.

"Don't lie to her, Sara," Linda said sharply. "You're not better. And you know it. The herbs they're giving you aren't working. You look worse than the last time I saw you. Are you eating at all?"

"I haven't been that hungry, and natural remedies have always been enough for our community," her mom said, but her voice lacked conviction. "I'm just getting older."

"You're forty-seven, Sara."

Linda's words actually surprised Emmalyn. She'd almost forgotten that her mom was only forty-seven. She looked more like sixty.

"I'll be all right." Her mom's mouth quivered. "I'm sorry, Emmy. I know I failed you."

She was shocked to get an apology. Maybe her mother's resolve was not as strong as it had once been. "If you want to make it up to me, you'll let Aunt Linda take you to the hospital to get some care."

"We can go today," Linda said.

"I don't have anything...no money, nothing."

"You don't need anything. You have us. We're your family, Sara. We always have been."

"I—I don't know." Her mother gave them both a terrified look. "How can I leave? I don't know any other life. It's too late. It's been too long."

"I didn't know any other life when I had to start over, Mom. And I was a child. But you had a life before you went to Haven.

And you can have one now if you come with us. I want you to get better. I hate seeing you like this."

"I would think you would hate me for more than my appearance."

"I have a lot of emotions about you," she said, unwilling to pretend she didn't. "But you're my mother, and if there's a chance we can start again and you can get better at the same time, I want to take it. But you have to want to take it, too."

Her mother gave her a look of anguish. "I'm scared, Emmy."

"I know, but you're not alone. Aunt Linda and I will help you get better. You can do this. But you have to decide now."

"Emmalyn's right," her aunt said. "This is your second chance, Sara. Please take it."

Her mother hesitated and drew in a breath that seemed to come from deep down in her body, shaking her limbs. She held it for a long second and then let it out. "Okay."

Emmalyn couldn't quite believe her answer. "Okay?"

Her mother nodded, her face tight, her eyes wide with fear.

"Let's go," her aunt said.

They started walking, each taking one of her mother's hands, positioning themselves on either side like protective sentinels.

Hunter met her gaze, assessed the situation, and immediately followed. Every step they took was filled with tension. She was afraid her mother would change her mind and bolt, or that someone from the commune would see them and try to stop them. But they made it to the parking lot without anyone shouting or coming after them.

"I'll take her in my car," her aunt said. "I'm just over there." She pointed to a gray SUV in the second row, which was only a few vehicles away from Hunter's car, so they headed in that direction.

Ten steps away from the car, a male voice rang out, and they froze.

"Sara, stop!" a man shouted.

Emmalyn turned her head to see a tall man with a graying

beard approaching them. Despite the years, she recognized him immediately—Jeremy. His eyes were as cold as she remembered, his mouth set in a thin, disapproving line beneath his beard.

"Get back here, Sara."

"I—I have to leave," Sara mumbled so quietly there was no way Jeremy could hear her.

"You're coming with me," Jeremy said.

As he stepped forward, Hunter jumped in front of him.

"She's not going anywhere with you," Hunter said forcefully.

Jeremy looked Hunter up and down, probably noting his height and strength advantage, his military bearing and the hard set of his jaw. "This doesn't concern you," Jeremy said. "They're trying to take my wife."

"Sara can make her own choices. If she wants to leave, she leaves," Hunter returned.

Jeremy's lips tightened. "You can't do this, Sara. I'm your family."

"I'm her daughter," Emmalyn said fiercely. "And she's coming with me. Get in the car, Mom." She looked at her mother, who gazed back at her in conflict. "Please," she added.

The simple word seemed to convince her. Linda opened the back door and then grabbed her mom's hand and got her into the car while Hunter prevented Jeremy from getting any closer.

"You'll be sorry, Sara," Jeremy warned. "This isn't the end. And when you come back, things won't be good for you."

Her aunt slammed the door shut so her mother could no longer hear Jeremy's threats.

"Leave her alone," Linda told Jeremy. "She's done with you."

Jeremy's anger flared, and he took another step in their direction.

"Don't," Hunter ordered. "Walk away."

Jeremy's expression tightened, but he clearly realized he was no match for the younger, taller, stronger Hunter. After a tense moment, he stepped back.

Emmalyn hadn't planned on going with her mom and aunt,

but she didn't want to leave them alone in case Jeremy tried to follow them. Hunter gave her a subtle nod, so she got into the back seat with her mom. Linda started the car and drove past both men, dust swirling up behind them, finally blocking them from view.

Turning back to her mother, she saw her visibly shaking. She put her arms around her as tears streamed from her eyes. "It's okay, Mom. You did it. You're free now."

Her mother didn't answer, but it didn't matter because she'd finally gotten her back, and she wasn't going to let her go. She met her aunt's gaze in the rearview mirror and saw tears on her aunt's face as well. This rescue had been a long time coming, and it was all because Linda had never given up on her sister.

After a few minutes, Hunter called her on the phone.

"I'm right behind you," he said. "I don't think that guy is following you, but I'm keeping an eye out."

"Thank you," she said gratefully.

"No problem. Where are you going?"

She paused at the question. "Hang on. Aunt Linda, would Jeremy know where you live? Should we go to my apartment?"

"I'm house-sitting for a friend for the next few months. The address is 211 Franklin Place in La Jolla," Linda said. "I don't think anyone from Haven would know my address, but I wanted to be sure, so I'm staying elsewhere for a while."

"You thought of everything," she murmured, impressed with her aunt's planning.

"She always did," her mom said. "Linda was better at planning ahead than I was."

She got back on the phone and gave him the address.

"I'll see you there," Hunter said.

"Was that the man who stopped Jeremy?" her mother asked as she ended the call.

"Yes. He's a...friend."

"Well, he has my gratitude," Linda said. "I'm not sure we

could have gotten away without him. I didn't think Jeremy would be at the market, Sara."

"He decided to come at the last minute," her mother replied. "I didn't have time to tell you. He's going to come after me, or he'll send someone. They don't let people just leave."

"They don't have a choice," she told her mom. "You're done with them. This is a new chapter."

"Maybe. But I don't know how long this chapter will last. I think something is really wrong with me," her mother said.

Her lips tightened as she looked into her mother's very sickly face and hoped that this rescue hadn't come too late.

CHAPTER ELEVEN

The next hour passed in a blur as they got to the house in La Jolla, which was a beautiful three-bedroom property on a bluff with a view of the ocean. It seemed like the perfect place for her mother to get her strength back. Hunter stayed out on the deck while she and her aunt helped her mother shower and change. Then Linda put out a platter of deli meats, bread, fruit, and vegetables, a celebratory lunch that was just another example of her determined optimism to get her sister back.

Emmalyn had always been grateful for everything her aunt had done for her, but now she realized she'd gotten a lot of her determination from her as well. When she'd left her mom to live with Linda, she'd traded a very weak role model for a very strong one, something else she needed to be thankful for.

As they sat down at the table, her mother was subdued, but she did eat, which was a good sign. Emmalyn felt bad about subjecting Hunter to a somewhat awkward lunch, but he'd told her he had nowhere to be until three, so he was staying until then or until she was ready to leave.

"So, Hunter," Linda began, breaking the silence. "Emmalyn said you're a neighbor."

"That's right."

"What do you do for a living?"

She tensed at Linda's question, knowing how sensitive Hunter was to answering questions about himself.

"I'm a helicopter pilot in the Marine Corps," he replied. "I was injured several months ago, and I've been recuperating at Ocean Shores."

"Oh. I'm sorry to hear you were hurt," Linda said. "But thank you for your service."

He tipped his head. "I'm back to one hundred percent now. Just waiting to be officially reinstated."

"Will you be deployed after that?" Linda asked.

"I'm not sure where they'll send me. But I'll go wherever they need me. That's the job."

His words reminded her that their friendship had an expiration date, but she couldn't worry about that now. As her mom lifted her water glass with a shaky hand, she said, "Mom, are you okay?"

"I don't know if I made the right choice," her mother said. "I've lived on the farm for so long. I don't know how to be in this world. What will I do for money, for a place to live?"

"You'll live with me," Linda said. "Money won't be a problem. You don't need to worry about that. I can take care of you, Sara. You just have to let me."

"And let me," she added.

"I don't want to burden either of you." Her mother's gaze softened as it settled on her. "It sounds like you have a good life, Emmy. I don't want to mess that up."

"I won't let you mess it up," she said. "I'm not a child anymore. I'm in complete control of my life and my happiness, and I want you to be in control of yours. Aunt Linda and I aren't trying to take over where Elias and Jeremy left off. We want to be there to support you in rediscovering your life."

"If I'm going to be well enough to have one," her mother said darkly.

"Well, you have a better chance now of that happening," she said.

"It was good you went to live with Linda," her mother said, meeting her gaze. "She taught you how to be strong. I've made so many mistakes in my life. Having you wasn't one of them, Emmy, but taking you to Haven was. You liked it there in the beginning. It was fun to be on a farm, to play with the animals and the other kids. But I could see as you got older what kind of life you would have, and I didn't want that. That's why I let you go."

"You should have come with me, but that's in the past. We need to look forward, not back."

Her mother slowly nodded. "I know you're right. I'm just not sure I can do that. I feel so strange, so out of my element." She put her napkin on the table. "I'm tired. Do you mind if I lie down in the bedroom?"

"You should rest," she said as her aunt concurred.

Seeing her aunt's worried look follow her mother into the house, Emmalyn said, "Do you think she's going to stay here? Or will she panic and find a way to get in touch with someone at Haven to come and get her?"

"She doesn't have a phone or any money. I don't think she can just walk out of here, but I'm going to keep an eye on her," Linda replied.

"It was smart of you to bring her to a place that doesn't belong to you. They might come after her."

"They might come after you, Emmalyn," Linda said. "Jeremy saw you. He might track you down, try to use you to find out where your mom is."

"Well, I'm not scared of him. I used to think he was so powerful but seeing him today—he just looked like an angry but weak man. He cowered in front of Hunter."

"He might come with reinforcements," Linda warned. "Or a weapon. We're just lucky he didn't have one on him at the market."

"I understand, but I'll be fine. Don't worry about me. You need to focus on Mom and getting her to a doctor."

"I already have an appointment set up for tomorrow. I was being optimistic," she added with a sheepish smile. "I figured if she didn't come, I'd cancel it like the others I've made for her in the past. But seeing you did the trick."

"I'm not sure about that. She's finally more scared of dying than leaving."

Her aunt nodded. "It was still good for her to see you."

"I'm glad it worked out. Can I help you clean up?"

"No. I've got it from here, Emmalyn. You don't have to do anything else, but you are welcome to come and see her whenever you want. It's up to you."

"We'll talk," she promised, giving her aunt a hug before they left.

As Hunter drove away from the house, she felt as if a weight had slipped off her. "Thank you," she said gratefully. "Not just for preventing Jeremy from grabbing my mom, but for supporting me and my crazy, dysfunctional family."

"You are an interesting trio," he said lightly.

"Interesting is a nice word for it."

He flung her a smile, then said, "You and your aunt are two of the bravest women I've ever met."

"My aunt is, for sure."

"So are you, Em. Your mother is lucky to have both of you. I hope she'll be able to get better and find a new life for herself."

"I hope so, too, but I'm not convinced she won't run back to them at her first opportunity."

"Well, you can't prevent that. If she does, it's on her."

"I know." She let out a sigh. "My mom has always been my secret shame. That's why I turned her into a heroic person in my stories. But you saw who she really is today. She's very weak."

"She is who she is, Em. She made choices a long time ago that changed the course of her life. Whatever shame there is or isn't—it's not yours. It's hers. You were a kid. She made the decisions for both of you."

"I know. I just wish she was a better mom. That sounds terrible, doesn't it?"

"It sounds like the words of a disappointed daughter, but one who has every right to feel that way."

"Thanks." She paused. "What's your mom like?"

"She's a strong person, very loyal, protective, much like your aunt. She held the family together when my dad was deployed, and she ran a tight ship. Because she also had to work, she had a lot of rules, and my brother and I were expected to follow them. We were also expected to contribute, so there were plenty of chores, and grade expectations were high."

"She sounds great."

"She was good, but she could be rigid. She liked to have control, and when she didn't have it, it really rattled her. That caused a lot of problems in her marriage to my dad. My father's job always took precedence, and she couldn't control where he was going to be sent or how long he would be gone, or anything really."

"That must have been difficult and lonely, too."

"I think she was very lonely. And that made her angry. When my father was home, they fought a lot. He would go against the rules she had set, and that would piss her off because he didn't respect how she was running the house, and she didn't think he appreciated her hard work." He paused. "But things got worse when my dad was injured during one of his tours, and he came back with not just physical injuries but also mental issues."

"That's terrible," she murmured, wondering if his dad's issues had weighed on him when he'd gotten injured.

"It was bad for a few years. My father didn't want to admit he had PTSD. He started drinking and self-medicating. My mom couldn't convince him to get help, and that made her frustrated and angry. They really started to hate each other then. It was not a fun place for any of us to be. The day I graduated from high school, my mother told me she was leaving my dad. That she couldn't do it anymore. She'd waited as long as she could. My older brother was already in college, and I was on my way. It was time for her to have a life. I couldn't disagree."

"It still must have been difficult to have your parents break up."

"It was kind of a relief, to be honest. She got married again when I was in my early twenties. Her second husband is a dentist. He doesn't go anywhere without her."

She smiled at that. "And your father?"

"He eventually got help, and then he retired. He moved in with a very nice woman a couple of years ago. She runs a café, and my dad, who never did a dish in his life that I remember, is now wearing an apron and helping out the restaurant." Hunter shook his head in disbelief. "They both did better the second time around. I'm just sorry we all had to spend about ten years in hell before they broke up."

"They were trying to keep the family together."

"I'm not sure it was good to grow up in that kind of constant conflict, but I appreciate the efforts they made."

"And your brother. Where is he now?"

"Brett is currently stationed in Germany."

"Is he a pilot as well?"

"No. He is boots on the ground and loves the action up close and personal. My dad was the same way. I was the only one who wanted to fly."

"Have they ever visited you at Ocean Shores?" she asked curiously. "Not to sound like a nosy neighbor, but I've never noticed you having any visitors."

"They've never been there. And everyone at Ocean Shores is a nosy neighbor," he said with a teasing smile.

"Why haven't any of your family members come around? You've been going through such a hard time. It sounds like you all care about each other."

"We're very independent. We live separate lives now. We have for years."

"Still..."

"They all came to the hospital after the crash. I was airlifted to Germany. My brother was already there. My father and mother both came to see me, but I was in a bad mental space, and I didn't want them sitting by my bedside. I wanted to be alone. I was in too much pain to deal with them, so I told them if they wanted to help me, they should go away."

"I wouldn't have gone even if you had told me that."

He gave her a quick look. "Why not? It's what I wanted."

"Because you clearly weren't thinking straight, and they must have known that."

"Well, they did stay for a few days, but eventually they took me at my word and left. They do check in."

"And what do you tell them when they check in?" she asked. "Let me guess. You're fine. You're healed. And you don't need any help."

"Good guess."

"But none of that was true for a long time, Hunter."

"There was nothing anyone could do to help me, Em. I had to get better on my own. And I did." He paused. "Just like you did. We're both survivors."

"That's true."

Silence fell between them for a moment, then Hunter said, "I understand a little of what your mother is feeling now."

"You do?"

"Yes. She knows she's going to have to change her whole life, and even though a part of her wants to be free, there's a part of her that feels like she doesn't deserve to be free after the bad choices she made. After she let her daughter go."

"I think she's convinced herself that by letting me go, she saved me."

"She probably had to convince herself of that. It was the only way she could live with herself."

He had a point. "That's pretty insightful," she said.

"I have my moments."

"Do you think she'll try to go back to Haven?"

"I don't know. Sometimes it's easier to go backward than forward."

She thought about that, wondering if he was talking more about himself than her mother. "Do you think returning to your job is a step forward or backward?"

He didn't answer right away, then he said, "I'm not sure. But I'm going to find out."

———

When they got home, they found Paige, Henry, and Olivia sitting at a table in the courtyard, eating ice cream. Kaia and Lexie were stretched out on loungers by the pool while Gabe and Madison were in the water, tossing a beach ball back and forth. Josie, Frank, Maggie, and Skye were at another table playing bridge. Skye was apparently the latest person to be roped into being a fourth for their card game.

Seeing all her friends having a good time on a beautiful Sunday stripped the dark thoughts from Emmalyn's mind. This was what she loved most about Ocean Shores and the family she'd found there. Even when she felt out of sorts, as soon as she came home, she felt better. Smiles, laughter, and conversation lightened the tangled and deep emotions of the last few hours.

As they joined Paige and the kids at the table, Olivia burst into a long, rambling story about the movie, with Henry joining in to add his excited thoughts. Clearly, the kids had had a great time.

When Olivia finally came up for air, Hunter said, "Thanks for taking Olivia, Paige."

"She was a delight, and Henry was happy to have a friend," Paige replied. "They want to go swimming, but I thought I should wait and ask you before they went in the pool."

"Can I go, Hunter?" Olivia asked, a plea in her gaze.

"Sure. As soon as you finish your ice cream," he replied. "And I'd be happy to watch both of them if you want a break, Paige."

"Well, I have to put some laundry in, so I wouldn't mind you keeping an eye on them for a few minutes, if that's okay."

"No problem."

"I'm done," Olivia said, popping the last of her ice cream into her mouth and jumping to her feet.

"Great. We'll get changed and meet you back here." He paused. "Do you want to join us in the pool, Emmalyn?"

"Uh, I don't feel like swimming, but I'll hang out for a bit." The last thing she wanted to do was go upstairs and be alone in her apartment, where she would have way too much time to think.

As the four of them went to change into bathing suits, she made her way over to Lexie and Kaia, taking a seat on the lounger next to Kaia.

"You're getting red," she told her friend.

"As always," Kaia said with a sigh as she sat up. "The curse of a redhead. I'll take a dip, then lather up again."

As Kaia joined Madison and Gabe in the pool, Lexie smiled and said, "You should put on a suit. It's hot out here."

"I got a lot of sun yesterday at the beach."

"I heard you took a surf lesson. Liam was excited about that."

"It was more of a boogie board lesson and geared to six-year-olds, so I don't think anyone should be too excited."

"Well, you have to start somewhere. Speaking of starting somewhere..."

She shook her head. "Don't get any ideas, Lex."

"How can I not? You and Hunter are spending a lot of time together. Paige said you were going to a farmers' market, but that was hours ago, and I couldn't help noticing neither of you came back with anything."

"That's true. We just looked around and ate some lunch." She didn't want to get into the longer story now, but maybe someday she would tell her friends about her past. Just not today.

Lexie smiled. "No one cares if you are interested in each other. You know that, right?"

"For no one who cares, you have a lot of questions," she returned.

"Well, I'm curious. Hunter has always been a mystery."

"I'm just helping him with Olivia."

Lexie gave her a doubtful look. "Olivia was with Paige, and you were with Hunter, so...it's not just about Olivia."

"Maybe it isn't all about her," she conceded. "I'm enjoying getting to know Hunter, but he's on his way out. Once he's cleared for duty, he'll be gone."

Lexie nodded with understanding. "I get it. It's better not to invest too heavily in someone who has a foot out the door."

"Exactly."

"But in the meantime, you can have fun."

Lexie echoed Paige's earlier words. She didn't know if she could call the time they'd spent together fun, but there was still the afternoon, and it was a beautiful day. "Maybe I will go change into my suit," she said.

"Excellent idea," Lexie said. "I'll save you a seat."

CHAPTER TWELVE

Monday morning, after the best weekend he'd had in months, Hunter dropped Olivia off at school, then headed to the medical center for his final physical therapy session. It was probably the first time in months he wasn't feeling stressed about the workout. And it was because he hadn't spent the weekend isolated and alone, consumed with his dark thoughts.

Instead, he'd taken surf lessons, bonded with Olivia, helped Emmalyn navigate the situation with her mother, and spent time getting to know his neighbors. While he'd done a lot of those activities in the service of Olivia or Emmalyn, they'd actually served him more because they'd brought him back to life. Now he was looking forward to showing his therapist and himself that he was ready for the upcoming tests.

Jessica greeted him with her usual no-nonsense smile. "Last day, Kane. Let's make it count."

He went through the familiar routine of stretches and exercises, pushing himself hard. At the end of ninety minutes, he was drenched in sweat, muscles burning, but he felt stronger than he had in months.

"Very good," Jessica said with an approving nod as she handed him a towel. "I think we're finished, Captain."

"It's almost hard to believe."

"Believe it. Even when you were frustrated with your progress, you never quit. And this is the result."

"I didn't do it alone. We both know you had to kick my grumpy ass more than once."

"I'm used to grumpy asses," she said. "But it's good to see you looking...lighter. I hope that's not just because you're happy to see the last of me."

"It's definitely not that."

"Well, whatever it is, it's good. You have a lot of tests to get through, and a positive mental attitude can only help."

"Hopefully, I can hang on to it." He said goodbye, then headed into the locker room to take a shower.

Thirty minutes later, he was dressed and ready to move on. As he left the locker room and headed toward the lobby, a familiar voice called his name. "Kane?"

He turned around and saw Mike Ramsey, a fellow pilot who had been injured in a different mission three months before his crash. Their recoveries had overlapped for a few weeks before Mike had returned to duty.

"Ramsey," he said, shaking his hand. "What are you doing back here? I thought you'd seen the last of this place a long time ago."

"Mandatory three-month follow-up, but everything is good." Mike's gaze ran across his face. "You look better than the last time I saw you, Kane."

"Final PT session today."

"That's great news. Want to grab a coffee?"

"Sure."

Several minutes later, they took their coffees to a table in the cafeteria. "Are you back with your unit?" he asked Mike.

Mike's expression shifted subtly. "I'm with the 463rd now. Good group, but different."

Hunter understood the sentiment. He knew he'd be reassigned as well. His team had a new leader now, and he would likely be assigned to a different unit. After years of forging unbreakable bonds through countless missions and shared dangers, he'd be starting over with people he didn't know and would have to learn how to trust.

Mike took a sip of his coffee, then added, "I couldn't wait to get back to duty, but when I did, it felt strange. Physically, I was fine. But I'm not the same person I was. I don't know if that's a good thing or a bad thing."

Hunter was surprised by his admission. Most soldiers who returned to duty proclaimed to be even better than they were before.

"Don't get me wrong," Mike continued. "I'm very good at my job. I make mission decisions with no hesitation, no weakness. But my outlook is different than it was. I can't really explain it."

"You don't have to explain it. I get it. You can't go through what we've both gone through without being changed in some irrevocable way. But maybe we are better for having to fight for survival...not just our lives but also our careers."

"I'd like to think so." Mike paused. "It was even worse for you because you lost Gary. He was one of a kind, wasn't he? Courageous, sometimes reckless, always friendly, and man, could he talk about nothing and make it sound like something."

He smiled, thinking about Olivia. "His daughter is a lot like him."

"That's right. He had a kid. How's she doing?"

"She's hanging in there."

"And Gary's wife?"

"Bree is having a hard time," he said, not wanting to get into the particulars. Not that he knew the particulars since he hadn't spoken to Bree since she'd left. She'd refused to return any of his calls or answer his texts.

"That's rough. So, when's your medical evaluation?" Mike asked.

"Wednesday is the physical. Psych evaluation next Monday."

Mike nodded. "The physical part's easy. It's the head stuff that's tricky." He paused, taking another sip of coffee. "Have you ever considered not going back?"

"No. Did you?"

Mike shook his head. "I'm not trained for anything else."

"I feel the same way."

"I figured. We're cut from the same cloth, both lifers."

For some reason, the word *lifers* bothered him, even though he'd always thought of himself that way. He'd gone into the military with the idea that it would be his career, just like his dad and his brother. But it could be a rootless life and somewhat insular, and he was starting to realize how good it felt to have a group of friends from different walks of life.

This past weekend, he'd spent time with Liam, a former professional surfer. He'd talked to Paige about her nursing job and learned that Lexie had given up a high-powered attorney job to become a freelance photographer, something she loved doing even if it didn't make the same amount of money.

He'd also realized how often he judged people on one or two characteristics that didn't define them at all, like Emmalyn, who had so many layers underneath her sweet smile that he couldn't wait to keep unraveling them.

"Anyway," Mike said, interrupting his thoughts. "I gotta run. If you ever need to talk to someone who gets what you're going through, I'm around. Give me a call. We can get a real drink."

"Thanks," he said, but he knew he wouldn't call Mike. He needed to get through these challenges on his own, not because he was refusing help, although it was partly that. But it was because no one else could make him feel ready. He had to do that himself.

However, he could find comfort in the fact that Mike had returned to duty. It wasn't impossible, but Mike's injuries had not been as extensive as his, nor had the circumstances of his crash, which had occurred on a training exercise due to technical issues. His helicopter had been shot out of the sky and his best friend had died. He'd been lucky to survive. Now he had to make sure he didn't waste that luck.

———

Monday afternoon, Emmalyn drove to La Jolla after school got out. She'd texted with her aunt and knew her mother had gone to the medical appointment Linda had made for her and had done some tests, but she didn't know any of the results yet.

On the way to the house, she stopped to pick up flowers and a dark chocolate bar that she remembered being one of her mom's favorites. She had no idea if she even ate chocolate anymore because sweets had been restricted at the farm. But she wanted to do something to make her feel special. Her mom was in such a fragile state; it was hard to drum up the anger she'd once felt toward her. Now it was pity and sadness for so many wasted years.

When she arrived, her aunt answered the door, giving her a smile that looked a lot brighter than it had yesterday.

"Emmalyn, I'm glad you came."

As she stepped inside, her mother got up from the couch and came over to see her. She was wearing a pair of jeans and a sweater, looking more normal than she had in years. She was still very pale with dark circles under her eyes, but her hair had been washed and somewhat styled, and her aunt had clearly lent her mother some makeup.

She held out the flowers. "These are for you."

Surprise and joy spread across her mom's face. "They're so pretty."

"Why don't I put those in a vase?" her aunt suggested, taking the flowers from her hand.

She reached into her bag as her aunt took the flowers into the kitchen. Smiling at her mom, she said, "I also got you this candy bar. I remember sharing one with you a long time ago. I think you said it was your favorite. I hope my memory is right."

Her mother's lips trembled as she took the candy bar and stared at it. "I don't think I've had one since then. You were probably four or five."

"Maybe we can share it again. Chocolate is my weakness."

"It was once mine. But it's been so long, I barely remember what chocolate tastes like. Maybe a little later. I just had a snack."

"Of course."

"Why don't we all sit down?" her aunt suggested as she returned to the room with the flowers in a vase.

Taking the seat on the couch next to her mother, she said, "What did the doctor have to say?"

"She thinks my thyroid could be low," her mother said. "And I might possibly have an autoimmune disease, but they won't know until they get my tests back. They took a lot of blood."

"They want her to rest and improve her nutrition until we know what else might be going on," her aunt added.

"Well, I'm glad they're going to do a thorough review." She hoped whatever was ailing her mother was something that could be managed with medications and lifestyle changes.

"It felt so odd to be in a doctor's office again," her mom said. "I haven't talked to a doctor since I moved to the farm. That was so long ago..." Her voice trailed away.

Emmalyn jumped into the silence. "You can't look back, Mom. I know it won't be easy, but your health, your life, could depend on it. And I want you to have a full and long life, one I can be a part of."

She was a little surprised at the words that came out of her mouth. Her mother also looked at her in shock.

"You do, Emmy? After I let you go?"

"Well, I can't lie and say I don't have mixed emotions about us, but I am grateful you let me go because I got away from

Haven, from people who weren't going to give me a chance to grow up, to be educated, to be free."

"I thought Haven would give us the family we needed. We wouldn't be alone anymore, and you would have other kids to play with. Some of that came true."

"There were other kids there, but we had little time to play. I missed out on so much in the seven years I was there. I found out how much when I went to live with Aunt Linda, and I saw how the rest of the world lived. Do you know how far behind I was in school? I had to work so hard just to catch up."

"I tried to teach you some things."

"I know you did, but it wasn't enough." She took a breath. "But like I said, I don't want to keep rehashing the past. I'm happy you're here."

"It does feel nice to be in this beautiful home with a view of the ocean and wearing clothes that are soft and comfortable," her mother admitted. "I've been unhappy for longer than I've been willing to admit, even to myself. I figured that was my penance for missing my chance to leave when Linda first came to get us."

"You're here now, Sara," Linda cut in. "That's what matters. We're going to get to the bottom of your health issues and make things right. You still have a lot of life to live."

"I'm not sure I deserve it."

"You deserve it," she said. "We all have things to work through, but we can only do that if you stay the course. I don't want you to get some medicine and then go back to Haven. What we're doing for you can't be for nothing. If you leave, if you walk away from us again, it's going to feel like the worst kind of betrayal, and it will hurt so much." Her eyes blurred with tears as she could still feel the emotion of the last time her mother had turned her back on her. "Please don't do that to either of us."

Her mother stared at her with painful emotion. Then she

said, "I won't go back. I won't hurt you again, Emmy." She turned to her sister. "Or you, Linda."

For the first time in years, she felt a glimmer of hope that perhaps she could find a way to have a relationship with her mother. But she also knew that her mom was a weak person who didn't always keep her promises, so only time would tell.

CHAPTER THIRTEEN

Time moved both incredibly slow and incredibly fast with a six-year-old, Hunter thought as he fed Olivia spaghetti for dinner Monday night and tried to engage her in conversation. Since he'd picked her up at three o'clock, she'd been up and down in her mood, complaining one minute, laughing the next. He'd taken her for a walk on the beach and thrown a beach ball around with her, which had been fun for a while, but as soon as they'd returned to the apartment, she'd started asking him when her mom was coming back. The only thing that had distracted her was the show he put on the television. Maybe it was bad to put her in front of the TV, but there was only so much he could say when she asked about her mom.

Now, he still had the evening to get through, and he had to tackle homework in the next hour, too. He'd put that off because she'd been in such a bad mood, but he couldn't let her go to school tomorrow without doing the spelling words and very easy math problems she'd brought home.

A knock at his door brought a wave of relief. He'd once dreaded the friendly knocks from neighbors wanting to invite him to things. Now, he was ridiculously happy about the interruption. He was even happier when he saw Emmalyn on his doorstep.

His stomach clenched at the sight of her pretty eyes and warm smile. She got more attractive every time he saw her. He'd missed her today, too, which was ridiculous since they'd spent most of the weekend together. He should have been relieved to have a break, but he wasn't.

"Oh, you're eating," Emmalyn said as she came into the apartment and saw Olivia at the table.

"We're pretty much done," he said.

"Hi, Olivia," Emmalyn said.

He was surprised to see Olivia barely mutter hello and then start playing with her fork again. If even Emmalyn was getting the silent treatment, he was in big trouble.

She gave him a questioning glance.

"I think Liv is having a bad day," he said quietly.

"Well, we all have bad days." Emmalyn moved to the table and sat down in the chair next to Olivia. "Want to talk about what's bothering you, Liv?"

He'd asked Olivia to talk about what was bothering her at least ten times, so he didn't think Emmalyn would get an answer. To his shock, Olivia suddenly burst into tears, words pouring out of her.

"I have to draw my family for homework," Olivia sobbed, getting out of her chair to press herself into Emmalyn's arms.

"Okay," Emmalyn said as she hugged her. "What's the problem?"

"I don't have a family anymore. My daddy is gone and so is my mom. But if I don't do it, I'm not going to get a star," she added, sobbing and hiccupping in between her words.

He felt a stabbing pain at her words. He'd had no idea that was what was bothering her, but it made perfect sense. No wonder she'd been sad all day. She'd been reminded of everyone she'd lost.

"Oh, sweetie," Emmalyn said in a soothing voice. "It's going to be okay. You can still draw your family."

"But they're not here."

Emmalyn put her hand on Olivia's chest as she gazed into her eyes. "They're here in your heart. And it's not just your mom and dad who are your family. You can draw your grandparents."

"Mommy said Nonna and Papa can't take care of me anymore. They're gone, too."

He drew in a sharp breath, his heart aching for her.

"Well, family is not just about parents and grandparents; it's about people who love you, who take care of you." Emmalyn tilted Olivia's chin up, gazing into her eyes. "And you get to choose who else you want to be in your family."

"I can choose?" Olivia asked, her eyes wide.

"Absolutely. Some families are born, and some families are found. Like when I moved here to Ocean Shores, I found a new family in my friends: Lexie, Kaia, Paige, Josie...everyone who lives here."

"So, they could all be my family, too?" Olivia asked. "What about you and Hunter?"

"We can absolutely be your family," Emmalyn replied, her gaze moving to him.

"I am so glad you're here with me, Liv, that your mom brought you to stay with me. I was really sad when your dad died, and I think your mom must have known that. She knew I needed some company. I needed a sweet, smart little girl like you to be in my family, just like your dad was."

"I guess I could draw everyone," Olivia said.

"That would make a great picture," Emmalyn told her.

"And I can put Daddy in it, even though he's in heaven?"

"Your dad should be right at the front," he said as Olivia's gaze sought his.

"Okay. Can I do it now? Can I be done eating?"

"Sure. Do you need paper?"

"I got some at school. It's in my backpack."

As she ran into the bedroom in a much-improved mood, he gave Emmalyn a grateful smile. "You're like a magician. You can turn tears into smiles."

"Maybe with six-year-olds." She gave him a compassionate smile. "It sounds like you two had a rough afternoon."

"She wouldn't talk to me. She did mention she was missing her mom, but since I couldn't give her any answers on when her mom would be back, she stopped talking about that, too. I didn't know how to get her to open up. But you said one thing, and she spilled her guts."

"I have had some practice," she said. "I'm sure you did your best."

"My best wasn't that good. Her mother should be here," he said quietly.

"Well, sometimes moms aren't always there."

"Speaking of which, how's your mother doing?"

"She went to the doctor and had a lot of tests. They don't have a diagnosis yet, but there seem to be possibilities that are not as serious as others, so I'm hopeful that's the way it will go."

"How is she dealing with being away from her home?"

"She's up and down. She's trying to convince herself she made the right decision, but she's scared, and I think if Jeremy showed up at her door...she'd be tempted to go back. I asked her to promise me that she wouldn't, and she did make me that promise, but..."

"You don't believe her?"

"I want to believe her, but trust has to be earned. Let's just say I'm guardedly optimistic. How did your day go?"

"I finished my last physical therapy session. I also ran into another pilot who had been injured and returned to duty. It was nice to see someone succeed who has gone down the road I'm about to travel."

"That's good. What's the next step?"

"A very detailed physical on Wednesday." He paused. "I need to ask you for a favor."

"Seriously? The man who never needs help wants a favor?"

"Yes. I have to do blood tests at eight a.m., and I'm going to need to leave here by seven thirty that day. I asked Paige, but she said she drops Henry off at daycare at seven thirty, and I don't know if I can get Olivia into that. Is there a chance you could take Olivia to school?"

"Of course. That's barely a favor. I'm going there anyway."

"You'll have to hang with her for a while before school."

"It's fine. I'm happy to do it."

"Thank you. You've already gone above and beyond for me."

"What I've done for you doesn't come close to what you did for me yesterday, Hunter. I might not have gotten my mom away from that market if you hadn't been there."

"I'm glad I could help."

"And I'm happy to help you, too. I like Olivia, and you're doing a good thing here. You're giving her the security and love she needs."

"I want to do right by Olivia. Not only for her, but for Gary and also for Bree. But I can't help Bree if she doesn't come back."

"Hopefully, she will return soon."

Olivia ran back into the room, bringing a piece of blue construction paper to the table. She placed it in front of them. "Is it okay?" she asked.

The drawing was done with the bright, bold strokes of a child's hand. In the center was a building with lots of doors and windows—clearly Ocean Shores—and surrounding it were four figures. A tall man with red hair and black dot freckles stood at the top of the page, surrounded by clouds and a bright sun. Below were three more stick figures: a woman with brown hair, a man with black hair, and a woman with yellow hair.

"That's Daddy," Olivia said, pointing to the figure in the clouds. "He's watching over us from heaven. And that's Mommy. Then you and Emmalyn." She looked at them anxiously. "Is it good?"

His throat tightened as he stared at the simple, heartfelt drawing: Gary watching over the four of them, a makeshift family that somehow made sense in Olivia's eyes.

"It's beautiful, Livvy," Emmalyn said, her voice a little thick. "Thanks for putting me in your family."

"I was going to do everyone, but I ran out of room," Olivia said practically. "Do you like it, Hunter?"

"I love it," he said, impulsively wrapping his arms around her and giving her a hug.

"You're squishing me," she protested.

He laughed, then let her go. "Sorry."

"Can I watch a show now?"

"No. You still have to do your spelling words and your math. Why don't you bring those out here, and we'll do them together?"

"Before you go, Liv, I'm going to say goodnight," Emmalyn said, giving Olivia a hug. "I'll see you tomorrow."

As Olivia went into the bedroom, he walked Emmalyn to the door, opened it, and stepped out onto the landing with her. It was twilight now, the stars just appearing in the sky, the day's temperature starting to cool down. He wished he could spend more time with her. Maybe she felt the same way as she didn't appear to be in a hurry to leave.

"It's a beautiful night," she said.

"It is," he returned, but he was talking about her and not the night.

She flushed under his gaze. "You're staring."

"I know."

"We can't..."

"Can't do what?" he challenged.

"I just want to be friends with you, okay?"

He met her gaze, seeing the same conflicted emotions, the unspoken acknowledgment of the sparks between them. It wasn't okay at all but he couldn't say that, because he couldn't offer an alternative suggestion.

"Goodnight, Hunter," she said when he remained silent. Then she turned and left.

He was really starting to hate watching her walk away from him. But sooner rather than later, he might have to walk away from her, so maybe she was right. Maybe it was better this way.

CHAPTER FOURTEEN

Wednesday morning, Hunter couldn't wait for Emmalyn to show up, not just because he had to get to his physical, and he needed her help to get Olivia ready for school, but because he hadn't seen her in thirty-six hours, and it felt far too long. He'd even hung out with Olivia in the courtyard yesterday evening, watching Olivia and Henry in the pool while Paige took a workout class, in the hopes of seeing Em, but she'd never shown up.

The thought that she might have been on another date didn't sit well, which was ridiculous, since he had no reason to be jealous. And he'd never been a jealous guy. He'd always figured if someone didn't want to be with him, it was better to find out early, but maybe that was because he'd never really cared that deeply about anyone. Not that he cared that deeply about her. He just liked her more than he'd expected.

Even without Emmalyn showing up, he'd enjoyed the previous evening. He'd spent time with Gabe and Max Donovan, who went back and forth between Hollywood and Ocean Shores as he worked on a screenplay for a movie that needed a rewrite to fit a new actor. Talking to a chef and a writer had reminded him of how narrow his worldview had gotten. It had been interesting to learn more about the trials and tribulations they were working past to get a restaurant off the ground and a movie made.

Checking his watch, he realized he needed to get breakfast going. Olivia had told him that her mom always made her pancakes on Wednesday mornings, and he'd decided to give it a shot. He couldn't remember ever making pancakes, but how hard could it be? He had a box of mix, water, and an egg, as well as maple syrup that he'd picked up at the market last night. He could do this.

After mixing the batter as directed, he turned on the skillet, spraying it with some sort of healthy oil. Then he spooned out the batter, watching the first pancake drip into the second. He made a slight adjustment for the third one, but it also ran into the others, making one oddly shaped and way too big pancake, but whatever. He could break them up when they were done.

When it looked like the batter was thickening, he flipped the pancake over and frowned. It was burned on the edges with long brown streaks through the middle of the cake, somehow looking both well-done and raw at the same time.

As he put the large, ugly pancake on a plate, Olivia came into the kitchen. "What's that?" she asked with a disgusted shake of her head. "That doesn't look like Mommy's pancakes."

"I'll make more."

"Can you make them better than that? Why is it just one big one? I like little ones."

"I can do little ones. Why don't you finish getting dressed?"

She gave him a doubtful look, then headed back to the bedroom.

A knock came at the door, so he turned off the stove and moved quickly into the living room to let Emmalyn in.

"Good morning," she said, looking pretty and fresh in a skirt and sleeveless sweater, her hair pulled back in a ponytail, her hazel eyes sparkling. "Do I smell pancakes?"

"Something went wrong," he grumbled.

"Uh-oh," she said, following him to the kitchen.

"I followed the instructions, but I got this." He held up the plate, seeing her bite back a smile.

"That was your first one, right?"

"Yes. I'm not sure I should try for a second. I obviously did something wrong."

"The first pancake always comes out like that, especially if you haven't made pancakes before. The trick is to get the griddle really warm before you start cooking. You put the flame at a low to medium heat level." She turned the flame back on. Then she moved to the fridge and grabbed some butter. "I also like to use a little butter on the pan versus a spray." She dabbed some butter onto the griddle.

"Okay. Should I do the batter now?" he asked.

"Not yet. We're still heating the pan and letting the butter melt so it doesn't burn before the pancakes cook."

"Got it," he said, realizing his mistake was that the oily spray had probably burned, which had given his pancake the weird streak marks.

Em waited another minute, then spooned out the batter into three perfect circular pancakes. "As soon as the pancake fills with little air holes, it's time to flip." A moment later, she flipped them over, and they were a perfect golden brown.

"Amazing."

She laughed. "Your second one would have been better even without my instruction because the griddle would have been at a more even temperature. You can't give up too soon."

"I wasn't going to give up. Quitting isn't really in my nature."

"Mine, either. Mostly because I always want to believe there's a perfect pancake coming, or whatever it is I'm trying to make happen."

"So, pancakes are a metaphor for life," he said with an amused smile.

"And also really delicious, especially with butter and syrup."

As she put her perfect pancakes on the plate, he called

Olivia, who was very excited to see both Emmalyn and the kind of pancakes she was expecting.

"These look yummy," Olivia declared, dousing them in syrup.

He probably should be controlling that, but she was happy, and her sugar high would happen at school, so he wasn't going to worry about that.

"Shall I make the rest?" Emmalyn asked. "Are you going to have some, Hunter?"

"No. I'm fasting for my blood work, but you're welcome to eat."

"I already had breakfast. I'll just cover the batter and put it away."

He felt so domesticated as he watched her moving around his kitchen. With Olivia sitting at the table, he had the strangest thought that this could be his actual life if he wanted it. Not with Olivia, who needed to be with her mother. And probably not with Emmalyn...although, she was a big part of his interest in the picture in his head.

The closing of the refrigerator snapped him out of his reverie. This wasn't his life. He wasn't a family man. He was a pilot, someone who was always taking off and going somewhere else, and he didn't want to worry about who he was leaving behind.

"I've got this," Emmalyn said, "if you want to get going."

He really should get going before he forgot *why* he was going.

"Thanks." He turned to Olivia. "I'll see you after school."

"Okay," she said with her mouth full.

He exchanged a smile with Emmalyn, his gut twisting once more as he found it far too difficult to drag his gaze away from her.

"Is there something else?" she asked, a question in her eyes. "Do you need me to bring Olivia home from school?"

"I'm not sure when I'll be done."

"I'll plan on bringing her back unless you text me otherwise."

"Thanks, Em."

"You're more than welcome. I hope the tests are all good."

"Me, too." But he wasn't thinking about the tests when he left the apartment; he was still thinking about her.

———

Hunter got his focus back as soon as he entered the bustling medical center, which had become his second home the last seven months. While it was a great facility, he really couldn't wait to be done. He checked in at the lab first and did his blood work and other tests. Then he headed upstairs to see his physician. It was after nine when he was ushered into an exam room with Dr. Marquez. He'd seen him a few times during his recovery period, but not for the past three months.

"Captain," Dr. Marquez said, shaking his hand. "You look better than the last time I saw you."

"I'm back to normal," he said confidently.

"How's the leg? Any pain, weakness, issues with your lower back or hip?"

"No pain, no weakness, no problems at all."

"Glad to hear it. I'm going to run you through a variety of tests to see if your body is as strong as your confidence," Marquez said with a smile.

"It is. I've been working hard for a long time. I'm ready."

"I can see that, Captain." He paused. "I know you have a lot to prove and feel your entire career is on the line."

"It *is* on the line. That's not a feeling; that's a fact," he pointed out.

"I understand the stakes, and I want you to succeed as much as you want to succeed. So don't look at anything we're doing as adversarial. We're on the same team."

"I understand."

"Then let's get started."

The next three hours were challenging. He ran on a treadmill with electrodes attached to his chest, monitoring his heart rate and oxygen levels for both sprints and long-distance running. He did flexibility tests that pushed the limits of his recovered muscles, reaction time assessments that measured his responses down to the millisecond, and a battery of vision and hearing checks that were more comprehensive than any standard physical.

By the end, he was sweating and tired but still confident. His body had responded well to every challenge. The months of physical therapy had paid off; he was in peak condition, perhaps even better than before the crash in some areas.

He was told to grab lunch and report back to Dr. Marquez at three, where he would go over his results. He'd hoped to move straight through to that meeting, but apparently, the blood work wouldn't be back before then. Knowing he wouldn't be able to pick up Olivia, he texted Emmalyn and confirmed that he needed her to bring Olivia home. Then he headed to the cafeteria and grabbed a chicken Caesar salad and a bottle of sparkling water.

A few minutes later, he got a text from Emmalyn. *No problem. How's the day going?*

He texted back: *Good. Just waiting for the results. Can't see the doctor until three.*

No problem. We should celebrate tonight.

We'll see. He was confident, but he needed to get the official results before he could even think of celebrating.

I'm going to keep positive thoughts.

He appreciated her supportive text. He could use all the positivity he could get.

When he reported back to Dr. Marquez at three p.m., he had to wait another excruciating twenty minutes before he was invited into his office to review the results.

"I'm impressed," the doctor said, giving him a smile. "Your recovery has been exceptional, Captain." He looked at the computer screen on his desk. "Blood work is perfect. Cardiovascular and lung function are excellent, flexibility is within optimal parameters, strength and reaction times are slightly above your last pre-injury exam."

"So I passed?" he asked, still needing to hear the words.

"Yes."

He stood up and shook the doctor's hand. "I appreciate all the help I got here from you and your team. I wouldn't be feeling as good as I am without the excellent medical care I received."

"You're very welcome," Marquez replied. "And I hope I never see you here again."

"I hope the same thing."

As he walked out of the medical center into the bright afternoon sunlight, he drew in a deep breath and let it out, feeling a tremendous amount of relief. One hurdle cleared.

He pulled out his phone and texted Emmalyn: *Physically cleared.*

Her response came almost immediately: *So happy! Olivia and I are going to swim with Henry and Paige if that's okay with you.*

Absolutely!

See you soon.

The simple message gave him far too much pleasure, and he had to remind himself that Ocean Shores wasn't his long-term home, and that Emmalyn and Olivia weren't his family.

CHAPTER FIFTEEN

Hunter jumped into the pool around four thirty with a big splash that delighted Olivia and sprayed Emmalyn with cool water that she laughingly wiped out of her eyes as he came to the surface.

"Nice," she said dryly.

"Sorry. I needed to let off some steam."

"I'll bet. Long day but a good ending."

"A very good ending," he agreed.

She was happy to see the sparkle of happy relief in his dark-brown eyes. He swam over to Olivia and Henry and picked each one up and tossed them across the pool as they screamed with delight.

"Hunter is actually astonishingly good with children," Paige said. "Considering how he used to be before Olivia arrived, I would never have guessed."

"He looks so much lighter now," she said.

"He's finally healthy again, not just physically but emotional-ly," Paige commented.

"I'm so glad to see it."

"You're getting invested in him."

"More than I want to be," she admitted, pausing as Ben got into the pool. "Hi, Ben."

"Ladies," he said, then dunked his head under the water. "I needed that. Hot day today."

"Were you working?" Paige asked.

"Yes, since about four o'clock this morning."

"That's a long shift," she said.

"We finally broke open a long-running investigation, so it was worth it. Who's interested in a game of pool volleyball?" he asked.

"I'd go for that," Paige said.

"Emmalyn?"

"You two should play."

"Let's get a fourth," Ben said. "Hunter, we need another player."

"I'm there," Hunter said as Henry and Olivia moved into the shallow end and grabbed their boats from the edge of the pool. Hunter gave her a smile. "Are we partners, Em?"

"I'm probably the worst one. Paige played volleyball in high school."

"Well, I would still pick you first," he said with a laugh.

Ben drew a net across the deeper end of the pool, and the game was on.

She and Hunter clashed a few times as they went after the same ball, and one time, she nearly slipped underwater when their arms collided. His hand shot out to steady her, gripping her waist, the heat of his palm searing on her bare stomach. Her breath caught as she looked up, finding his dark eyes locked on hers.

"You okay?" he asked, his voice low enough that only she could hear it.

"Fine," she managed, very aware of his fingers still at her waist, of how close they were standing. "Just clumsy."

"I've got you." Something in his expression made her believe he was talking about more than just keeping her from falling.

"Hey, Hunter!" Ben called from across the net. "Ball's coming your way!"

Hunter released her instantly, both of them turning to see the beach ball arcing toward their side of the net. Hunter lunged, sending it back with far more force than necessary, straight at Ben's face, but Ben made a quick move, avoiding contact with the ball.

"Competitive much?" Ben laughed.

"Sorry," Hunter replied with a wolfish grin that made something flutter in Emmalyn's stomach.

She'd never seen Hunter like this—playful, relaxed, yet with that underlying intensity that seemed hardwired into him. Even in a casual pool game, he approached each volley as if it were a tactical mission, positioning himself strategically, calculating angles, driving them toward victory with a single-minded focus that was both amusing and oddly attractive.

But what struck her most was also how he'd seamlessly integrated Olivia into his life. Between volleys, he'd check on her, making sure she was still happily playing with Henry. No hovering, no constant questions about whether she was okay—just a watchful eye and the occasional encouraging nod when she asked a question or told him something.

"Your serve, Em," Hunter called, tossing her the ball. She caught it, her fingers slipping slightly on the wet surface. "Better make it good," he added with a wink. "We're only up by two."

She took a breath, focusing on Ben's position across the net, and served. The ball sailed over the net in a perfect arc. Ben lunged for it but missed, and the ball hit the water with a satisfying splash.

"Yes!" Hunter's hand shot up for a high five, and she met it, laughing at his enthusiasm. His fingers lingered against hers for a heartbeat longer than necessary, and the same electric awareness she'd felt earlier sparked between them.

"You two are lethal together," Paige observed from across the net, her expression speculative.

"Hunter doesn't know how to lose," Emmalyn said,

attempting to deflect attention from whatever was happening between them.

"Is that a problem?" Hunter asked, his gaze suddenly intense on her face.

"No," she replied honestly. "It's actually kind of—" She stopped herself before saying *sexy*.

"Kind of what?" he pressed, moving slightly closer.

"Impressive," she finished, feeling heat rise to her cheeks that had nothing to do with the warm evening air. "But we haven't won yet." She turned her attention back to Ben, who served the next ball.

The game continued, but something had shifted between them. She found herself hyperaware of Hunter's movements, of the water droplets trailing down his tanned shoulders, of the way his muscles flexed when he reached for the ball. Several times, their eyes met across the small distance, and she had to force herself to remember they were in the middle of a game, with friends watching.

They'd agreed to end the game with the first to fifteen and finally they were up fourteen to thirteen. "Let's finish this," Hunter said as he served the ball.

The next volley battle that followed was fierce. Ben and Paige were just as competitive as Hunter was. She was probably the one who cared the least about winning, but she got caught up in Hunter's excitement and found herself playing with an intensity she had never experienced before.

As the ball lofted over the net, Hunter called, "I got it," but she was going for it, too, and couldn't stop herself. They collided and the force of their collision sent them both underwater.

She came up sputtering, finding herself practically in Hunter's arms. His hands were at her waist again, steadying her, his face inches from hers. For a suspended moment, the rest of the world faded away—the sounds of splashing, of Olivia and Henry playing, of Ben and Paige laughing... All she could focus on was Hunter's dark eyes and the sensation of his hands on her body.

"Did it go over?" she asked breathlessly.

He smiled. "I don't know."

"It went over," Ben said with a grumpy scowl as he and Paige came under the net to congratulate them. "I still don't know who actually hit it, though."

"Doesn't matter. We won," Hunter said.

Paige laughed. "You are cutthroat, Hunter. And Emmalyn, you are no better. I didn't think you were that into beach ball volleyball."

"I didn't think I was, either," she admitted. "I got carried away."

"Yeah, I could see that," Paige said with a knowing smile as she moved toward the kids.

Ben jumped out of the pool and checked his phone. "Looks like our Chinese food delivery is almost here. I'll meet the driver." He threw a towel around his shoulders and walked toward the parking lot.

"Time to get out," Paige told Henry and Olivia. "We need to dry off so we can eat."

"Can we have five more minutes?" Henry begged.

"Two minutes," Paige negotiated as she got out of the pool.

"Same for you, Liv," Hunter said as he moved toward the steps.

Emmalyn swam to the ladder and got out. She reached for her towel on a nearby chair, and as she turned to wrap it around her, she ran into Hunter again, this time with no water to buffer the contact. His chest pressed against hers for a brief moment, both of them still wet, her towel caught between them.

"We have to stop meeting like this," he said, his voice a low rumble that she could feel as much as hear, his sexy smile sending a tingle down her spine.

She gave a nervous laugh, taking a step back. "Sorry, I didn't see you."

"I'm not complaining." He reached out to tuck a strand of wet hair behind her ear. "You look fantastic in that bikini by the way."

She blushed. "Uh, thanks."

"Hunter! Look what I can do!" Olivia called, having climbed out of the pool. She was attempting to wrap her towel around herself like a cape.

The moment shattered, and Hunter stepped away. But the look he gave Emmalyn before turning to help Olivia conveyed everything unsaid between them—the attraction, the tension, the possibility... Whatever they had going on, it was no longer just friendship. She just didn't know what it was.

CHAPTER SIXTEEN

Thursday and Friday felt endlessly long for Hunter. While he got in a run each morning followed by weights and stretching, he had too many hours to fill while Olivia was at school, and he looked forward each day to picking her up. But she wasn't really the distraction he wanted most—that was Emmalyn.

After their pool volleyball game Wednesday night, which had amped up the chemistry between them, she'd backed away. She'd told him she had to get to school early the next day and stay late the following two days because she was working on the book fair and ice cream social scheduled for Friday afternoon.

He was sure that was true, but he was equally sure she was trying to avoid him. She'd been just as aware of him as he'd been of her, and she clearly didn't know what to do about it. He didn't know what to do about it, either, but he still wanted to see her. They'd spent so much time together the past week, he actually missed her, and that was an unusual feeling.

But now that Friday afternoon had arrived, she wouldn't be able to avoid him any longer, because he'd promised to take Olivia to the book fair when he picked her up from school.

When school ended, he met up with Olivia in the playground, where she was eager to hand him her backpack and lunchbox. They walked out to his car so he could put them away, then headed toward the library, where the book fair was being held.

Olivia grabbed his hand and pulled him through the hallways with determined strides, telling him they had to get to the auditorium before all the good books were gone. When they arrived at the auditorium, the room had been transformed into a bookstore, with colorful displays and tables throughout the space. A banner hung over the entrance: "Fall Into Reading Book Fair."

"There's Henry," Olivia announced, pulling him across the room.

"Hey, Hunter," Paige said. "Ready to spend all your money?"

"Apparently," he replied as Olivia and Henry started grabbing books off the table. "I've been informed that unicorn books are absolutely essential."

"Henry's the same way with dinosaurs," Paige said with a laugh. "This place is dangerous."

"Have you seen Emmalyn?" he asked, trying to sound casual.

"She's doing a read-along in her classroom in fifteen minutes. I told Henry he could pick out three books before then."

"That sounds like a good plan," he said. "Olivia, do you want to go to Emmalyn's read-along?"

Olivia nodded vigorously. "Can we buy books first?"

"Sure," he said as he took the books from her arms and headed toward the nearest volunteer, who was swiping credit cards on a mobile device. After that, they joined Paige and Henry and made their way to Emmalyn's classroom, joining a stream of children and parents heading in the same direction.

Emmalyn's classroom was exactly as he would have expected —bright, colorful, and organized, but also with the controlled chaos that seemed to define her. Children's artwork covered the walls, alphabet letters strung across the ceiling, and a reading corner was set up with pillows and a small child-size sofa. In the center of the room, a rocking chair sat on a colorful rug surrounded by small chairs and cushions.

And there was Emmalyn, greeting children as they entered, her face lighting up with genuine warmth for each one. She wore a blue dress with tiny yellow sunflowers printed on it, her hair pulled back in a loose braid. She looked completely in her element, confident and radiant in a way he hadn't seen before.

Their eyes met across the room, and her smile faltered slightly before recovering. She gave him a small wave, then turned to help a child find a seat.

"Let's sit there," Olivia said, pointing to a spot near the front.

Hunter followed her, feeling awkwardly large among the tiny chairs and tables. As Olivia and Henry sat on the carpet together, he ended up sitting cross-legged on the floor behind the circle of children, with Paige sitting next to another mother a few feet away.

"Hello, everyone!" Emmalyn called, clapping her hands to get the children's attention. "I'm so happy to see so many of your smiling faces." She moved to the rocking chair in the center, gathering the children closer. "Today, we're going on an adventure with one of my favorite books. It's called *The Gruffalo*, and it's about a grumpy buffalo. Has anyone heard this story before?"

Several hands shot up, including Olivia's.

"Wonderful! Then you can help me tell it," Emmalyn said. She opened the book, revealing colorful illustrations of a forest scene. "Deep in the woods, a little mouse took a stroll..."

As she read, Hunter found himself captivated, not just by the story but by Emmalyn herself. She changed her voice for each character, her expressions animated and engaging. The children were enthralled, leaning forward to see the pictures, gasping at the right moments, laughing at others. She had them participating, repeating key phrases, predicting what might happen next.

This was a side of Emmalyn he hadn't seen—the consummate professional, completely assured in her role, expertly managing a room full of excitable children with joy and ease.

Watching her with these kids, he could see why she'd chosen teaching. She was a natural.

After finishing *The Gruffalo*, she read a second book about magic, followed by a story that had the children repeating animal noises. By the end, even the most fidgety children were engaged, hanging on her every word.

"And that's our story time for today!" Emmalyn announced after the third book. "I hope you all find some wonderful books to take home. Remember, reading takes you on adventures every day!"

As the children dispersed, many stopping to give her hugs before leaving, Emmalyn's gaze found his again. This time, her smile seemed more genuine but still a little guarded.

"That was amazing," he said, standing up as she approached. "You're incredible with them."

"It's my job," she replied modestly, but there was a gleam of pride in her eyes.

"Emmalyn!" Olivia exclaimed, throwing her arms around her. "I've missed you!"

"I've missed you too, sweetie," Emmalyn said, returning the hug.

"Hunter bought me all these books!" She gestured to the stack he was still carrying.

"I see that." Emmalyn laughed. "You're going to be very busy reading!"

"Nice job, Emmalyn," Paige interrupted. "You are so good at keeping the kids engaged."

"Thanks."

"Can Olivia join us at the playground for a bit?" Paige asked him. "The kids want to play before the ice cream social starts."

"Please?" Olivia begged, looking up at Hunter.

"Go ahead," he said. "I'll be right out."

As the children left with Paige, Hunter found himself alone with Emmalyn for the first time since Wednesday night. The classroom suddenly felt much smaller.

"How's it going?" she asked as she put away the books she'd just read. "Everything okay with Olivia? Have you heard from her mother?"

"Olivia is good. We're finding our rhythm. Haven't heard from Bree, which is disturbing. But she has to come back sometime, right?"

"I'm the wrong person to ask that question."

"How is your mom? Have you been spending time with her?"

"No. I've been busy getting set up for the book fair. I know she's still doing some tests, but she's hanging in there. My aunt says she's eating and sleeping better, so it's going well so far. We still need a diagnosis. Hopefully, that will come soon."

"I'm glad things are going well."

"Me too. It's still weird, though. Having her back in my life after so long." She met his eyes. "Life can change so quickly, in both bad ways and good ways."

"That's true. I certainly never expected to be taking care of a six-year-old, that's for sure."

"Olivia adores you, Hunter. You know that, right?"

"I'm not sure she adores me, but she seems to tolerate me."

"Her feelings are much stronger than that."

"I hope that's true," he said as their gazes clung together. "What about your feelings?"

She sucked in a quick breath. "I don't know what you're asking me."

"Yes, you do." He took a step closer to her, the tension building between them. "There's something happening between us. I know you can feel it."

"Maybe I do like you more than I thought I would. But you're leaving, so what's the point?" she challenged. "You're going back to your life, and I'm staying here in mine."

He couldn't argue with her logic, but he wanted to. He also wanted to touch her, to taste her sweet lips, to feel her mouth under his.

She must have read his mind because her eyes widened and

her lips parted. Before he could second-guess himself, he reached out to brush a strand of hair from her face, his fingers lingering against her cheek.

"Hunter," she whispered, half warning, half plea.

He decided to only answer the plea and not the warning. He leaned down and captured her lips with his. The kiss was tentative at first, a question, but when she responded by sliding her hands up to his shoulders, it quickly deepened into something urgent and electric.

He backed her against the bookshelf, one hand cradling her face, the other at her waist, pulling her closer. She tasted like coffee and cinnamon and something uniquely her that made his head spin. All the tension that had been building between them —in the pool, during quiet moments at dinner, across crowded rooms—crystallized into this single point of contact, this kiss that felt both inevitable and surprising.

When they finally broke apart, both breathless, he rested his forehead against hers, unwilling to move away completely. "Whatever this is—it's damn good," he murmured.

"That's the problem," she said, her cheeks flushed, her voice breathless.

"Maybe it's not a problem."

Before she could respond, the classroom door swung open.

"Emmalyn, the ice cream social—" The woman who'd entered stopped talking as she took in the scene. "Oh! Sorry. I didn't mean to interrupt. I was just going to ask if you could help with the ice cream."

"I'll be right there," Emmalyn said, stepping away from him.

The other woman disappeared as quickly as she'd come.

"I have to go," she told him.

"I understand, but this isn't over, Em."

"It should be, Hunter. Not just for me, but also for you. You don't need any more complications in your life, do you?"

He didn't know how to answer that, but it didn't matter because she was already out the door. As he stood alone in her classroom, surrounded by children's artwork and alphabet letters, the taste of her still on his lips, he wondered how he was supposed to walk away from someone who was so wrong but felt so right...

———

After helping to clean up after the ice cream social, Emmalyn finally headed home around seven thirty Friday night. It had been a long day, and she was exhausted. Despite her weariness, her nerves still tingled from her unexpected make-out session with Hunter. She still couldn't quite believe it had happened.

She'd wanted to kiss him for a while, but she'd been trying to make the *just friends* tag ring true. That had gone out the window with one staggeringly good kiss, and she really wanted to kiss him again, just to make sure she hadn't imagined how great it was. But that would take them further down the wrong path, and she really shouldn't go there. Getting further involved would only make saying goodbye more difficult, and she didn't want to get her heart broken. She didn't want to care about someone who had already told her he was going to choose a different life.

It wasn't anything close to the same thing as what had happened with her mother, but some of the worrying emotions felt familiar. She needed to date people who were going to stay in this town that she loved and be part of her friend group and her life. People like Steven, except she hadn't felt any heat with Steven, and she hadn't even thought about him since she'd texted him the day after their date and gently told him she wasn't interested in dating him.

Maybe if she'd met Steven before Hunter's personality had done a 360, it would have been different. She would have thought Steven was nice and they had a lot in common. But that's not the way it had gone down. She'd been intrigued and captivated by Hunter ever since Olivia had arrived, and the more she got to know him, the more she liked him.

He'd supported her on a difficult day with her mother, and he'd listened to her story about her past without judgment. He'd also turned out to be more fun than she'd ever imagined and a good father figure, too. This man, who had finally returned to the world, had a lot going for him. But the fact that he was better now was also the reason she'd be losing him.

But not yet, she told herself, and as she walked into the courtyard and heard voices, she couldn't help hoping Hunter was part of whatever was happening. Her heart sped up as she saw Hunter, Paige, and Ben sitting at a table while Henry and Olivia were sitting on the ground by the pool playing with Henry's dinosaurs.

Ava and Liam were at another table with Gabe and Madison while Frank Wickham was doing laps in the pool and Maggie and Josie were sitting on loungers, sipping glasses of wine.

"Emmalyn," Paige said, waving her over. "Frank bought pizza." She pointed to the large pizza box on the table. "There are still a few pieces left. Are you hungry?"

"I actually had pizza at the school. One of the PTA moms brought it in as we were doing inventory for the book fair."

"Was it a successful event?" Paige asked.

"It was. Looks like sales exceeded last year, and we ended up with only a few books that weren't bought, so they'll go in the library."

"You must be tired," Hunter commented, his warm gaze on her face.

"I am, but it was a good day for the school and the kids, so worth it."

"At least sit down and have some wine," Paige said, lifting the bottle of wine in front of her. "I'm betting you could use a drink."

"I wouldn't mind a glass," she admitted.

"Have a seat," Hunter said, pushing out the empty chair between him and Ben.

"Thanks." She gave Ben a smile as she sat down, thinking he

was a good-looking guy, too, and very single. Maybe she should get to know him instead of Hunter. Ben had recently moved into Ocean Shores, and he loved it. His sister lived in the building, too, so Ben would probably be staying. But despite his attractive features, she didn't feel anything for Ben, but that was probably because Hunter was sitting on her other side. Hunter was now laughing at something Paige had said, and the sound of that laugh instantly made her turn her head.

He gave her a smile, his gaze darkening as he took her in, an intimate look in his eyes that told her he was remembering their earlier kiss. Her breath quickened, and she forced herself to look away. Turning to Ben, she asked him how his day was.

"It was quiet, which is never a bad thing in my line of work," Ben replied.

"Has it been an adjustment, joining a new department?"

"Not bad. Everyone is friendly. It's definitely a more chill environment, which I was ready for."

Kaia had mentioned Ben had gone through some rough stuff in LA, but she hadn't elaborated, and Ben didn't seem interested in going into more detail.

"Hunter, my dinosaur broke, can you fix it?" Olivia interrupted as she came over with a dinosaur made of blocks, two of which seemed stuck together, making the dinosaur lopsided and unable to stand upright.

"Let me look," Hunter said.

She smiled to herself as he worked on the dinosaur with the same intensity he seemed to bring to every part of his life. He was the kind of man who wanted to do everything well. When he'd fixed the dinosaur, he got up and walked with Olivia to where Henry was playing while Paige excused herself, having gotten a phone call.

"And then there were two," Ben said lightly, clinking his glass to hers. "I actually wanted to speak to you, Emmalyn. I saw a guy outside your apartment earlier today. I asked him what he was doing there, and he said he was looking for you."

Her body stiffened. "What did you say?"

"Nothing. I told him I didn't know who you were."

"What did he look like?"

"Older, fifties probably, gray hair, weathered skin. He had a lean, rough look to him. Does that ring a bell?"

"Unfortunately, it does," she murmured, her gut clenching at the thought of Jeremy coming to her home.

"Are you in trouble, Emmalyn?" he asked, his gaze direct and pointed.

"I shouldn't be, but maybe."

"You don't have to tell me, but I'd be happy to help if I can."

Since they were currently alone at the table, she gave him the short version. "My mother recently left a very controlling group of people...a cult, you might say. One of the men saw me taking her away, and I think Jeremy probably tracked me down because he wants to find her.

Ben had a neutral expression on his face, not reacting at all to the emotional part of her statement. Instead, he said, "Does this cult have a name?"

"They go by Haven. The group lives on a farm in a remote area in the hills of north San Diego."

"And what's Jeremy's last name?"

She thought for a moment. "I think it's Warren, but I'm not sure that's his real name. The group has been living off the grid for years. The leader calls himself Elias Ray, but again, I don't know if that's his given name."

"Do you know if they're involved in any illegal activities?"

"No, but I wouldn't be surprised if they were. The men often disappear for days at a time. Who knows where they go." She paused. "I left the group when I was twelve, but my mother stayed until last weekend." She drew in a breath and added, "And no one here knows anything about that, so..."

"Don't worry. I won't say anything. But I'm concerned about this man tracking you down."

"I guess I wasn't that hard to find."

"Would your mom be willing to talk to me about them? If they are involved in criminal activity, I might be able to use that to make sure this man doesn't bother either of you again."

"She's fragile right now. It was hard for her to leave. I'm still afraid she might go back. I don't think she'll tell you anything about them, and I don't really want to ask her. I need to handle this myself."

"I'll do a little research on the group. In the meantime, I would keep your door locked and be very aware of your surroundings wherever you go. Do you have my number?"

"I have it from the group chat."

"Good. If this guy bothers you in any way, call 911, then call me."

At his words, a chill ran down her spine. She didn't want a confrontation with Jeremy, but Ben was right; she needed to be ready. Jeremy probably would return. "I'll do that if he shows up again. And I appreciate your help."

"I'll see what I can find."

Hunter came back to the table, giving her a questioning look as he took in the seriousness of their expressions. "Everything okay?"

"Fine," she said, taking a sip of wine. "Looks like you got the dinosaur fixed."

"He's now able to stand upright and do battle," he said as he sat down again.

"I have to take off," Ben said, pushing back his chair. "See you later."

"Have a good night," she said.

As Ben left, Hunter gave her a pointed look. "Something was going on with you two."

"You're very suspicious."

"I'm right, aren't I?"

"Ben said he ran into a guy outside my apartment, who was looking for me. Based on his description, I think it was Jeremy."

Hunter's lips tightened, and his gaze darkened. "That's not good."

"Ben told him he didn't recognize my name. But I think Jeremy will probably be back."

"I don't think you should be alone tonight."

"I'll be fine."

His frown deepened. "I wish I could stay with you, but—"

"You have Olivia, and I don't know that Jeremy is dangerous. He's probably just going to try to bully my mother's address out of me. That won't happen."

"You don't know if he's dangerous or not. People who live off the grid like him could easily have a weapon and no respect for laws or authority."

"Possibly, but I don't want to work myself up about it. I told Ben about the group, and he's going to look into them, see if they have any history of criminal activity."

"Well, that's good, but that won't solve your immediate problem. Maybe you should go to the house where your aunt and mother are staying."

"If I do that, there's a chance he could follow me there, right? I'll be fine. I have a dead bolt on my door. My windows lock. I'll be safe. If someone starts pounding on my door, I'll call you."

"You better. I mean it, Em. You call me immediately."

She was touched by his concern. "I will. I have Ben's number, too. I feel safe here. I'm not going to let Jeremy ruin that."

"I'm just sorry you have to deal with this."

"Whatever I have to deal with is worth getting my mom away from them."

"That's a generous sentiment considering your relationship with your mom."

"Maybe so, but it's better to forgive than to live in anger and unhappiness. What's the point of that?"

He nodded, a thoughtful expression on his face. "As someone who has been living in anger and unhappiness, I would have to agree that there is no point. But it's not always easy to get out of that state. I might still be there if not for Olivia..." He paused. "And you."

She shivered despite the warm evening air. "I haven't done anything, Hunter."

"You've done more than you think. You were there for me when I didn't deserve it."

"Well, look at you now. You're a changed person. You're part of the group. You're smiling. It's good to see the change in you. And if I had a small part in that, I'm glad."

"Should we talk about what happened in your classroom earlier?"

"No, we shouldn't," she said quickly, taking another sip of her wine. "It was just a moment. It doesn't need discussion."

"Usually, I would agree, but maybe not in this instance. If I need to apologize..."

"You don't. I was okay with it."

"Just okay?" he asked with a small smile.

She couldn't help smiling back at him. "Maybe better than okay. But—"

He groaned. "I really hate that word *but*."

She didn't have a chance to tell him it shouldn't happen again because Olivia suddenly screamed, and they both jumped to their feet.

It took a second for her to realize that Olivia hadn't screamed from fear but delight as she ran toward a slender brunette woman and threw herself into her arms.

Olivia's mother had finally returned.

CHAPTER SEVENTEEN

Hunter stiffened, then moved forward, his profile tense. Emmalyn knew he'd wanted Bree to come back, but she suspected he had a lot of anger toward her and the position she'd left him in. Everyone in the courtyard had gone quiet with Olivia's scream, all eyes on the drama unfolding.

"Mommy, you're holding me too tight," Olivia complained.

Bree eased up on the hug, giving her daughter a teary smile. "Sorry. I'm just so happy to see you." She got to her feet, her gaze moving to Hunter. "I'm back."

"I see that," he said, his voice guarded.

"Mommy, I want you to meet my friends." Olivia grabbed her mom's hand as she pulled her toward the pool. "This is Henry. He goes to my school."

"Hi, Henry," Bree said.

Henry smiled but didn't say anything.

Olivia threw out a bunch more names to her mother as she pointed to various people in the courtyard, then she said more loudly, "Emmalyn," and dragged her mother in her direction. "This is my mommy."

"Hi," she said. "Olivia has told me a lot about you."

Bree gave her an uncertain look. "Hopefully, not all bad."

"Definitely not," she assured her.

"Let's go inside," Hunter interrupted in a sharp, forceful voice that reminded her of the old Hunter. "We need to talk, Bree."

"I know," Bree said, meeting his gaze.

"Emmalyn, are you coming with us?" Olivia asked.

"No, honey. You need to be with your mom. I'll see you later."

Hunter looked back at her. "I meant what I said earlier," he reminded her. "If you need me, call me."

"I'll be fine," she said, watching them walk into Hunter's apartment and shut the door.

It felt a little odd to be on the other side of that door. She'd been in the middle of everything going on, but now she was on the outside. It was where she belonged. None of this was her business, but she couldn't stop caring about Olivia because her mother was back, and the door was closed.

Paige came up to her. "So that's Olivia's mother, huh?"

"Yes."

"Hunter didn't tell me much about where she was. He just said she was grieving her husband and needed some time. Does this mean Olivia is going to leave?" Paige asked. "Henry will be so disappointed. He adores her. They've become best friends."

"I don't know, but things will change." The pretend family life she'd been living with Hunter and Olivia was going to end, and she would miss that.

On the other hand, she and Hunter would no longer have a six-year-old chaperone within earshot...so things might get interesting in a different way.

———

"Still as spartan as ever when it comes to decorating," Bree commented as she gazed around Hunter's apartment, which was actually far more cluttered than it usually was because Olivia had been accumulating more stuff by the day and most of it was spread around his living room.

"Mommy, come see my bedroom!" Olivia tugged her mother's hand, pulling her toward the bedroom. "Hunter got me unicorn sheets, and he put all my drawings on the wall!"

Bree followed her daughter into his bedroom, and he could hear Olivia telling her everything as fast as she could. It was almost as if Olivia wasn't sure her mom would stay long enough to hear all her stories, so she had to get them out fast. He hoped that wasn't the case, because Olivia needed to be with Bree.

He walked toward the bedroom, hovering in the doorway as Olivia showed her mother her family picture, saying that Daddy was looking down from heaven on all of them.

He could see the emotion in Bree's eyes when she realized she was in the picture with Hunter and a woman she'd just met. She shot him a look. "Who exactly is Emmalyn?"

"She's a friend."

"Emmalyn is so nice," Olivia added. "She made pancakes for me just like yours."

Bree gave him another questioning glance, then turned back to Olivia. "Pancakes? Does Emmalyn stay over?"

"She lives upstairs," Olivia said, then grabbed her mom's hand and pulled her back to the bed. "I named my monkey Captain Bananas, after Daddy."

"After Daddy?" Bree asked in confusion.

"Because of the monkey Daddy made friends with," Olivia explained. "Hunter told me all about him."

"Okay," Bree said. "I don't think I heard that story."

"Hunter could tell it to you."

"Why don't you give your mom a chance to catch her breath?" he said. "It's almost bedtime. Get in your PJs and brush your teeth, and then you and your mom can talk before you go to sleep."

"You're not going to leave, are you, Mommy?" Olivia asked,

worry in her eyes, as if she was afraid that if she took her gaze off her mother, she would disappear.

"No, I'll be here after you change," Bree said.

Olivia looked relieved, but he didn't like Bree's answer. She should have said she wasn't going anywhere ever again.

They walked into the living room as Olivia went into the bathroom.

"Is Emmalyn your girlfriend?" Bree asked.

His jaw dropped. "Seriously? That's the first thing you want to ask me?"

"She seems to be very close to Olivia."

"She's been helping me out since you dropped Olivia off and disappeared more than a week ago. You shouldn't have done that, Bree. It wasn't fair to Olivia."

"You mean it wasn't fair to you."

He shook his head at her hard words. "No. This isn't about me. I can take whatever you want to dish out. I know you're angry and in pain, and I'm in the middle of that. But Olivia was confused when you left her with me. And you should have returned my calls. I had to take her to a new school. I had to get her a backpack and a lunchbox. How could you just leave her without any information or instructions?"

"I'm sorry. I was overwhelmed and panicked. I thought I left you a list, but I wasn't thinking clearly. I just had to be by myself for a little while. I couldn't breathe. I couldn't function. I was falling apart, and I had no one else to leave Olivia with. I knew you would take care of her."

"How are you feeling now?"

"Better. I found a new therapist, and I've spent the last week talking to her a lot. I've been writing in a journal and trying to actually sleep at night and just breathe." She paused. "I know you think I'm selfish, that I abandoned Liv, but I knew I wasn't right in the head, and I just had to take time for myself. I never had a chance to grieve Gary because Olivia needed me so much, and then my parents started falling apart, and I felt really lost and also pissed off at the situation I was in. Gary wasn't supposed to leave me alone. He always promised he'd come back, and I know it's not his fault, but I've had trouble accepting what happened."

He could relate to that. "I've had trouble, too." His heart went out to her as he saw the genuine anguish in her eyes. "I should have saved him."

"It doesn't sound like you could have done that," she murmured.

"I wish I could have found a way."

Her gaze locked on his. "I really hated you for being alive when Gary was dead."

"I know. I hated myself."

"But it wasn't fair to you. It wasn't your fault. I shouldn't have fallen apart the way I did. I'm a military wife, or I was. I was used to taking care of Olivia on my own because Gary was gone so much. But after he died, I found out our finances were in bad shape. I had to move in with my parents because of that. But then, my dad was drinking too much, and my mother was covering it up, and I knew they weren't capable of babysitting. I couldn't trust them with Olivia. I didn't think I could trust anyone." She let out a breath. "And then I heard Gary's voice in my head saying there's one guy you can always trust. Stop being mad at him for something that wasn't his fault and ask for help."

He could actually hear Gary saying it exactly like that. "I'm glad you came to me with Olivia, but you could have stayed and let me help both of you. Your actions really confused Livvy. And that was wrong, Bree."

"I know. How has she been?"

"Well, she's been okay. The first few days were bumpy. Emmalyn was a godsend. She's a kindergarten teacher at Ravenswood, so she helped Olivia get acclimated. And my neighbors have also rallied around. Olivia made a friend in Henry, and she hasn't had a lot of time to be sad, but it still comes at her, especially at night. She asks me a lot of questions about Gary and about you."

"I'm a terrible mother."

"You were in crisis, and you put Olivia somewhere safe. I get it now. But you have to do better, Bree."

"I know that, and I will. I feel stronger. I can do this. I can raise her."

"Good. Because she needs you as much as you need her." As he heard the sink turn off, he added, "She's almost done. We should talk more later. You are staying, aren't you, Bree?"

"I want to stay, but you don't exactly have the room."

"You can sleep with Olivia. I've been on the couch, and I'm fine with that."

"Okay. I'd like that. I've really missed my girl."

"She's a wonderful kid, Bree, a mix of you and Gary."

She teared up at his words. "Sometimes, she's so much like Gary, it makes me want to cry, but then I try to be happy because it means he lives on in her."

"And in you. What are your plans beyond tonight?"

"I'm not sure. I need to find a job and a place to live. Since Olivia is in school not far from here, I thought I'd try to stay in this neighborhood."

"That would be good. Olivia has already made friends in school, and she loves her teacher." He paused. "There might be an apartment in this building. I can find out."

"I'm not sure how much I can afford."

"I'll help you figure it out. You don't have to do this alone."

"You'd do that for me after I dropped my kid on you without any warning?"

He gave her a small smile. "To be honest, after the shock, I realized it wasn't the worst thing in the world. She's a great kid."

"Are you talking about me?" Olivia asked as she ran into the room with a bright smile.

"I am," he said. "I was just telling your mom what a good girl you've been."

"Are you going to tell me a story tonight, Hunter?"

"I'll let your mom do that. I'll see you in the morning." He gave Olivia a kiss on the cheek, feeling a wave of relief when she walked into the bedroom with her mother. He'd been worrying about what he would do if Bree didn't come back before he finished his tests and possibly got reassigned, but now that wouldn't be a problem.

As the quiet of his apartment settled around him, he really wanted to talk to Emmalyn, but he needed to stay and speak more to Bree when she was done putting Olivia to bed.

Pulling out his phone, he sent her a text: *Bree is staying the night, and then we'll figure out what's next. She says she's got her head together now.*

Emmalyn's answer came quickly: *I'm glad. Olivia needs her mom. I hope she doesn't have to leave Ravenswood.*

Bree wants to get a job and a place to live around here. I'm going to ask Josie if there's anything open in the building.

It would be great to have them here and good for Olivia not to have to make another big change. But maybe Bree should settle somewhere closer to family since you might be leaving soon.

He actually hadn't thought about that. Would it be good for them to get an apartment here when he could be gone within a couple of weeks?

But Henry, Paige, Emmalyn, and all the other residents who had been so kind and friendly to Olivia would still be here. They would make Bree part of the family, just as they'd done for him. It was strange to think about them living here without him, but Ocean Shores had always been just a temporary pit stop. He was going back to his career, a job he loved, that he was good at, that had always been his identity. If he had to trade Ocean Shores for that, well, he'd make that deal. But the problem wasn't just the building, the neighbors—it was Emmalyn. She was the one he didn't want to trade.

Another text came in from Emmalyn: *On second thought, I*

think living here would be good for Bree. I found a family here, and it seems like she needs one, too.

She does. I wish we could talk more, Em. Tomorrow...

She gave him a thumbs-up, which made him frown because he felt like he was back in the friend zone, and that was the last place he wanted to be.

CHAPTER EIGHTEEN

Saturday morning, Hunter knocked on Josie's door around nine. If Bree couldn't live at Ocean Shores, he would need to help her find something else, because they couldn't go on sharing his small apartment indefinitely.

Josie answered the door, wearing a colorful kimono robe, and holding a mug of something that smelled like coffee and whiskey, although it seemed a little early to be drinking. But he wouldn't be surprised if Josie mixed alcohol into her morning coffee, as she always seemed to be exceptionally happy.

"Well, well, Hunter Kane," she said, her brow arched in surprise. "You're the last person I expected to see. You've been my lowest maintenance tenant since you moved in. Until recently, I sometimes forgot you were even here. What can I do for you?"

"I heard there might be a unit available to rent."

She nodded. "There is. It's a two-bedroom. Are you looking to move into something bigger? Because I heard you might be leaving us altogether."

"This is for a friend of mine. You were at the pool last night when Olivia's mom, Bree, showed up. They need a place to stay, and I think Ocean Shores is where they belong."

"Well, Olivia is a sweet little girl, and she's gotten to be good friends with Henry, but didn't her mother drop her off with you without much warning? That doesn't sound like a very responsible person."

He realized that the Ocean Shores grapevine had probably been gossiping about Olivia since she'd arrived. "Bree has had a rough year. She lost her husband, Gary, my best friend and copilot, seven months ago in the same crash in which I was injured."

"I'm sorry about that," Josie said, her smile dimming as she gave him a kind look. "Why don't you come inside, and we'll talk? Would you like some coffee?"

"No, I'm fine," he said as he stepped into her home. He was momentarily distracted by the insane amount of color everywhere, and the smell of oranges and cinnamon, or maybe it was incense. Whatever it was, it was intense. The décor was bohemian and artsy, which fit her personality, but it was also even more extreme than he would have guessed.

As his gaze swept the room, a wall of photos caught his eye—film stills, magazine clippings, and a framed image of a younger Josie, radiant in a red gown, holding an Oscar. A brass nameplate at the bottom read: *Josie Bell, Best Supporting Actress—Heart of the Wolf.*

He blinked. "Wait. *Heart of the Wolf?* I know that movie. That was *you?*"

She gave him a half smile. "Yes. I played a single mom whose kid adopts a wolf. Hollywood loved it. Got me a little gold man and a messy divorce at the same time."

"I had no idea."

"My past has never been a secret."

"The Oscar and your divorce were tied together?"

"Sadly, they were. But I left LA and came here, and life eventually got good again. Now, tell me more about Bree. Does she have a job?"

"She's looking for one, but I'll cosign on the apartment. I'll give you however many months you want up front. I need them to be safe and secure in their housing for at least the next year. Olivia just started first grade at Ravenswood, and she's doing well. I don't want to mess that up."

"You're really looking out for them, aren't you?"

"Yes. Because that's what my friend would have expected from me, and what I expect from myself."

"That's very generous. Has Bree done any work in the past, or has she been a stay-at-home mom?"

"She was a stay-at-home mom for the past several years. With Gary gone a lot, it was better for Olivia if Bree was there to take care of her. But before that, Bree worked as an admin, and I think she also has retail experience. Hopefully, she'll be able to find a job around here soon."

"Maybe one of the tenants will know of something. You should ask around."

"That's a good idea."

"All right. Why don't I show you the unit, and then you can make a decision? Do Bree and Olivia want to come along?"

"They actually went down to the beach park this morning. I wanted to check things out before I got their hopes up. Olivia loves it here. I know she'll want to stay, but I wasn't sure if it was possible."

"It's definitely possible. Let me just change, and I'll be right with you."

As Josie disappeared into her bedroom, he looked back at the wall, reading some of her clippings. Josie might have only won a single Oscar, but she had been in several other blockbusters with well-known movie stars of her generation. He wondered how she'd gone from celebrity stardom to running an apartment building at the beach. That was probably a well-known story, but he had never asked about Josie or about anyone else, really. He'd just started getting to know them. And this wall of history made it clear that he probably didn't know nearly as much about anybody as he thought he did.

Everyone was more than they appeared to be at first glance.

Emmalyn was a prime example of that. She was friends with everyone in the building, but the only one who knew about her past was him. Maybe Ben knew something now, and maybe Em would continue to open up. He thought that would be a good thing, because she really shouldn't be embarrassed about her past. She'd made a life for herself after everything she'd been through, which was incredibly impressive.

"I'm ready," Josie said as she reentered the room, wearing white linen pants and a short-sleeved floral shirt, her dark-red hair brushed and pulled back with a clasp. She grabbed a key ring off a hook by the kitchen wall and led him out the door.

The apartment was on the second floor, just above the laundry room and across the courtyard from Emmalyn's unit. The two bedrooms were rather small, but Bree and Olivia could each have their own space, and their bedroom windows looked out to the beach, which was a definite plus. The one bathroom was accessible from the hallway and should work for the two of them. There was a gray couch sitting in the living room, but otherwise, the apartment was empty.

"What do you think?" Josie asked.

"It's great," he said. "I'm surprised it's been empty for a while."

"Some people who want two bedrooms also want two bathrooms. This unit unfortunately only has one."

"It will work for them. Bree and Olivia will be back in about an hour. Would it be okay if I bring them here to take a look?"

"Of course. I'll leave you the key," she said as she took it off the key ring. "Just get it back to me this afternoon, and I hope Bree will take it."

"She will."

"You better check with her before you make any commitments. I know you want to help her fix what's wrong, but she may want or need to do that herself."

"Her options are limited, but I see your point," he said, knowing that what Josie was really telling him was to include

Bree in on the decision so she would feel invested. "What about the couch? Will it be staying?"

"I can have someone pick it up, unless you think Bree might want it?"

"I think she might."

"You can let me know when you bring the key back."

As Josie left, he walked around the unit one more time, becoming even more convinced this was the right spot for Bree and Olivia to start over. Maybe he wouldn't be here more than a few more weeks, but the others would be. Olivia would still have Henry, Paige, and Emmalyn as well as all the others. Not that Bree knew any of those people, but he thought he could get Olivia to convince her if she had any doubts. Not that he should be using a six-year-old to forward his agenda, but desperate times called for desperate measures. And he wanted to get them set up before he had to leave.

The thought of leaving didn't give him as much excitement as it used to. But he'd get that back once he knew for certain the future he'd been working toward was actually going to happen.

He walked out of the apartment and locked the door. Then he decided to circle the building and stop in at Emmalyn's to say hello. As he walked down the corridor and around the corner, he heard a man's voice. Sharp. Demanding. Threatening.

Then Emmalyn yelled, "Get out."

What the hell?

He turned the next corner and ran toward her apartment.

"I said get out," Emmalyn cried again.

A terrible crash lit up the air. Ben came out of the apartment a few doors down.

"What's going on?" he asked.

"I don't know."

As they reached the door, he heard a man say, "You bitch!"

The door was slightly ajar. He pushed it open, shocked to see Jeremy standing across from Emmalyn, blood dripping down his face, the same blood that was on a large ceramic apple-shaped vase in Em's hand.

Emmalyn was breathing heavily, but there was a determined glint in her eyes, and she was clearly positioned to attack again.

"Get away from her," he told Jeremy as he moved to Emmalyn's side.

Ben blocked Jeremy as he tried to leave. "Not so fast," Ben said.

"Get out of my way," Jeremy snapped as he suddenly reached around his back and under his shirt.

"Gun," Hunter said quickly, jumping in front of Emmalyn as Ben grabbed Jeremy, shoving him face up against the wall and removing the gun from his waistband. "I'm a police officer," Ben told him. "And you're under arrest."

Jeremy froze at Ben's words.

Ben looked back at Emmalyn. "I assume this is Jeremy Warren?"

"Yes," she said.

"I ran a check on you, Mr. Warren, or should I say Daniels? It doesn't matter. You have outstanding warrants in both names."

"Does that mean you can take him to jail?" Emmalyn asked.

"I can, and I will," Ben replied.

"I didn't touch her. She hit me. I'm going to sue your ass," Jeremy said.

"I'm sure you'll try," Ben said in a cool voice. "Hunter, there are zip ties in my kitchen, first drawer under the microwave. Door is open."

He nodded and quickly left the apartment to get the ties. When he returned, he handed him the ties and watched as Ben fastened Jeremy's hands behind his back. Then Ben read him his rights and marched him out of the apartment.

When they'd left, he turned to Emmalyn, who was still clutching the apple vase. "I don't think you need that anymore," he said gently, taking it out of her hands.

"It was the closest thing to me," she said.

"What exactly happened?"

"Jeremy was waiting for me when I got home from the market. I was fumbling for my key, and I didn't see him. He came out of nowhere. I opened my door and stepped inside, and he was right behind me. I didn't have time to yell or call anyone."

He felt a wave of rage and guilt, seeing the fear in her eyes and realizing how badly she could have been hurt. He should have checked on her earlier. He should have made sure she wasn't alone. "I'm sorry you had to deal with this on your own."

"I let down my guard for a minute. I was stupid."

"No. You were brave."

"I couldn't tell him where my mother was. And I wasn't going with him. Whatever was going to happen was going to happen here." She paused to take a breath, then blew it out. "I think he was surprised I didn't cower in front of him. That's what he's used to. But I wouldn't give him the satisfaction of seeing fear in my face. He's a bully, and I needed to stand up to him."

He was more than a little impressed by her courage and her willingness to act. She hadn't panicked when Jeremy had pushed his way into her apartment. She'd stood up for herself. And for her mother.

The first time he'd seen her, he'd thought she was a sweet, soft, innocent person who probably hadn't had to endure one cloudy day in her life. He had been very wrong about that. He had also underestimated how strong and fiery she could be. And he had to admit that this side of her made him like her even more.

"You did good, Em."

"Thanks for coming to my rescue."

"I heard you yell."

"I'm surprised you heard me downstairs. I didn't think I was that loud."

"I was on the second floor, checking out the empty unit for Bree and Olivia."

"Oh. Is that going to work out?"

"If Bree likes it, yes. She's at the park with Olivia. I need to get her approval, but I can't see a reason why she'd say no."

"Olivia would love to stay here, and it would be good for her to be close to you."

"And to you," he said, gazing into her eyes. "She likes you a lot, Em." He paused. "And she's not the only one. When I think about what could have happened here..."

"I'm okay, Hunter. And if I wasn't, it wouldn't be on you. You're not responsible for me. I've been taking care of myself for a long time."

"I know. And clearly, you're very capable of doing that. But I still hate to think of you being hurt." He stepped forward, framing her face with his hands as he stared into her eyes. "I just want you to be safe and happy."

She gave him a soft smile. "I'm both of those things."

He smiled back at her. "Good."

"Although, I could be a little happier," she murmured, her gaze moving to his lips, then back up to his eyes. "I know I said I didn't want to start anything..."

"Em, we've already started," he said as she wrapped her arms around his body, and he pressed his mouth against hers.

Kissing her was exactly what he needed and what she seemed to need, too, as they lost themselves in each other.

And then there were voices outside and pounding on the door. They broke apart as he heard Kaia say, "Em, are you there? What's going on?"

"I better open the door," she said.

He gave her a nod, his mouth still tingling as she let Kaia and Lexie in.

"Ben said someone tried to attack you," Kaia said, her gaze sweeping Emmalyn's face. "Are you okay? What happened?"

"It's a long story," Emmalyn replied. "But I'm fine. Everything is good."

"Was it someone you knew? Did he follow you home?" Lexie

asked, worry in her gaze.

"It was someone I knew. He wasn't after me. He wanted to use me to find my mother."

Hunter suddenly realized that Emmalyn's carefully constructed life was about to unravel. "Maybe you should take a break," he interrupted. "Catch your breath."

She gave him a smile of gratitude. "It's okay. I want to tell them. They're my friends. You should probably go find Bree and Olivia."

"All right," he said, seeing the certainty in her eyes. "I'll check in with you later."

He left her apartment, knowing she wanted and needed to tell her friends what was happening, and he thought it was good she was finally ready to share her past.

He just wished the timing had been better.

Or maybe the timing had been exactly right, because they were careening down a road neither of them was sure they should travel.

———

It was easier than Emmalyn had expected to tell her story to Kaia and Lexie, who quietly listened without commenting.

"I'm so sorry," Lexie said when she'd finished. "I had no idea you had such a hard childhood."

"I didn't, either," Kaia put in. "I can understand why you didn't want to talk about it. I have to say, I always thought there was something a little off about your past. You made random comments about not listening to music or watching TV or learning how to swim. But you never seemed interested in confiding in us, so I didn't want to ask."

"It was hard not to tell you. I just didn't want anyone to judge me by my past. I've been ashamed of my mother and the way we lived for a long time. It became a habit to lie about her, one I couldn't break. But everything came to a head this past week."

"We all have things in our past we don't want to talk about," Lexie said. "But for the record, you turned out really well considering what you went through."

"Thanks."

"So what's going to happen to the man who came here today?" Kaia asked.

"Ben said he had an outstanding warrant. I don't know what that's about, but hopefully, Ben can hold him for a while. Maybe I can also get a restraining order or something."

"Ben will help you figure out what to do," Kaia said confidently. "It's good he was here."

"And Hunter, too," Lexie said. "How did that happen?"

"He was looking at the empty apartment. I guess Bree, Olivia's mom, might want to rent it so that they can stay here."

"Oh, that would be great," Lexie said with an excited gleam in her eyes. "I'll follow up with him on that. But didn't you say that Hunter was probably going to leave? Will they want to stay here if he's gone?"

"I hope so. Olivia has made friends with Henry, and I'm close to her, too. I know Olivia's mother, Bree, has been going through a hard time since her husband died. I want to support both of them. I think we should do everything we can to make Bree feel welcome."

"As we always do," Lexie said.

"It sounded like Hunter already knew your story," Kaia interjected, a curious gleam in her eyes.

"He did. He was with me when my aunt rescued my mother. I guess I left that part out."

"How was he with you?" Kaia asked.

"I told him what was going on and he offered to go with me to the market."

"The farmers' market," Lexie echoed. "Where you didn't buy anything. Wow, I had no idea you had just been through something so intense. I thought you were just sneaking around with Hunter."

She smiled. "It was more than that." She sighed as Kaia and Lexie exchanged a pointed look. "I know you both think there's something going on—"

"Because there's something going on," Kaia interrupted.

"Maybe there is," she admitted. "But I'm pretty sure it's just going to be a short-term thing, so no one needs to get excited about it."

"Are you trying to convince us or yourself?" Lexie asked.

"Maybe all of us. I wish things were different, but timing is everything, and it's not working in my favor."

"Does he have to leave? Couldn't he be stationed at Camp Pendleton?" Kaia asked.

"I don't know. He seems to think he will be assigned elsewhere, but he's not even sure if he's going to get cleared for duty, so there's a lot up in the air."

"Then just let things be whatever they are meant to be," Lexie suggested. "Until you know what's going on, you just have to live your life."

"But living my life in the short term could hurt in the long term. I like him...a lot."

"It sounds like you've already gotten to a place where the hurt is going to be there regardless," Lexie said quietly.

"But if I stay away from him, I'll start to care less, won't I?"

Kaia gave her a sympathetic smile. "I don't think that's how it works, Emmalyn. My advice—you're already involved, so I'd just double down and try to enjoy the hell out of things until they end and hope maybe they won't." She paused. "Are you and Hunter coming to Maverick's tonight for Liam's birthday?"

"I'm coming. I don't know about Hunter."

"Well, now that Olivia's mother is back, maybe he's free, too," Lexie said. "I'll make sure he knows about it when I talk to him about the apartment."

"You two do not need to try to get me and Hunter together," she said. "Like I said before, I don't even know what I want."

"Well, maybe you need to find out," Kaia said.

CHAPTER NINETEEN

Maverick's Bar and Grill was glowing like a lighthouse on the bluff, its patio strung with warm lights that bobbed in the ocean breeze. Emmalyn's steps slowed as she neared the bar Saturday night. It was so peaceful outside; she wasn't sure she was ready for a crazy night at Maverick's. But it was Liam's birthday, and everyone always showed up for birthdays, so she really needed to be there. But she'd had such an unsettling day.

Her phone suddenly buzzed, and her gut tightened as Ben's name flashed across the screen. "Hello? Ben?"

"I wanted to fill you in on what's happening with Jeremy."

"I have been wondering." She'd hoped to hear from Ben much earlier than now.

"I wanted to be able to give you as much definitive and helpful information as I could before I called."

"So there is helpful information?"

"Yes. It turns out the group your mother escaped from is heavily involved in smuggling guns and drugs. The commune is just a front for their criminal activities. While the members of the commune seem to live below the poverty line, the leaders have banked a great deal of wealth."

"That's ironic since they're so against materialism for everyone else who lives there."

"Well, this is just the start of a long investigation. The San Diego PD will be heavily involved, as the group resides in their jurisdiction. But the main takeaway for you is that Jeremy will not be released on bail. You and your mom are safe. If that changes, I will let you know immediately."

"Thank you so much, Ben. This is the best news."

"No problem. Are you at the bar?"

"Just about to walk in. Are you coming?"

"Working tonight. Have fun."

"Thanks."

She felt immense relief at the news that Jeremy was behind bars and the group was being investigated. It was ironic that Jeremy's attempt to get her mother back was what had finally gotten him arrested. Putting her phone back into her bag, she walked into the bar, feeling much more relaxed and ready to just enjoy herself.

As she walked past the weathered surfboard at the front door and into the bar, she was immediately enveloped in the warm, friendly, buzzing atmosphere. Old surfboards hung from the wooden-beamed ceiling, and black-and-white photos of legendary surfers covered the walls. The weathered wood floors had been worn smooth by years of sandy feet and dancing, and the salty sea air mingled with the scent of beer and the burgers being served from the kitchen. Maverick's wasn't fancy, but it had soul—a perfect reflection of their coastal community.

As she moved farther into the room, Brad waved to her from behind the bar, a towel slung over his shoulder like always. His brother, Tyler, was mixing drinks at the far end—his charm out in full force as he served drinks to a trio of attractive young women.

Kaia, Lexie, Ava, Madison, and Serena had snagged a table near the old classic jukebox that didn't actually play but was part of the vibe. They were nursing cocktails and catching up on gossip, while Liam and Gabe were at the bar, picking up drinks from Brad.

"We saved you a seat," Kaia said as she reached them.

"Thanks," she said, taking one of the three empty chairs at the end of the long table. "I thought you might be in the back room."

"It's more fun out here," Ava said. "Liam likes to be in the center of the action, and since it's his birthday..." She shrugged as she smiled. "Gotta keep him happy."

"Oh, please," Serena said, rolling her eyes at her sister. "Your fiancé couldn't be any happier. Liam is one of the most cheerful people I've ever met. It's a miracle that someone as sour as you could land someone like him."

"I sometimes think that, too," Ava admitted, accepting her sister's teasing comments with a smile. "We definitely didn't start out on the right foot when you accidentally forgot to tell me he'd be staying at your apartment while I was housesitting for you and taking care of Miss Daisy."

"I thought you needed someone to loosen you up, and it worked."

"I have to admit, you did me a favor," Ava conceded. "We are definitely opposites, but I think we're starting to rub off on each other, in a good way. Or maybe he's just rubbing off on me."

"Well, it would be nice if Liam would introduce us to some of his fellow hot Australian surfers," Kaia complained.

"That might happen next month," Ava said. "There's some big surfing competition happening, and Liam said some of his buddies are coming to town."

As the conversation flowed around the table, Liam returned with a tray of drinks, one of which he placed in front of her, a fruity concoction with an umbrella. He gave her a smile. "Brad saw you come in. He said you'd probably like this. It's a very light shot of tequila with a bunch of blended fruit."

Brad knew her too well. She was a wimp when it came to

anything stronger than wine, but sometimes it was more fun to sip a cocktail.

The bar grew more crowded as the night progressed. Gabe and Liam sat down with them, as well as two other guys she didn't know but who were friends of Liam's. It was a fun group, and she was having a good time, but someone was missing, someone she really wanted to see.

As people changed seats, Lexie slid into the one next to hers. "I told Hunter to come. Have you talked to him?"

"We texted, and he said he would try, but he's helping Bree and Olivia get furniture. I guess they don't have anything, and they definitely need two beds."

"I talked to them when they signed the rental agreement. Bree said she had to sell some of her furniture when she moved in with her parents, so she needs to start completely over."

"We should help her. I bet some people in the building have an extra chair or desk they don't need."

Lexie smiled. "That's a good idea."

"I'll check in with everyone tomorrow, see if we can find some furniture to get her started."

"Well, check with Hunter first and see what they bought today."

"I will. I'm glad it's going to work out. Olivia really needs some stability, and I hated the idea of her having to move so soon and start over at a new school when she was just getting comfortable at Ravenswood."

"It works out for us, too. We can report full occupancy to the owner when he comes in tomorrow."

"You don't really think he'll sell, do you?"

"I hope not. We'll have a better idea after his visit." Lexie paused, her gaze moving past Emmalyn, a smile parting her lips. "Look who's here."

Emmalyn turned her head to see Hunter walking toward them. He looked devastatingly handsome in dark jeans and a navy button-down short-sleeve shirt that stretched perfectly across his broad shoulders. His dark hair was slightly damp, as if he'd just showered, and as he drew closer, he smelled faintly of soap and something woodsy that made her pulse quicken.

"You made it," Lexie said.

"Sorry I'm late."

"You're not late. Have a seat," Lexie added as she jumped to her feet. Emmalyn took another long sip of her drink as Hunter sat down.

"I heard Bree is taking the apartment," she said.

"Yes. She's relieved to have one less decision to make, and Olivia is over the moon."

"Lexie mentioned that Bree doesn't have much furniture. I don't know what you bought today, but I was thinking that I could ask around and see if anyone has anything extra that they don't want. Just to help her get started."

"That's very nice of you. You're always thinking about ways to make people comfortable."

"It's a lot to start over."

"We bought bedroom furniture today, but Bree doesn't want me to pay for everything, so she'd probably appreciate some hand-me-downs."

"I'll work on that tomorrow then." She paused as the music suddenly grew louder, and half their group moved to the dance floor.

"Shall we join them?" Hunter asked.

"I'm not much of a dancer."

"Neither am I, but we're not performing for anyone." He got up and held out his hand.

How could she resist? She followed him onto the crowded dance floor, a little disappointed when he let go of her hand. But the music was fast, and it was fun to move to the beat, to stop thinking for a while and just let loose.

She felt emboldened by the music, the alcohol, and all the events of the day. She didn't want to be defined by her past, by old habitual thinking that she was a little weird, that she wasn't like everyone else, that she didn't know what they knew, that she was somehow stunted because of her childhood. But she wasn't that awkward kid; she was a grown woman, a teacher, someone who encouraged bravery and individuality, and today she'd stood up to one of the biggest bullies in her life. That thought made her smile. And as Hunter grinned back at her, she thought they'd both changed a lot in the past week, and in a good way.

The music suddenly shifted to a slow song, something sultry, something yearning. Hunter grabbed her hands and pulled her close, putting his arms around her as they swayed to the music. They might not be good dancers, but they were good at this, their bodies moving together in a perfect rhythm, making her think about other ways they could move together.

Hunter's hand slid up her back, his fingers grazing the nape of her neck, and she suppressed a shiver as she looked into his darkened gaze.

"Emmalyn," he began, his voice rough with emotion.

She didn't know what he was going to say because the music suddenly stopped, and then Brad's booming voice rang through the bar. "Cake time!"

They broke apart to see Serena and Ava setting an enormous sheet cake on the table. As Ava lit the candles, she and Hunter joined the group encircling the table.

Liam put his arm around Ava and gave her a kiss. Then the group sang "Happy Birthday" before Liam blew out his candles. A round of applause followed along with questions about what he'd wished for.

"I don't need to wish," Liam responded, gazing at Ava with love in his eyes. "I already have everything and everyone that I need."

"That's so sweet," Serena said. "But you could still wish for a million dollars."

"Money isn't everything."

Serena rolled her eyes, then began cutting the cake.

"What would you wish for, Em?" Hunter asked curiously, "if those were your candles?"

"I don't think I should tell you," she murmured.

A sexy smile parted his lips. "Maybe I could help make your wish come true."

Heat ran through her. "That's a pretty confident statement, considering you don't know what my wish would be."

"I'm hoping it's the same as mine."

The intensity in his gaze nearly buckled her knees. Suddenly, the bar felt too crowded, too loud, too everything. And really the only person she wanted to talk to was him.

"Do you want to get out of here?" she asked impulsively.

"God, yes," he breathed, relief evident in his voice.

They said quick goodbyes, making excuses about being tired and needing to check on Olivia and Bree. If their friends saw through the transparent lies, they were kind enough not to comment.

The night air was cool against Emmalyn's flushed skin, but as Hunter took her hand, she felt another wave of heat. She had no idea what was coming next, but right now she was just going to enjoy the walk. Because everything felt right in the moonlight, the beach stretching out beside them, waves breaking gently against the shore. She was lucky to live here and lucky to have Hunter at her side, at least for tonight.

"Won't you miss this?" she found herself asking. "This night, this setting," she added hastily. "I wasn't talking about me."

His hand tightened around hers as he gave her a hot look that sent shivers down her spine. "I will miss everything, including you. But nothing is decided."

"I know. I'm just thinking ahead."

"I'm trying not to do that because life has a way of throwing all my plans out the window."

"Well, that's true," she said. "You seem very relaxed tonight and at peace with yourself, Hunter. Is it because Bree is back?"

"I'm happy she has returned to take care of her daughter, but the past week has also changed my perspective. I see things more clearly now."

"I like this version of you, Hunter. I never would have imagined that the angry, scowling man I met months ago would be laughing, making new friends, even dancing..."

"I was in such a dark hole; I couldn't see my way out. And part of me didn't want to get out. I didn't want to smile or be happy. It felt like a betrayal."

"Because Gary was gone," she said, understanding him so much better now. "You were punishing yourself."

"I was, but talking to Olivia about her dad helped me remember Gary in a way that didn't bring pain with it. Telling her about him made me realize how much he would have gotten on me for wallowing in my pain. He would have told me to shake it off, move on, that I was wasting my life."

"You weren't wasting your life; you were grieving. And probably not just for Gary but also for yourself, for the life you were worried you might have lost."

"There's no guarantee I haven't lost it. I've passed one test, but there are more to go."

"But you're feeling confident, right?"

"I am, but I've never been in this position before."

"Haven't you? I'm sure you had to prove yourself at the beginning."

"That was different. I was cocky as hell. I was always the best at everything I did because coming in second was unacceptable."

She smiled to herself, thinking she could have guessed that. "Did that drive come from your father? Were you trying to live up to him?"

"To him and to my older brother. But I didn't want to be as good, I wanted to be better," he said honestly.

"Were you?"

"I thought so, until I got shot out of the sky and realized I wasn't as invincible as I thought."

"I can't imagine what you went through."

"You don't want to imagine it," he said. "Let's talk about something else."

"Okay. It was fun dancing with you. You have some moves."

He gave her a disbelieving smile. "I'm not sure about that, but you were definitely feeling the beat."

She'd been feeling him as much as the beat, and as they neared Ocean Shores, she wondered just how far she wanted to take that feeling, because they were almost home.

When they entered the courtyard, it was empty, which wasn't surprising since many of the residents were still at the bar.

As they neared her apartment, Hunter said, "You're over-thinking, Em."

"How do you know?" she asked.

"Because you are suddenly very quiet," he replied as they arrived at her door. "And you get this little crease between your eyebrows when you're worrying about something."

"I do?"

"Yes." He reached out to smooth the spot with his thumb. The casual touch sent electricity dancing across her skin. "That's better. You know that nothing will happen that you don't want to happen."

"I'm conflicted as to what I want to do and what I should do," she said.

"I get it," he said with a nod of understanding. "I can't make you any promises. I don't want to lead you on. But I do care about you, Em. And there's a fire between us that gets hotter every day."

"I feel the same way," she admitted. "And I'm not asking you for promises. It's not on you, Hunter. It's on me."

"Your decision," he agreed.

She studied his face in the soft light of the hallway—the strong line of his jaw, the intensity and desire in his dark eyes, the hint of uncertainty beneath his confident exterior. This man who'd been so closed off, so damaged when she'd first met him, now stood before her, offering something she hadn't known she wanted until now.

"It doesn't have to be complicated," he added.

He'd been open and honest, completely transparent. No promises, no platitudes—just the truth. And maybe that was enough.

She took her keys out of her purse and opened the door. Then she turned to face him. "I'd like you to come in."

He let out a breath. "Good, because I'd like to come in."

As she stepped back, he moved into her apartment, then kicked the door shut and pulled her into his arms. She met his kiss with the passion that had been building between them for days. She might not have him forever. But she had him tonight, and she was going to make it a night to remember.

CHAPTER TWENTY

Emmalyn woke up slowly on Sunday morning, awareness coming in gentle waves. First, the warmth surrounding her, then the unfamiliar weight of an arm draped across her waist, and finally, the soft, steady breathing of the man beside her. She kept her eyes closed, savoring the moment, allowing herself to remember the night before—Hunter's hands on her skin, his mouth against hers, the way he'd looked at her as if she were the only person in the world who mattered. It had been everything she'd imagined and so much more. There had been tenderness amid the passion, laughter amid the intensity, a connection that went beyond the physical.

Finally, she opened her eyes and looked at him. In sleep, the hard lines of his face had softened, and his lips were slightly parted. She resisted the urge to trace the outline of his jaw with her finger, not wanting to wake him. Instead, she simply studied his face, committing each detail to memory.

He was handsome. Strong. Complicated. A man who had seen darkness but was fighting his way back to the light.

She'd watched him with Olivia, witnessed his patience and kindness, his steadfast determination to do right by his friend's child. She'd felt his protective instinct when Jeremy had threatened her, seen his vulnerability when he'd spoken of his crash and the loss of his best friend. A knot formed in her throat as she realized just how much she'd come to care for him in such a short time. It wasn't just attraction or chemistry—though they had plenty of both. It was deeper. She trusted him. And that terrified her more than anything.

Trust had always been her Achilles' heel, the thing she guarded most fiercely. Her mother had chosen a cult over her and had let her go when she was only twelve years old. That experience had taught her a brutal lesson—not to count on anyone. She couldn't give someone the power to hurt her. And she had never given anyone that power, until last night.

Of course, there had been other men in her past. But no one like Hunter, who had slipped past all her defenses days ago. She wouldn't regret the night no matter what happened, because they'd shared so much passion, laughter, and talking. She'd really loved the talking because it hadn't been about anything deep or traumatic. They'd spoken about favorite books, movies, and travel spots. Their conversation had flowed so easily, and when exhaustion had finally caught up to them, they'd fallen asleep in each other's arms.

But now reality had returned. They'd had their night, and maybe that was all they could or should have. Even if he didn't leave for a few weeks, it was going to be torture to be with him when she knew it was all going to end. At some point, she had to get her guard back up. *Didn't she?*

This already wasn't some casual fling she could walk away from unscathed. She was in too deep. She knew that. She'd known it before she'd slept with him. No regrets, she reminded herself. She just needed to move on.

With exquisite care, she slipped out from under his arm and eased off the bed. Hunter stirred slightly but didn't wake. She grabbed the first clothes she could find—a T-shirt and a pair of yoga pants—and padded out of the bedroom, closing the door gently behind her.

In the kitchen, she went through the familiar motions of making coffee, finding comfort in the routine, but deep down she knew that while everything looked exactly the same as yesterday, her life had changed.

Leaning against the counter as she waited for the coffee to brew, she wrapped her arms around herself. Hunter's scent still clung to her skin, a reminder she couldn't escape even if she wanted to. And that was the problem. She didn't want to escape. She wanted to crawl back into bed with Hunter, to pretend the outside world didn't exist, that the future wasn't looming with all its complications. But that wasn't real life. Real life was standing in her kitchen, trying to figure out how to protect her heart from a man who had already stolen it.

———

Hunter reached across cool sheets where Emmalyn's warmth should have been. He opened his eyes, confirming what he already knew—she was gone. The disappointment was immediate and surprisingly sharp.

He lay there for a moment, staring at the ceiling, replaying the night in his mind. The way she'd looked at him in the bar, the electricity of their dance, the breathless walk home. And then, finally, alone together, the last barriers between them had fallen away.

It had been incredible. Not just the physical connection, though that had exceeded every expectation, but the sense that they'd crossed some threshold together. He'd never experienced anything like it before. Sex had always been straightforward for him—pleasurable but uncomplicated. This had been different because Emmalyn was different.

He wished she hadn't already gotten up, that they could have escaped into each other again before they had to deal with the real world. But the scent of coffee drifted in from the kitchen, revealing her whereabouts.

Sitting up, he ran a hand through his hair. His clothes were scattered across the floor, mingled with hers in a way that brought a smile to his face. He pulled on his boxer briefs, jeans, and shirt, then made his way to the door.

The sight of her in the kitchen stopped him in his tracks. Her T-shirt clung to her breasts, the yoga pants outlining the rest of her beautiful body. Her wavy blonde hair was tousled from sleep and from his hands. She was achingly beautiful, and the rush of emotion he felt was both exhilarating and terrifying.

She turned and saw him, and the expression on her face was both happy and wary.

"Morning," she said. "I made coffee for you." She quickly filled a mug and brought it to him.

"Thanks." He took the mug from her hands, then set it on the counter and reached for her, pulling her up against his body. "I need something else first."

Desire flared in her eyes, which was all the invitation he needed to lean in and kiss her, savoring the heat between them and the taste of coffee on her lips. As he ended the kiss, he said, "I wish you'd stayed in bed longer."

"I didn't want to wake you." Her voice was light, almost deliberately casual, as she pulled away from him. "You looked peaceful and also tired. I thought you could use the sleep."

"For future reference, if it's a choice between sleep or you, I'll always choose you."

His words hung in the air between them, and he saw the flicker in her eyes—the recognition that his statement about the future had brought up the one thing neither of them could change.

"Emmalyn," he began.

She immediately shook her head. "Let's not do that, Hunter."

"Do what?"

"Talk about last night. It was great. It was awesome. And I don't want to ruin the memories by analyzing anything. Okay?"

He didn't want to say it was okay, because she was acting like it was over between them, and they still had time. "Nothing is going to happen for a while, Em. We can make more memories."

She shook her head. "No, we can't. *I can't.*" She gave him a helpless shrug. "It's going to be hard enough to say goodbye now, and it would be even worse if we get closer. So, let's just stop with this one beautiful night together."

He didn't want to stop with one night. He didn't want to contemplate never being with her again, but it wasn't fair to ask her for more when he had so little to give back to her.

"So I was thinking today, I'll check in with the other residents and see who might have extra furniture for Bree," she said, changing the subject.

He didn't want to talk about furniture or Bree, but he could see the determination in her eyes to act like they were just friends again. "You don't have to do that."

"I want to."

"Okay." He picked up the coffee mug and took a sip, searching for something to say that wouldn't make things worse. But what could he say? That he'd never felt this way before, and it scared the hell out of him? That wouldn't get him anywhere, because ultimately it wasn't his choice to go or to stay. If he wanted his career back, he would go where the Corps needed him to go. That was his life.

"Can you find out what Bree really needs? I'm not sure she would tell me directly, then I can focus on those specific things?"

"I can talk to her," he said.

"Great. Do you want something to eat?" she asked. "I could make breakfast before you go."

The problem was that he didn't want to go. He met her gaze. "I don't want it to be like this with you, Em. It suddenly feels awkward and tense."

"I'm sorry. I did have fun last night. I hope you know that."

"It's just over," he finished on a harsh note.

"It has to be."

"It doesn't have to be now."

"It does for me." She gave him a somewhat sad smile. "I'm going to take a shower. I'll see you later, and I'll try not to be awkward. I don't want that, either. We'll just be friends again. Okay?"

"Sure," he said. "Friends." But as she left to take a shower, he knew there was no way that would work.

———

Friends with Hunter? Who was she kidding?

Emmalyn scrubbed her scalp hard as she washed her hair and cursed herself for telling Hunter one night was enough and that was the end of it. She didn't want to be his friend; she wanted to be his lover. She wanted to spend every minute of every day and every night with him until the Marine Corps forced them apart. But her fear and panic had pushed stupid words out of her mouth and now she couldn't go against her terribly bad plan because she'd made such a big point about ending their short-lived fling immediately.

Although, she could definitely persuade him otherwise. It wasn't like he wanted it that way.

But it was smarter to end things now. She was already emotionally involved. Getting closer to him would only make saying goodbye harder. It was just sad to think she'd finally met someone with whom she had great physical chemistry as well as a truly remarkable emotional connection, someone she had trusted with her most personal story, someone she could count on—at least, until he had to leave.

And he would leave, no matter how much he might want to stay with her. Hunter's dream was to return to his unit, to his life. He'd worked hard to rehabilitate and recover. Passing his tests and being cleared to fly again and return to active duty was what he wanted the most, and she couldn't wish failure on him just so he could stay with her. She cared about him too much to not want him to succeed.

She just needed to deal with the situation as best she could. Since she'd already taken a stand, she had to stick to it.

Or maybe she could change her mind...

She sighed at her turbulent thoughts, knowing she would have to take things one day at a time. She certainly wasn't going to solve anything in the shower. She rinsed her hair, then dried off and got dressed. By the time she returned to the living room, Hunter was long gone, and her apartment felt emptier than it ever had.

She couldn't sit around and feel sorry for herself. She'd learned a long time ago that the best remedy for depression was to do something for someone else. She'd promised Hunter she'd look into getting Bree some furniture, and that's what she was going to do.

She made several calls. Unfortunately, neither Kaia nor Ava answered. But Paige picked up the phone with a cheerful, "Hello."

"It's Emmalyn," she said.

"How's it going?" Paige asked.

"Good. As I mentioned last night, Bree and Olivia need furniture. Do you have anything you're looking to get rid of?"

"As a matter of fact, I do. Henry's grandfather insisted on buying him a new desk for his room. I was just going to give the old one away, but Olivia can have it if she wants."

"That's great." She made a note on the pad in front of her. "I'll be in touch about when we can pick it up."

"Great. Talk soon."

She made a few more calls and came up with a television from Skye and a kitchen table and chairs from Maggie, who was itching to buy something new.

Hearing voices in the courtyard, she decided to go downstairs and see who else was around. Grabbing her keys, she walked outside, locking the door behind her. She didn't usually lock it when she was just in the complex, but after Jeremy's surprise arrival the day before, she wanted to be more careful.

Josie and Lexie were cleaning up the area by the barbecues.

"Good morning, ladies," she said.

Lexie looked up with a speculative smile. "Is it a good morning after a good night?"

She felt heat rush to her cheeks. "Let's just say it's a good weekend."

"I'm glad to hear that. You and Hunter disappeared from Liam's party pretty early, but with the way you were heating up the dance floor, I wasn't surprised."

"We were just—" Emmalyn began, then stopped herself. There was no point denying it. "Hunter's a great guy," she said with a helpless shrug.

Lexie smiled. "I'm glad you had fun."

"Me, too."

"I like Hunter," Josie put in. "More than I thought I would. He's really come to life the past week. That probably has something to do with you, Emmalyn."

"Probably more to do with Olivia. Speaking of which, I'm seeing who might have extra furniture or kitchenware for Bree. If either of you have anything you want to get rid of, they might want it."

"I just decluttered," Lexie said. "But Aunt Josie has a big storage unit full of stuff."

"I'll take a look," Josie promised. "After we talk to Grayson. I don't want to start pulling things out before he gets here."

"Grayson is the new owner, the one who might want to sell?"

"Yes, Grayson Holt. He is going to do a quick visit on his way to LAX for a flight to Europe. I'm hoping a face-to-face meeting and introducing him to our tenants will help him see Ocean Shores as more than just a line item on his spreadsheet," Josie said.

"I think that's him," Lexie said suddenly.

She turned to see a man walk into the courtyard. He was the kind of man who instantly drew attention, tall and good-looking but also appearing strikingly out of place in a southern California beach apartment complex in his tailored charcoal suit and polished shoes, carrying a sleek leather briefcase.

Josie straightened, then she gave him a wave, and he headed in their direction.

"Mr. Holt," Josie said as he reached them. "Welcome to Ocean Shores. I'm so glad you decided to come. I'm Josie, the manager. This is my niece, Lexie Price, and one of our tenants, Emmalyn McGuire."

He gave them a nod. "Grayson Holt," he said with a cool gleam in his arctic-blue eyes. "I'm afraid I don't have much time. I have a flight to LAX in a few hours, but my father wanted me to take a closer look at the property. Although, I've seen the financials, which tells me what I need to know."

"The financials don't tell the whole story," Lexie said, a slight edge to her voice.

He gave her a speculative look. "Perhaps not the whole story, but numbers don't lie, exaggerate, or spin, while people often do all three."

Lexie crossed her arms, giving him a dark look. "The kind of people who live here at Ocean Shores don't do any of those things, nor does the woman who manages the building. This isn't just a complex of apartments, Mr. Holt. This is a community. We are neighbors, friends, and family. And that's something that you don't find everywhere."

"Your community has no bearing on future decisions about the profitability of my family's investment."

"Well, it should," Lexie said. "Didn't they teach you about intrinsic value at Harvard?"

"Do you have a problem with me?" Grayson asked, giving Lexie a sharp look.

"Why would I?"

"You sound like an aggressive lawyer."

"Former. Georgetown Law," Lexie admitted.

Emmalyn watched their exchange with surprise and curiosity. Lexie rarely mentioned her previous career, and she didn't usually look at men with that particular blend of irritation and intrigue. Grayson Holt had definitely rubbed her the wrong way.

Josie cleared her throat. "Why don't I show you around, Grayson? May I call you Grayson?"

"Of course," he said as he followed Josie across the courtyard.

"What was that about?" she asked Lexie. "I thought we were supposed to charm him."

She let out an annoyed sigh. "I know. Aunt Josie is going to be pissed. But I have met so many men like him, smug and condescending. He just...bugged me."

"I can see that."

"I should go apologize."

"Maybe take a breath before you attempt that," she advised. "Let him meet some other people who aren't so angry."

"You're right. I hope I didn't mess things up."

"I doubt a few sharp words from one person will affect his decision. He seems very focused on numbers and facts."

"Our numbers are good," Lexie said.

"Then that's what you need to show him, because he clearly doesn't care that we have a community here."

"You're right. I'm going to get the file Ava sent me yesterday. She did a financial analysis for us. Maybe he can take that with him on the plane. At least it will give him something else to think about."

"Good idea."

As Lexie left, Hunter, Bree, and Olivia came out of Hunter's apartment. She straightened, putting a smile on her face as they came around the pool.

"Emmalyn," Olivia yelled, letting go of her mom's hand to run to her. "Did you hear that we're going to live here? We're on the second floor like you are. And we have two bedrooms. I get to have my own room, and Hunter says I can get new unicorn sheets that will fit my bed instead of his."

She smiled at that, thinking they'd been exceptionally lucky to find those sheets in a king-size. "I'm so happy you'll be staying."

"I can still go to Ravenswood and be friends with Henry and see you all the time."

"That's perfect," she said, moving her gaze to Hunter and Bree.

Hunter wasn't giving much away. Bree looked a little uncomfortable and possibly defensive. She couldn't do anything about Hunter's tension, but she wanted to ease Bree's. "Hunter mentioned that you might need a few things, Bree, and I asked around and some of your fellow neighbors have extra items they are happy to get rid of. You'd be doing them a favor if you wanted anything. So far, I've found a TV, a kitchen table and chairs, and a kid's desk. It's actually Henry's desk. He just got a new one."

"Hunter mentioned you wanted to help us get set up. That's very generous," Bree said, uncertainty in her dark eyes. "I don't quite know what to say. Why would anyone here want to help me? You don't even know me."

"Because we've all fallen in love with your daughter, and we want the best for both of you. Plus, a lot of us who live here have had to start over at one time or another. We know what it's like to have support when we need it, and we'd like to offer that to you."

Bree looked overwhelmed by her words, her gaze moving to Hunter.

He gave a nod. "I told you this place is great, Bree. They helped me heal, and maybe they can do the same for you."

"I hope you don't think I'm overstepping," Emmalyn added hastily. "You don't have to take anything, Bree. Maybe you want all new things. That's totally understandable."

"No. I appreciate anything that anyone wants to get rid of. That will help a lot."

"So I can have Henry's desk, Mommy?" Olivia asked. "Can we get it now?"

"No, we're going shopping for food," Bree said. "We'll get it later. Thank you, Emmalyn. Olivia has been raving about how nice you are. I can see she didn't exaggerate."

"It's not a big deal. I'm happy to do it."

"Let's go, Livvy," Bree said. "We need to get started on our errands."

They left, leaving her alone with Hunter again.

"Bree really appreciates what you're doing, Em."

"Like I said, it's really no trouble."

"What are you doing the rest of the day?" he asked.

"I'm going to visit my mom and my aunt."

"I hope they're both doing well. Are you going to tell your mother about the police investigation into Haven?"

"I'm debating how much I want to get into that. I can't believe she was involved in criminal activity, but I don't know. She's been with the group for more than twenty years. She probably knows a lot more than she would ever say."

"The police will probably want to talk to her."

"I know. I will tell her. I just want her to stay focused on getting better. I want her to see how good life is away from that horrible place."

He nodded, giving her a small smile. "She doesn't deserve you."

"I might agree with that," she said, happy as the tension between them finally eased. "What are your plans today?"

"I'm shockingly free again, now that Bree is back. Do you feel like some company? I wouldn't mind getting out of here, taking a drive down to La Jolla with you. Just as friends, of course. I'm going to follow your rules, Em."

Seeing the gleam in his eyes, she said, "I feel like you're mocking my rules, Hunter."

"I'm really not. I just like spending time with you. And I'm curious to see how your mother is doing."

"You really want to spend time with me and my dysfunctional family?"

"I do. I understand you want to cool things down between us, but we don't have to go from a hundred miles an hour to zero. There is a middle ground."

"I'm not sure about that, but..."

His eyes brightened. "I think I'm going to like this *but*."

"Why do you have to be so charming and nice?" she complained. "It would be easier if you went back to that dark, grumpy guy who didn't want to spend ten seconds talking to me."

"He's gone, Em. Not coming back. And you're a big reason why. So, how about we hang out together today?"

She couldn't help but give in, because she wanted to spend time with him, and he was making it impossible to say no by being so damn reasonable. "Fine, if you want to come with me as my friend, then I won't say no. But that's it. No kissing. No touching. Nothing else."

"Got it. Nothing will happen that you don't want to happen."

"That's what you said last night and look what happened."

He grinned. "Maybe because we both want the same thing."

"I never said we didn't," she muttered. "That's not the problem, and you know it."

"I might fail my tests, Em. The review board might not reinstate me. That is a real possibility. I might not be going anywhere."

She gazed into his eyes. "I want to be very clear about something, Hunter. I don't want you to fail. I want you to get your job back because you deserve it. If that means you have to leave, then that's okay. I'm not rooting against you."

His jaw tightened, as he gave a nod. "Thanks. I appreciate that." He paused. "Let me also be clear about something. I want to spend as much time with you as I possibly can. If that's friends only, I'll accept that. But I can't accept no contact. I can't act like I don't give a damn about you."

Her spine tingled at his words. They were coming very close to saying things that probably shouldn't be said, so she opted once again for the safer path. "All right. We'll be friends. And you can come with me if you want. I have to run upstairs and get my bag. I can meet you back here in about twenty minutes."

"See you then. And Em... It's going to be fine. I understand where you're coming from, and I'm not going to hurt you."

She was afraid it was too late for him to make that promise.

CHAPTER TWENTY-ONE

Just before noon on Sunday, Hunter followed Emmalyn through the sliding glass door onto the deck of the house in La Jolla. The view was stunning—unobstructed ocean views stretching to the horizon, waves crashing on the rocky shoreline below. A gentle breeze carried the scent of salt and flowers from the garden that wrapped around the property.

Linda had prepared an impressive lunch spread on the outdoor table: a platter of grilled vegetables and chicken, a colorful salad, and freshly baked bread.

"This looks amazing," he said.

"You didn't have to go to all this trouble, Aunt Linda," Emmalyn added.

"It wasn't any trouble. I'm just glad we can all have lunch together." Her gaze moved to his. "And I'm glad you could come, too, Hunter."

"I hope I'm not intruding."

"After what you did for us, you will always be welcome," Linda replied. Turning to Emmalyn, she added, "Your mom will be out in a minute. She's just getting dressed."

"How's Mom doing?" Emmalyn asked.

"She's still tired, excessively so. I'm not entirely sure it's all physical. I think she's going through some mental upheaval, too. Hopefully, we'll have more definitive answers next week as the tests come back." She paused as the sliding door opened, and Emmalyn's mother, Sara, stepped onto the deck.

Sara had on a loose-fitting short-sleeve dress that flowed to the ground and hid most of her figure but couldn't disguise her very thin, almost skeletal-looking arms. She'd put some makeup on her face, which helped with her pallor, although it didn't entirely mask the dark shadows under her eyes. Hunter honestly didn't know if she looked that much better than the last time he'd seen her. He hoped she'd get some answers soon.

"Emmalyn," Sara said, her face brightening at the sight of her daughter. "It's so good to see you."

"You, too, Mom." Emmalyn moved forward to give her mom a hug. "How are you today?"

"I'm better." Her gaze moved to Hunter.

"It's nice to see you again," he said.

"You, too," she replied. "I'm not sure I ever really thanked you for what you did at the market."

"No thanks necessary."

"Well, I do appreciate it. I'm happy Emmy has a friend like you."

He smiled without responding because that damn word was starting to really bother him.

"Let's eat," Linda said, urging everyone to take a seat. As she passed the food around the table, she said, "How's school going, Em?"

"Really well. We had our book fair on Friday, and it was very successful. I have a great class of kids this year. They're so sweet and innocent. I love being part of their first experience at school."

"You were always good with the little ones," her mother murmured. "They missed you when you left."

Emmalyn's smile faded. "I missed them, too. But I tried not to think of them too much, because it made me feel even more sad than I already was."

"I also missed you terribly, Emmy."

"Just not enough to come after me."

"I couldn't. After Linda took you away, I was always watched. For the next couple of years, I was restricted to the farm. Eventually, they realized I wasn't going anywhere, and they started to loosen their grip on me."

He could see Emmalyn biting back words that were probably harsh and a little unforgiving. He wondered if it wouldn't be better if she just said them. But that wasn't the kind of person she was. She knew her mother was fragile, and she wasn't going to put her mental or physical health at risk. He'd thought Em was such a softie when they'd first met, but there was a core of steel that ran through her.

"How's Ocean Shores?" her aunt asked, changing the subject.

"It's great," Emmalyn said. "You should come and visit me sometime, Mom. You can see my apartment, meet my other friends."

"I would like to do that, but I don't know when, or how long I'll have to stay hidden. I'm sure they're looking for me," Sara said.

Emmalyn gave him a quick look, a question in her eyes. He shrugged, not sure what to advise her to do. It was her call.

She wiped her mouth and put down her napkin. Then she turned to her mother. "There is something I need to tell you. Jeremy came to my apartment. He wanted to know where you were."

Her mother stiffened, her eyes widening in fear while Linda's expression turned angry.

"I didn't tell him," Emmalyn added quickly.

"Did he hurt you?" her mother asked. "Please tell me he didn't hurt you."

It was the first time he'd heard Sara express any real concern for Emmalyn, and he could see that Em was as startled as he was.

"He tried to slap me, but I hit him with a vase and told him to get out. Then Hunter and my neighbor heard the commotion and came to my rescue."

"Not that she needed rescuing," he put in. "She'd already handled Jeremy."

"Nobody handles Jeremy," her mother said, shaking her head, worry in her eyes. "I should go back. If I don't, you'll be in danger, Emmy. He'll keep harassing you until you tell him where I am."

"Mom, stop," Emmalyn said, cutting off her mother's panicked ramble. "I'm okay, and Jeremy is in jail. The neighbor who helped me is a police officer. He ran Jeremy's name, and it turned out that Jeremy had a warrant out for his arrest. Ben took him into custody. Jeremy is being held without bail, and the entire group is now being investigated. It's possible that the commune was a front for a smuggling enterprise."

He watched Sara carefully as she processed what Emmalyn was saying. He was looking for shock or surprise, but what he saw was acknowledgment, regret. "You knew," he said.

Her gaze darted to him. "I didn't know, not for sure," she said hastily.

"But you suspected," he said.

"Over the years, I wondered," Sara admitted. "I saw crates of guns, but I knew that the men wanted to be prepared in case anyone tried to take our land away from us."

"That's just a story you told yourself," Emmalyn put in. "But you had to know more. You were there for so long, and you were with Elias and then Jeremy."

"They didn't share their business with me. That wasn't my role, and questions were met with punishment, so I stopped asking." Sara drew in a shaky breath, then said, "What will happen to the women and children if the men go to jail?"

"They'll be taken care of," Emmalyn said.

"By who?" her mother asked. "Many of them didn't have families; that's how they ended up at Haven."

"I don't know exactly, but I'll talk to my friend, Ben, about it. I'm sure they'll be offered services to help them start over," Emmalyn said. "And maybe some of them do have extended families who can give them support. The important thing is that they'll be free to make their own choices."

"This is so much to take in. All of this is happening because I left," Sara said in bemusement. "So many lives will be changed because I walked away, and Jeremy tried to find me. I'm a little surprised he did that; he has someone else now. I'm sure it was just out of pride. He couldn't stand that I would try to leave. He always liked to be in control."

"He also probably didn't want you to talk to law enforcement," Hunter interjected. "Even if you didn't ask questions, you could provide information."

"That's probably true," Sara admitted. "Not everyone there was bad. I worry about some of my friends. I hope they'll be all right."

"They'll be better than they were," Emmalyn said. She gave her mother a pointed look. "There won't be a Haven to go back to, Mom, in case you ever have second thoughts. That's not going to be possible. The police will shut it down. It's over."

"I knew once I left Haven, I could never go back," Sara said. "I do miss my friends. And that farm was my home for the last twenty plus years, so I have mixed feelings about it being gone, but I know that I'm sick, and I have been for a while. I even got up the courage to ask Jeremy to take me to a doctor one day, but he refused. He told me the herbs would heal me. They didn't. And he didn't care." Sara paused. "I was too weak to fight him. But Linda's strength and your support finally helped me leave. I've never been as strong as either of you."

He could see Emmalyn holding back. She probably didn't like her mother saying she missed her friends or that she knew there were bad things going on at Haven, but she didn't have the courage to do anything about it. Emmalyn could not understand her mother's cowardice, and he had a problem with it, too. But Sara had also been beaten down over the past two decades, and he had a feeling that her life had been very, very difficult.

Linda cleared her throat. "I'm glad Jeremy is in jail and the group will be no more. I hope the men in charge pay heavily for their crimes." She paused, looking at her niece. "But I am sorry you had to deal with Jeremy, Emmalyn."

"I'm fine," Emmalyn said. "And I just want to put all of this behind us."

"I'll drink to that," Linda said, raising her glass of champagne.

The rest of them followed suit, including Sara.

After that, the conversation turned to other topics. Linda talked about her interior design business and a celebrity she was working for. Emmalyn related some funny things her kindergartners had said, and he shared a few stories from his life in the sky.

When they finally left, it was a little before three. As they got into the car, Emmalyn let out a breath of relief. As he looked over at her, he could see the toll the visit had taken, even though she'd shown absolutely no sign of her stress level while at the house.

"Tired?" he asked.

"Exhausted. It's just a lot of emotions. I have to keep them inside because I can't put anything else on my mom."

"I get that. But at some point, you need to let them out. It's not good to keep all that turmoil inside."

"Says the man who has done nothing but keep his emotions inside for months," she said dryly.

"Fair point," he conceded. "But it wasn't good for me. I think you need to blow off some steam."

"How would I do that? Scream? Yell? Cry?"

"I was thinking along the lines of hitting something."

She raised a brow. "Something like what?"

"You'll see. I have an idea, and I think it will be fun."

"What's the idea?"

"I want to take you to an arcade."

"An arcade?" A small smile tugged at her lips. "Are you twelve?"

"Sometimes," he said with a laugh. "There's one in Oceanside with batting cages. That's where I go when I need to let out some stress. You can pretend the ball is Jeremy or anyone else you want to smack, as long as it's not me. What do you say, friend?"

"I would have to say that... I have no idea if I can actually hit a baseball."

"Let's find out."

———

The Ocean Fun Zone was a sprawling entertainment complex with everything from batting cages to mini-golf and a massive arcade. It was busy for a Sunday afternoon, filled with families and teenagers enjoying the weekend.

As they entered the batting cage, Emmalyn took the bat from Hunter's hand somewhat reluctantly. She had never hit a baseball in her life. Nor had she ever been in a batting cage, although she had watched a few boys take some swings when she was in high school. But she'd only feigned interest in the sport because she'd thought they were cute.

Ironically, she was doing the same thing now. Hunter had looked so excited at the idea of helping her blow off some steam by hitting a baseball that she couldn't say no.

"Did I tell you I'm not very athletic?" she asked as he showed her where to stand in the cage.

"You can do it. It's just about timing."

"And coordination. Both of which I lack."

"You're not usually this negative," he said as he handed her a helmet.

"Really? I have to wear this?"

"Gotta protect that pretty head of yours," he said with a grin. "But don't worry. I'm going to put the pitch on slow. You won't get hurt."

She wasn't worried about the ball hitting her; she was worried about her hitting the ball, but it was too late to back out. Hunter gave her a few more instructions and had her take some practice swings, which did little to boost her confidence. But as she looked at the eight-year-old in the cage next to hers, she thought maybe she was being too much of a downer. That kid was having the time of his life. Maybe she would have more fun than she thought.

"Okay, you're ready," Hunter said as he backed away. "I'm going to push start. Just keep your eye on the ball."

"Got it, coach."

His warm smile suddenly made all this worth it. He wanted so badly to help her cheer up, that she needed to give it her best shot.

The machine whirred to life, and a baseball came hurtling toward her at what felt like a hundred miles an hour. She swung wildly, missing it by a foot.

"That was...enthusiastic," Hunter said diplomatically. "Try again. Don't rush. Let the ball come to you."

The next ball came. She swung. Missed.

"Okay, hang on." Hunter stepped forward. "Let's fix your stance." He positioned himself behind her, his arms coming around to adjust her stance and grip. His chest pressed against her back, his breath warm on her neck.

And suddenly, she couldn't remember what they were doing. But she did remember why they shouldn't be doing this. "Friends, remember?" she murmured, though she made no effort to move away.

"This is purely instructional," he replied, his voice tinged with amusement. "Bend your knees slightly. Turn your hips when you swing. Like this." His hands guided her through the motion, and she tried not to think about how good it felt to have his body aligned with hers.

"Got it," she said, feeling slightly breathless and needing him to move away before she dropped the bat, turned in his arms, and kissed him in a way that was not suitable for this family-friendly arcade. "I can take it from here."

Hunter stepped back, and she immediately missed his warmth. But she focused on the machine, getting ready for the next pitch. When it came, she told herself to wait, watch, and then swing. To her amazement, she actually made contact, and that success was more than a little satisfying. "I did it," she said, giving him a proud look.

"I told you that you could. Pay attention. The next one is coming."

Of course, she missed the next one because she was still too excited. But then she forced herself to concentrate as Hunter gave more words of encouragement.

"You've got it now," he said. "Pretend the next ball has Jeremy's face on it. And whoever else you don't like."

The image of Jeremy's smug face made her swing harder, and she hit the next ball even farther, as well as the one after that. While she missed as many as she hit, she had enough success to feel happy and breathless by the time their tokens ran out. Then she took off her helmet, dropped her bat, and gave Hunter a hug.

"Thank you," she said. "That was fun."

His hands lingered at her waist. "I'm glad you liked it." He paused. "I really want to kiss you right now."

"Friends," she reminded him.

"I'm beginning to hate that word," he grumbled, but he let go of her, and they left the cage so the next group could get in.

"What now?" she asked.

"Let's check out the arcade. We'll see what other games you can crush."

"I think crushing is a bit of an exaggeration," she said with a laugh. "And I want you to have fun, too. You didn't even take any swings."

"I had fun watching you figure it out," he said as they entered the building.

The arcade was loud and busy, kids darting between machines, clutching tickets and tokens. She couldn't remember the last time she'd been in an arcade, probably when she was a teenager. They spent the next hour working their way through the games, competing at Skee-Ball, which she won, racing games, which he dominated, and a zombie shooter game that had them both laughing as they tried to save each other from the digital horde. It was easy, uncomplicated fun—exactly what they both needed.

By the time they left the arcade, laden with a small stuffed unicorn Hunter had won for Olivia at the claw machine, the heavy mood from earlier had completely lifted. "Let's watch the sunset," Hunter suggested as the arcade was just across the street from the beach where locals and tourists were gathered on a bluff, watching the sun dip lower on the horizon.

"Okay," she said, happy to extend their time together.

They sat on a low fence along the edge of the bluff, watching the sun paint the ocean in shades of gold and amber. As they enjoyed the view, a small plane moved overhead, and she saw Hunter's gaze move upward.

"When did you know you wanted to fly?" she asked curiously.

"I was thirteen. My dad's friend was a pilot, and he took us up in his private plane. I loved being able to actually feel the flight. He let me take the controls for a second, and I had so much power at my fingertips; it was exhilarating."

"I would think it would be terrifying to be in a small plane."

"No. It was fun. I loved looking down on the world. After that, I begged my parents for flying lessons. My dad finally agreed when I was fifteen, and I was in heaven. By then, my parents were fighting incessantly and constantly talking about divorce. The house was a war zone. But up in the sky, none of that existed."

"So, when you went into the service, you knew you wanted to be a pilot?"

"I did. I had already gotten my pilot's license when I was seventeen, so by the time I joined the Corps, I already had experience in that area, which made me a good candidate for flight school."

"Why helicopters and not planes?"

"Because helicopters don't just fly; they dance," he said with a sparkle in his eyes.

"What does that mean?"

"The helicopter demands all your attention. It's hands-on flying, and it can do so many things that a plane cannot—take off vertically, hover in midair, slide sideways, spin in place. And you can land on a rooftop, in a valley, on a ship. You can get in and out of a rough situation very quickly."

"You really love it, don't you?" she said, seeing the truth in his eyes.

"Flying has always been my escape from the world down here."

"It seems like the world up there might be stressful at times."

"It can be," he admitted. "But when I'm on a mission, I have a bigger purpose. I'm doing something important, something that matters. I'm protecting the world below. I can't imagine not doing that anymore."

"Do you really have doubts, Hunter? You seem like you're fully recovered."

He didn't answer right away, then said, "My physical condition is up to par, but there will be more challenging combat-ready fitness tests to pass next week. And the psych evaluation will be important."

"You don't seem nearly as psycho as you used to," she said lightly.

He gave her a wry smile. "Thanks. I don't believe I have any lingering trauma from what happened, not anymore. The first month or two, I was afraid to close my eyes. I had nightmares every night. I relived that crash a thousand times. I couldn't get Gary's face out of my head." He paused. "The last nightmare I had was right before Olivia arrived, and I haven't had one since. I think talking to her about Gary made me think about him in other moments, good moments, not the worst day of his life, but the better days—for both of us."

"That's good."

"It is, but I don't know if anything will come into my head when I get back behind the controls, when I'm in a position to relive my last mission. I guess I'll find out."

"Did Gary also love to fly?"

"So much. He grew up in Oklahoma. His grandfather was a crop duster. Gary was flying from the time he was ten."

"You two must have been quite the pair."

"We were night and day in looks and personality. I was more serious, more rigid, more of a rule follower. Gary was easygoing, fun, and sometimes he was okay with good while I constantly strived for perfection. Not that he was ever bad at his job. He took that seriously. But I always felt like I had to do more."

"You put a lot of stress on yourself, don't you, Hunter?"

"I think you do, too," he said with a smile. "I saw you biting back a lot of words when you were listening to your mother defend herself."

"It's better for me to keep the stress now than put it on her. What would be the point? You heard her, Hunter. She just leans into the idea that she's a weak person and that makes her lack of action okay. I'm so tired of hearing her whine about being a coward. At some point, I want to say, 'Snap out of it. If you don't want to be a coward, don't be one.' But I can't do that, because... she is weak and sad." She gave a helpless shrug. "She's never going to change. I just have to accept her for who she is. It's just not easy."

"I know. That narrative is probably the only one she could

live with. You know what life was like at that place; I don't. But from what you've told me, the conditions were harsh, and the women and children worked hard. She probably regretted taking you there and then regretted not leaving with you, so she had to find a way to live with those actions. I don't think she's just weak; I think she was damaged. Maybe she felt abandoned by her parents, by your biological father. You've never mentioned who that is."

"I don't know who he is. My mom said she was a party girl and a couple of guys could have been my dad, but she didn't really know any of them, so she didn't say anything. That part I've made peace with. I can tell myself my dad never knew about me, so he didn't abandon me. He just didn't know I existed." She paused. "I guess we all tell ourselves a story that we can live with. And I'm sorry. I really didn't mean to get into all this again."

"No problem. I'm happy to listen."

"The sun is about to go down," she said, waving her hand toward the kaleidoscope of colors on the horizon.

"Another day in the books," he murmured, putting his arm around her shoulders. "Glad I got to share it with my friend."

She met his smile. "It turned out to be a good day. The batting cage was a great call. I felt more relaxed after I hit some balls."

"What are friends for?"

"You're really playing around with that word, Hunter."

"I can't seem to get it out of my head. I can't seem to get *you* out of my head."

"I feel the same way about you."

"We should rewrite the rules, Em. They're not working."

He was right, but she couldn't stop clinging to her one last defense. "I know, but...I can't."

"Well, if you change your mind..."

"I'm going to try not to, Hunter," she said. "At least not tonight. We should go home, back to our separate apartments. I have things to do, and you have a big day tomorrow."

"Tomorrow," he muttered with a little sigh. "I guess I'll find out then if I'm crazy or not."

"You're not," she said. "You really are a different person than you were after your accident."

"I hope the doctor agrees with you."

CHAPTER TWENTY-TWO

Hunter arrived at the medical center forty minutes before his scheduled psychological evaluation on Monday morning. He would meet with Dr. Elizabeth Chen, a military psychologist who specialized in aviation trauma. The early arrival wasn't about punctuality—though that was ingrained in him—but strategy. He wanted time to center himself, to get into the right headspace. After checking in, he sat down and pulled out his phone, scrolling through emails and texts without really seeing them.

His thoughts kept drifting to yesterday, to Emmalyn...the somewhat awkward lunch with her family, followed by the fun at the batting cage and the simple pleasure of watching the sunset with her. He found himself smiling at that memory and felt much more relaxed. Just the thought of Emmalyn could drive the tension out of his body.

A door opened, and a woman in her late forties with short black hair and rimless glasses stepped out. "Captain Kane?"

He immediately got up. "That's me."

"I'm Dr. Chen," she said, extending her hand.

"Nice to meet you," he said, shaking her hand before following her down the hall.

Her office was surprisingly warm, with bookshelves filled

with both clinical texts and what looked like poetry collections, a few plants thriving near the window, and a glass desk. She waved him toward the sitting area where two comfortable chairs sat on either side of a coffee table.

"Have a seat," she said. "Can I get you water?"

"I'm good, thank you."

She took the chair across from him and placed a tablet on her lap, then met his eyes directly. "I've reviewed your medical records and the incident report. Today is about assessing your psychological readiness to return to flight duty. Some of what we discuss may be difficult, but I need you to be completely honest. There are no right or wrong answers here."

He doubted that was true, but all he said was, "Understood."

"Let's begin. Tell me about the accident."

Despite having anticipated this question, his throat tightened. He'd rehearsed this story countless times in his head, trying to make it clinical, factual, but sitting here now, Gary's face flashed in his mind. But instead of seeing him the night of the crash, he saw his smile and heard his joking voice saying something like, "Sorry you have to talk to a shrink about me."

"Captain?"

"Sorry," he said, realizing he needed to stay focused. And he definitely shouldn't tell her he was hearing Gary's voice in his head.

For the next twenty minutes, he related the details of their humanitarian mission, the poor intel, the unexpected firefight, and the fatal crash, stumbling only once when she asked him where Gary had been sitting when the helicopter was hit. That did bring a bad image back into his head, but he pushed it away, answering her question with the brutal truth, that Gary had been sitting closest to the point of impact. She asked several follow-up questions, and when she was done, he let out a breath.

"Did you change your mind on that offer of water?" she asked, giving him a thoughtful look.

"No, I'm good. What else can I tell you?"

"Do you have nightmares, Captain?"

"Sometimes, but I haven't had one in several weeks now. They've definitely diminished over time."

"What about flashbacks? Does anything trigger memories of that night in your daily life?"

"No. I've never experienced that."

"When you have had a nightmare, what was happening in your dream?"

"It was usually about the crash, the knowledge that Gary was dead, and I was not."

"I understand he was a very good friend of yours, not just another team member."

"He was my closest friend, but I would have felt the same about any of my team members. I was the lead. It was on me to get everyone back safely, and I failed."

"But as you mentioned earlier, it was determined that the intelligence was wrong. So, don't you blame those responsible for that?"

"Sure. I definitely blame whoever screwed that up. I don't know who it was or if it was more than one person, but it was a mistake that cost my friend his life."

"Would you say you still have anger about that?"

"At times," he admitted. "But less and less each day."

"Why is the anger diminishing?"

"Because I've stopped focusing only on myself. I've been taking care of my friend's daughter. His wife and child have also been suffering his loss. His six-year-old kid has really helped pull me out of my funk. She has reminded me of the good times with her father, and now when I think about Gary, I don't see him dying; I see him living. And while there's still grief for his loss, I've been able to let go of the guilt and the anger because life goes on, and I want to be there for his widow, for his kid, and for the other people in my life. I can't change what happened, as much as I want to. So, I've accepted it, and I'm looking forward, not back."

She made some notes on her tablet, then said, "If you were cleared to fly tomorrow, how would you feel about getting in the cockpit?"

"I'd feel like I was home. I've always loved to fly. That hasn't changed."

"How can you be sure it hasn't changed?"

"I guess I can't be completely sure until I get behind the controls, but I don't have any fear of flying."

"What about fear of being shot at again?"

He gave the question consideration. "That's not something I worry about. It might never happen again, and if it did, I would deal with it in the moment as I've been trained to do. I know the risks of my job, and nothing that's happened has changed my willingness to take those risks. If I didn't think I was mentally fit to get back in the cockpit and put others' lives in my hands, I wouldn't do it. I would never put anyone else in jeopardy. Nothing is more important than a leader with a clear head."

"One last question, Captain Kane. If the review board doesn't clear you for flight duty, what then?"

"I..." He paused for a moment. "I don't know. The Corps has been my whole adult life. Flying has been...everything." He thought about it further. "But I'm starting to see that there might be more to life than what I do for a living. I'd find a way forward, even if it's not the path I expected. But that's not the result I'm hoping for."

Dr. Chen studied him for a long moment, then set the tablet aside. "Thank you for your candor today, Captain. You've demonstrated significant self-awareness and acknowledgment of the challenges you've been facing." She smiled. "There's also nothing like a six-year-old to take your mind off your own problems. I know. I have one of those at home. I'm glad that in helping this little girl with the loss of her father, you've been able to deal with the loss of your friend. That said, trauma recovery isn't linear. You may still have setbacks, and it's important to address them when they arise."

"I understand. My father suffered from PTSD, and I know the importance of working on my mental health as well as my physical health. Is there anything else?"

"No. I'm going to recommend you move forward in the review process. I don't see any red flags, but as you mentioned yourself, getting back in a helicopter will tell you more about how you actually feel than any conversation we might have. I would encourage you to be ruthlessly honest with yourself about any emotions you might have, because you have a very stressful job, and you're going to need to be at the top of your game to do it well."

"I'm very aware of that," he assured her.

She got to her feet. "Then I wish you luck, Captain."

"Thank you."

As he left the medical center and stepped into the bright California sunshine, he felt lighter than he had in months. He'd thought it would be a lot more difficult to talk about Gary, to relive the accident, but he realized now that all the nightmares, all the months of sleepless nights, all the stories he'd told Olivia had finally brought him to a place where he could remember that horrific night without having to relive it.

He still had to get back into a helicopter, which would be the final and ultimate test. But for now, he was going to hang on to the good feelings and hope he was doing as well as he thought he was.

———

"A little to the left!" Emmalyn called, directing Liam and Ben as they maneuvered Maggie's kitchen table through Bree's front door and put it in the open space adjacent to the kitchen. "That's it. Perfect," she said as Brad came in with the chairs.

As soon as she'd gotten home from work on Monday afternoon, she'd started coordinating the delivery of furniture to Bree's apartment. Paige had volunteered to watch the kids after school so Bree could get things organized without tripping over Olivia every other second.

Bree came out of the bedroom with Lexie, who had just delivered some of her beautiful, framed seascape photos to put up in the bedroom.

"What do you think of the table?" she asked Bree.

"It's great. Everything is wonderful." Bree looked around the group. "You are all so kind and generous. I can't quite believe it."

"Believe it. This is just the beginning," Liam told her. "Whether you want new friends or not, you've got them, Bree."

"I feel very lucky," Bree said.

"Is that it for us, Emmalyn?" Brad asked. "I need to get down to Maverick's."

"We're good. I appreciate the help."

"Oh, wait," Brad said, turning to Bree. "Are you looking for a job, Bree? Because I have some server shifts I'd like to fill at my bar."

"I do need a job, but I need to work while Olivia is in school."

"That probably won't work," Brad agreed.

"How about working at a sporting goods store?" Liam asked. "I run the Beach Shack, and I could use part-time help during the day."

"I have worked in retail. But I don't want you to make up a job for me," Bree said.

"Trust me, I'm not," Liam replied. "I only need someone from nine to two, and it's difficult to find people that only want those hours."

"Those would be perfect for me."

"Then come down to the store tomorrow, and we'll talk."

As the guys left, Lexie said, "Bree, I have an idea for some wall art for Olivia's room. Is it okay if I work on something, or do you have specific ideas for how you want to decorate?"

"I have no ideas. Decorating isn't really my thing," Bree said.

"A blank wall makes me stressed. I never know where to hang anything."

"Then I'll come up with some ideas," Lexie said. "Also, Aunt Josie is checking the storage locker for anything else that might be fun to incorporate into your new space. I will be in touch," she said as she left the apartment.

Bree gave her a helpless, bemused look. "I'm overwhelmed. I don't know how to thank everyone, especially you, Emmalyn. I know you were the driver behind all of this.

"We just want you to be happy and comfortable here."

"Hunter told me this place is different. I didn't believe him, but now I do," Bree said. "It's been a long time since I felt like I belonged somewhere."

"I know it's not easy starting over after everything you've been through."

"It's not. But it's necessary." She paused. "Hunter told me how much you helped him with Olivia, how you made her feel comfortable at school. You must think I'm a horrible mother for abandoning her the way I did."

She could see the guilt in Bree's eyes. "I think you were in a horrible situation, and you did what you had to do to get yourself together. You chose the right person to leave Olivia with. I have to admit, at first, I wasn't sure, because Hunter was a recluse before Olivia arrived. None of us knew him. He rejected all our efforts to be friendly. Everyone could see he was in a lot of pain, but he wouldn't let us help. Olivia's arrival broke down all his walls, and he had to let us in. I watched him change into a completely different person. He really stepped up. He wanted to take care of Liv to the best of his ability."

"I knew he was going through a hard time because he barely spoke to me the last few months, but I just couldn't deal with his pain and mine. I was also really angry with him," Bree said.

"You blamed him for what happened?"

"Yes. He'd always told me he'd have Gary's back. He promised me that Gary would always come home, and that's not what happened. But logically, I know it wasn't Hunter's fault. And the last thing Gary would want is for me to blame his best friend for something he couldn't control. I just needed someone to put my anger on, and Hunter was it. That was wrong."

"Hunter said he blamed himself, so I think you were both on the same page."

"He talked to you about it?"

"A little, not a lot."

"He must like you because Hunter doesn't open up to very many people."

"You've known him a long time, haven't you?"

"Eight years," Bree replied. "He was Gary's best man and is Olivia's godfather. He's been a big part of my life. And I feel bad for ignoring his pain, because it must have been as excruciating as mine. Gary and Hunter were so close. They were like brothers. And they brought out the best in each other." Bree paused. "I worried about Gary every time he deployed, but knowing Hunter was looking out for him always made me feel confident that they'd come back. Hunter was so good at his job. I knew he wouldn't make a mistake. He wouldn't miss some critical detail. I never should have blamed him. I've made a lot of mistakes. I don't deserve all this kindness everyone is showing me."

Seeing true regret in Bree's eyes, she said, "Of course you deserve kindness. You lost your husband. Whatever you said or did was out of grief, and Hunter would never hold that against you. And, frankly, I think you did him a favor by dropping Olivia off. It forced him to snap out of his depression."

Bree offered her a small smile. "He said something like that to me, too. I'm glad it helped."

"He's so much better now, Bree. He smiles and laughs and talks to people. It's been an amazing transformation."

"You care about him, don't you?"

"We're friends."

"Hunter doesn't look at his female friends the way he looks at you," Bree said with a knowing gleam in her eyes.

She gave a helpless shrug. "Maybe there is something between us, but he'll be leaving once he's cleared for duty. He could end up far away from here."

"He could, but he doesn't have to go alone."

She stared at Bree in shock. "What do you mean?"

"You know what I mean. You could go with him."

"But I—I have a life here. And I've known him for like ten days."

"I fell in love with Gary in five days. He used to say he fell in love with me in two. Our families thought we rushed into things, but we both knew we had something special. I thank God now that I acted quickly. You shouldn't waste time because you never know how much you're going to have."

As Bree finished speaking, the front door opened, and Hunter came in, carrying Olivia.

"Look who I found," Hunter said. "Paige was bringing her back, but I intercepted them."

Olivia squirmed out of his arms as she looked around the apartment in amazement. "We have so much stuff now, Mommy."

"We do," Bree said. "Lexie brought some photos for my room, and she's going to get some for yours, too."

"Can I see?" Olivia asked.

"Sure," Bree said, following her daughter into the bedroom.

As they left, she turned to Hunter. He looked pretty happy, so she dared to ask the question hovering on her lips. "How did the evaluation go? Or would you rather not say?"

"It went well," he told her, his smile broadening.

"Oh, that's great. Was it a difficult session?"

"Not as hard as I thought it might be. But I'm relieved to have it behind me."

"I'm sorry you have to keep reliving that night, Hunter."

"It actually gets a little easier each time." He paused, waving his hand at the room. "It looks like you've been busy here."

"Along with a lot of helpers. What do you think?"

"It looks warm and comfortable, just like the person orchestrating all this. Bree is a lucky woman."

"I'm happy to help." She felt a yearning for so much more than the conversation they were having. She wanted to really talk to him. She wanted to kiss him and touch him and do all the things that were out of the friend zone. She never should have put them there. But since she had, she needed to get out of this apartment. "I should go. I have things to do."

"Can we get together later, Em?"

She hesitated, tempted by the gleam in his eyes. "I want to, but I can't."

Disappointment shadowed his gaze. "Are you sure?"

"You have a lot going on this week, Hunter. You should focus on that."

"And when the week is over?" he asked.

"We'll see." She gave him a helpless smile.

"That's not a good enough answer, Em."

"It's all you're getting today."

"Okay, but I'm going to keep asking."

"My answer won't change," she said, hoping that was true, because Hunter was very hard to say no to.

He smiled and repeated what she'd just said, "We'll see."

———

Hunter couldn't stop thinking about Emmalyn as he took Bree and Olivia to a popular pizza place on the boardwalk that night. Em had put the brakes on their relationship, and he understood why, but he didn't like it. Unfortunately, he had to accept it for now. This week would provide answers that they both needed, so maybe it was best to take a little break.

After ordering, Bree allowed Olivia to put on headphones and watch a show on her phone while they waited for their pizza.

"Your apartment looks good," he said. "Maybe not totally your style..."

"It's fine," she said with a shrug. "I actually like that it doesn't remind me of my home with Gary. It makes it easier to start over."

"You've had to do that a lot, and I'm not talking about just this last terrible year," he commented, knowing that Gary, Bree, and Olivia had moved several times even before Gary's death. That was the life of a military family. It had always been much easier for him to move because he never had to leave anyone behind.

That freedom had allowed him to give all his attention to his career. But in retrospect, it had also been lonely. Not that he'd ever yearned for what Gary had. He'd grown up in an unhappy military family, and he couldn't see himself doing that again. But he was starting to realize how much he had limited his life by that choice.

"I have had to start over a lot," Bree said. "But I never minded when Gary was with me. It's different now. I've been so angry since he died, but my therapist helped me see how much that anger was hurting me and my daughter. The last thing I want to do is hurt Olivia."

"You're a good mother, Bree."

"How can you say that after I disappeared?"

"You needed help, and you asked for it."

"I didn't really give you a chance to say no."

"True," he conceded. "But it worked out for both of us, so let's just keep moving forward."

"Emmalyn mentioned that you think you'll be stationed elsewhere when you're cleared for duty."

"It's an unknown, but it's likely. My team has a new leader now. I'm sure I'll be assigned where they need me to go."

"You have to do what you have to do."

"Exactly. I'm still glad you moved into Ocean Shores. I think you'll like it there."

"I already do. The friendship, the kindness, the support—it's amazing. Brad offered me a job at Maverick's, and Liam offered me work at his store."

"Really? That's great."

"The store hours are better for me. Liam only needs someone during the hours Olivia will be in school. It's perfect. It may not pay that much but enough to supplement what else I have."

"I don't want you to worry about money. I've prepaid your apartment for six months, and then we'll talk after that."

"You didn't have to do that. I do have some money, just not as much as I thought I would."

"I want to do it, so don't argue," he said.

"All right. Thank you again." She paused, giving him a thoughtful look. "Are you worried you won't get cleared for duty?"

"There are a lot of hurdles to get over."

"I've never seen you fail at anything, Hunter. When you want something, you don't let anything or anyone get in your way."

"That might have been true before, but I've been humbled this past year. I'm not invincible, and I can't control everything. That's been a tough lesson to learn."

"But you'll still fight as hard as you can."

He nodded. "I will."

"Are you going to fight for Emmalyn?"

He started at her surprising question. "Why would you ask me that?"

"Because you like her, and I'm not buying the *just friends* thing. So, what's the deal? Are you going to ask her to go with you to your new assignment?"

"I can't do that. She has a life here. A career, friends, family. I couldn't ask her to give up all that. We've only been spending time together since you dropped off Olivia," he added, even though it felt like he'd known Emmalyn for years. He'd talked to her about his parents, his dad's PTSD, and his own issues. And she'd told him all her secrets about her past and introduced him to her family. They had a bond and a connection that went far deeper than anything he'd experienced before.

"Maybe it's not just your decision," Bree suggested. "Emmalyn might have an opinion."

"She had a rough childhood. Roots are important to her, and that's the last thing I can offer. You know how hard it can be to follow a military man around the world."

"I do. But I don't regret it for one second, and I'm glad Gary gave me the choice to decide what I wanted to do. He didn't try to make it for me. Just something to think about, Hunter."

Bree's words stuck with him throughout their meal and all the way back to Ocean Shores. But he couldn't ask Emmalyn to change her whole life for him. They'd known each other less than two weeks. They'd spent one night together. How could he ask her to give up everything? He couldn't. He just had to see what happened with his tests, and if he was cleared for duty, where that duty might take him. Then he'd consider if there was any possible way they could keep exploring what they had. There was a slim chance he could remain in this area. That would be the best scenario. Then they could both have what they wanted.

CHAPTER TWENTY-THREE

Tuesday and Wednesday passed in a blur for Emmalyn. To avoid thinking about Hunter, she'd kept busy with work, staying later in the afternoons than she usually did. She hadn't heard from Hunter since Monday night, but she knew he'd been taking combat fitness tests at Camp Pendleton the past two days. She really hoped he was doing well. His success would take him away from her, but she still wanted it for him. He deserved to get his career back. He'd worked so hard to make that happen. She just wished his career didn't stand in the way of their relationship. But as she'd learned many years ago, wishing was pointless.

After school on Wednesday, she drove to her aunt's house to check on her mom. Linda greeted her with a smile that felt lighter.

"Is there good news?" she asked hopefully.

"Come in. I'll let your mother tell you."

Linda led her out to the deck, where her mother was at the table sipping a cup of tea. She still looked pale, but there was a new alertness in her eyes, a subtle energy that hadn't been there before.

"Emmy," her mother said, standing to embrace her. The hug felt stronger than it had just days ago.

"You look better," Emmalyn said.

"I feel better," her mother replied. "The doctor finally told me what's wrong with me."

"Which is what?" she asked as she took a seat at the table with them.

"It's a combination of problems including malnutrition, hypothyroidism, and..." Her mother turned to her sister. "What was the other one, Linda?"

"Pernicious anemia," Linda said. "Her body doesn't absorb B12 properly. She's probably been deficient for years. She'll need thyroid medication and B12 injections, as well as vitamin supplements to get her other levels into an appropriate range, but it's all manageable now that she's getting treatment and improving her nutrition."

"Thank goodness. So, you're going to be okay?"

"Better than okay," her mother said, a cautious smile forming. "I already feel more clear-headed just knowing what's wrong. The doctor says the brain fog I've been experiencing was probably from the thyroid issue."

"That's wonderful news. Your future is looking bright."

"I'm beginning to feel that way." Her mother paused, then gave her a speculative look. "How's your future looking these days, Emmy?"

"Uncertain," she admitted.

"Because of Hunter?"

"Yes. I don't know what to do about him," she said with a sigh. "Things are complicated. If he passes his tests, he'll go back to active duty. He'll be reassigned, maybe deployed. He's a military man, who will always be leaving, and I can't handle that kind of relationship."

"Because he wouldn't be putting you first," her mother said with a surprising amount of insight. "And you've already been hurt so badly by someone who couldn't do that."

"You could have done it; you just didn't," she said, the accusation slipping past her lips before she could stop it. But maybe she'd kept her mouth shut for too long.

Her mother stiffened, but she took the hit. "I'm sorry, Emmy. You're right. I could have acted differently. I didn't have the courage to do that."

"No, you didn't. But what you did isn't influencing my decisions now." Even as she said the words, she wondered if that was true. Maybe subconsciously she was avoiding being hurt because she didn't want to feel abandoned as she had before.

"I hope that's true," her mom said. "Because I would hate to think you're missing out on something special because of me."

"Whatever I decide isn't going to be about you."

"Fair enough. I just want you to be happy, Emmy."

"I want the same for you. Obviously, our relationship is going to be a work in progress, but I'm glad we get a chance to do that work."

"Me, too."

"I was thinking we might take a walk along the beach," Linda interjected. "Now that we know we're safe from Jeremy and the others, and your mother is feeling better, there's no reason not to get out. It would be nice, don't you both think? The sand in our toes, the wind in our face, the sun on our heads..."

Her aunt had been trying to bring them together for so long that she didn't have the heart to say she was tired.

"It does sound nice," she said. It would also be a way to postpone going back to Ocean Shores, which had once been her peaceful place but now seemed fraught with emotion.

———

Hunter flopped down on his couch just after seven on Wednesday night. He was so exhausted he wasn't sure he could get back up again. The grueling combat fitness tests had pushed him to his limit. Somehow, he'd made it through. Taking out his phone, he texted Emmalyn. He hadn't talked to her in two days, and it felt like forever.

Just got home, he texted. *Are you around?*

She answered almost immediately. *Just got back from seeing my aunt and my mom. How did your day go?*

Instead of texting her back, he called her.

"Hi," she said. "How were the tests?"

"They were rough. Harder than I expected."

"Did you pass?" she asked, a wary note in her sweet voice.

"I did. My numbers weren't as good as my last tests, but good enough."

"You're only going to get stronger."

"I would think so," he agreed. "How was your day? How's your mom?"

"My day was fine. My mom has two very treatable conditions, which is great news, so with medication, a better diet, and more sleep, she should improve quickly."

"That's great."

"It really is. I feel like we can all breathe easier now. We took a walk on the beach, and I could see my mother finally starting to feel her freedom."

"I'm so happy for all of you."

"Me, too. It's all because of my aunt. She never gave up on getting my mother out of there. My mom might be weak, but my aunt is a lion."

"You take after her."

"I hope I do."

"I'd like to see you, Em. It feels like way too long."

"Not tonight," she said quickly. "I need to get some sleep, and I think you probably need that as well. You have even bigger tests coming in the next few days."

As much as he hated to admit it, she was right. "I do. And to be honest, I'm not sure I can get up from the couch I'm on."

"You should go to bed."

"I miss sleeping with you."

"We didn't do a lot of sleeping the night we were together, Hunter," she said dryly.

He laughed. "True. But you know what I mean."

"I do. But I want the best results for you, so I'm going to help you by saying goodnight."

"You know I don't like to take help."

Her laugh warmed his heart. "I know that very well. You know, every year I read the kids in my class a story about a bear who gets a nail stuck in his paw. And he doesn't trust anyone, so he limps around in pain and frustration because he can't get the nail out by himself. And then one day, he lets someone help him, and he feels so much better. The nail is gone, and so is his pain, and he can be himself again."

"I'm guessing I'm the bear."

"You were until Olivia arrived. Until you had to let me help you. Now, you're yourself again, and the real you is so much better than the wounded bear who locked himself away in his apartment for seven months."

"I didn't think anyone could help. It wasn't just about trust. I thought it was impossible to feel better."

"And yet here you are—feeling better."

"Better than I would have imagined," he admitted. "Those dark days are behind me."

"So tomorrow and the next day, through whatever tests you have to face, just be yourself, Hunter. I am completely confident that will be good enough. Now I'm going to let you go so you can sleep."

He didn't want her to let go. He didn't want to stop talking to her. But he also needed to prove her right. If he was going to be his best self, he needed to sleep. "Good night, Em."

"Night, Hunter. I know you're not going to need it, but good luck."

"Thanks." As he hung up the phone, he thought of so many

other things he could have said and wanted to say, but tonight wasn't the time. He just had a bad feeling that there was never going be a right time.

CHAPTER TWENTY-FOUR

Thursday afternoon, Hunter donned his flight suit, then reported to the simulator bay where a perfect replica of his helicopter's cockpit waited, hatch open. Lieutenant Commander Wong, a tall man with sharp eyes, stood at the control panel.

"Captain Kane," Wong greeted him. "Are you ready?"

"Yes, sir."

"Good. Today's session will run approximately two hours. We'll start with standard flight procedures, then progress to increasingly complex scenarios. Some will mirror aspects of your accident. Our objective is to assess your technical skills and your psychological response to stress triggers. Any questions before we begin?"

"No, sir."

Wong gestured to the simulator. "Let's get started."

Hunter climbed into the cockpit; the familiar environment was both comforting and unsettling. He secured his harness, positioned his headset, and began the pre-flight check sequence. His hands moved over the controls with practiced precision, muscle memory kicking in despite the months away. "Communications check," he said into his headset.

"Communications functional," Wong's voice replied. "Beginning startup sequence. Your first task is a standard patrol along the coast, light winds, clear visibility."

The screens around Hunter came to life, displaying a detailed simulation of Camp Pendleton's coastline. He completed the startup procedure, feeling the simulator rumble to life beneath him. As he lifted off, a sense of rightness settled over him. Whatever else had changed, this hadn't—he belonged in the air.

The first hour progressed smoothly. Hunter executed a series of increasingly challenging maneuvers, navigation exercises, and tactical scenarios. Wong occasionally inserted minor emergencies—instrument failures, weather changes, communication issues—which Hunter handled efficiently. Then came the pivot.

"Captain, new scenario," Wong announced. "Humanitarian mission, mountainous terrain, local intelligence reports area clear of hostiles."

Hunter's heart rate spiked as the simulator screens shifted to display a landscape eerily similar to the one from his final mission with Gary. His palms grew damp against the controls.

"Report status," Wong prompted.

Hunter forced himself to breathe steadily. "Approaching drop zone. All systems normal. Visibility good. Proceeding as planned."

He guided the helicopter toward the designated landing zone, scanning the ridgelines as he had that day. The simulator pitched slightly, mimicking turbulence.

"Incoming fire from ridge position three miles southwest," Wong announced. "Multiple hostiles, heavy weapons detected."

His vision narrowed as memories ran through his head, but he forced himself to stay in the present. "Taking evasive action," he reported, his voice tight but controlled. His hands moved over the controls, banking the helicopter sharply away from the simulated threat.

"Tail rotor failing," Wong announced. "Hydraulic pressure dropping."

Hunter's breathing quickened, but he kept his focus. This

wasn't like before. He knew what was coming. He could handle it.

"Implementing emergency protocols," he said, fighting to maintain control of the rapidly destabilizing aircraft.

The simulator bucked and pitched as he guided it toward the clearing, alarms blaring, systems failing one by one. Sweat rolled down his temples, but his hands remained steady. He brought the helicopter down hard but controlled, nothing like the catastrophic crash.

As the simulator settled, Hunter realized he was gripping the controls so tightly his knuckles had gone white. He consciously relaxed his fingers, taking deep, measured breaths.

"Excellent work, Captain. Please exit the simulator."

Hunter disconnected his harness and climbed out.

"How do you feel?" Wong asked.

"Good," he said.

"No flashbacks?"

"Nothing I couldn't handle."

The lieutenant commander nodded. "That's what we needed to see. You're cleared for flight evaluation tomorrow, 0900 hours, with your CO."

"Thank you, sir."

As he left the room, a mix of emotions swirled through him. Relief that he'd passed the simulator test. Pride that he'd maintained control. Anticipation about tomorrow's actual flight.

He pulled out his phone and called Emmalyn. She didn't answer. She was probably still working, so he left her a short message. "I passed. I'm on my way back to Ocean Shores. Hope to see you there."

———

There was a crowd at the pool when Hunter got home Thursday evening, and he was happy to see Bree and Olivia in the middle of it all. Gabe was cooking up tacos again, reminding him of the first taco night he'd attended two weeks ago. Since then, his life had completely turned upside down, or maybe it was right side up.

As usual, his gaze swept the group for Emmalyn, and he felt a wave of relief when he saw her sitting on a lounger talking to Kaia. He didn't know if her awareness of him was as acute as his for her, but when she turned her head and saw him, their gazes locked together. So much passed between them in that one shared look of remembered intimacy that his body tightened and his nerves tingled.

He made his way around the pool, waving to Olivia and Henry, who were playing in the shallow end and greeted Bree and Paige before joining Em and Kaia. "Hello, ladies," he said.

Kaia shaded her gaze with her hand as the setting sun streamed into the courtyard, casting both her and Emmalyn in a soft glow of light. "Hunter, I hear congratulations are in order."

"I hope it's okay I shared your good news," Emmalyn said quickly.

"It's fine," he replied. "Mind if I share your lounger?"

She moved over to make room for him. "I was so happy to get your text. Was the simulator difficult?"

"It was more challenging than I anticipated, but I kept my head."

"I knew you would."

"It seems like they've tested the hell out of you," Kaia put in. "The Marine Corps is tough."

"They are, and that's one of the great things about it. I know whoever I'm serving with is the best of the best, and hopefully, they feel the same way about me."

"Is tomorrow the first day you'll be back in the air since the accident?" Kaia asked.

"Yes."

"Are you nervous?"

"A little," he admitted. "I know I can do the job. I just have to prove it."

"Nerves are good," Kaia said as she sat up to get her face out of the sun. "Sometimes, being nervous makes you sharper, more focused. Whenever I'm in a high-pressure situation, where the stakes are high, I tell myself to trust my training and do what needs to be done. I have no doubt that's what you'll do tomorrow, Hunter."

He met her gaze with a smile. "Thanks. I appreciate the vote of confidence."

"You're welcome." She pulled a cover-up over her bikini. "Who needs a margarita?"

"I'll take one," he said.

"Emmalyn?"

"Sure. Do you want help carrying them back?" Emmalyn asked.

"Don't worry, I can handle it. Margaritas coming up."

As Kaia left, Hunter turned to Emmalyn. "God, it's good to see you, Em."

She flushed under his close gaze. "It's good to see you, too."

"How was your day?"

"Oh, the usual. Caden brought in his pet lizard without telling me. It got out of his backpack, and we had to spend half the morning trying to find it. Then it landed on Bella's leg, and she screamed and cried for ten minutes. When that was finally over, Dominic told the class his mommy had a sleepover with his baseball coach. And Kristina mentioned that her grandma stays at home all day and drinks vodka. Apparently, she's Russian and here on a month-long visit."

He smiled. "Wow. That's a usual day?"

She grinned back at him. "Pretty much."

"I'm beginning to think you're the one in the high-pressure job."

"Hardly. You, Kaia, and Ben—you all do really important things. You fight for our country. They save lives every day. I'm just a kindergarten teacher."

"Are you kidding? You're teaching kids about the world.

You're giving them skills they can use for the rest of their lives. Don't ever downplay what you do, Em. It's important."

"Well, thanks. I appreciate that."

Kaia came back with margaritas and also with Lexie. They accepted their drinks as the two women sat on the lounger across from them.

"Congrats, Hunter," Lexie said. "Kaia gave me the update."

He hadn't realized how many of his neighbors were following his journey, and he was touched by their interest. "Thanks. How are things going around here? Didn't I hear something about the new owner coming by?"

"He stopped by for a very short visit last weekend. I sent him an analysis of our business that Ava created for us, and he has backed off on his plan to sell, at least for now. He said he's busy with a merger, and he doesn't have time to deal with this, so we can revisit things in a few months, but we still need to get some of our operating expenses in a better place."

"Does that mean our rent will go up?" Kaia asked.

"Probably not any of your rents, but some of the tenants who have been here for over ten years may have to start paying a more equitable rate. Ava made some suggestions that we're going to take a closer look at, but we have a little breathing room, which is great."

He was happy to hear there wouldn't be any immediate changes. He might not be here much longer, but he wanted Bree and Olivia to have a stable living situation for at least the school year.

"Tacos are ready," Liam called out from across the pool. "Come and get them."

Kaia and Lexie jumped up while he and Emmalyn stayed where they were.

"I'll let the crowd clear out," she said.

"Me, too." He gave her a smile. "I've missed you, Em. Tomorrow night, I'll be done with everything. Can I take you out to dinner?"

Indecision played through her eyes, but finally, she said, "I'd like that."

Relief ran through him. They might be coming to an end, but he wasn't ready for that end to be now. "It's a date." As he finished speaking, a splash of water hit the side of his face. He turned his head to see Olivia giving him a mischievous grin.

"Hey, you got me wet," he told Olivia.

"You should come swimming," Olivia said. "The water is warm."

"Maybe another time. How was school today?"

As Olivia launched into a long story about her new friend, Lucy's cat, Emmalyn excused herself, and his gaze followed her.

The courtyard was crowded now with so many of his new friends and neighbors talking, laughing, and living life. As Emmalyn joined the crowd, she smiled and exchanged a hug with Ben. He knew it was probably just a thank-you for all the help Ben had been giving her, but he couldn't help feeling a twinge of jealousy. He had no right to feel that way. He had one foot out the door, but the thought of Em with someone else was very hard to swallow.

He reminded himself these were her friends, that she could have dated any of the single guys before now, but Ben had only moved in a few months ago. And there was another guy sharing Skye's apartment who was new. Plus, Liam had some Australian friends over, and they were charming the women with their accents and good looks. He frowned when one of those guys said something to Emmalyn and she laughed. His gut clenched again.

"Hunter," Olivia said. "Are you listening to me?"

He refocused on Olivia's annoyed face. "Sorry, what did you say?"

"I asked if you'd come over tonight and tell me another story about Daddy before I go to bed?"

"Sure, I can do that."

Her face brightened. "About a monkey?"

"Maybe something else," he replied, not sure exactly what he would tell her, but he had a million stories about Gary.

"You need to get out and dry off," Bree told Olivia as she joined him. "Then we'll get a taco before we head upstairs."

As Olivia swam to the steps, Bree gave him a smile. "I heard your good news, Hunter. I'm happy for you."

"I still have to fly tomorrow, and that will be the first time in a long time that Gary won't be by my side."

"He'll be there, Hunter," Bree said. "You'll take him with you, and you won't let what happened to him stop you from flying, because you and Gary were born to fly. And Gary will be there in your head, cheering you on every step of the way. You just have to be willing to hear him. You can't let the pain keep him out of your head. Trust me, I know."

A knot grew in his throat. "I will take him with me. And I'll fly for both of us."

"That will be enough."

"I hope so."

CHAPTER TWENTY-FIVE

Friday morning dawned clear and bright, perfect flying weather. Hunter arrived at the airfield at 0900, his stomach tight with anticipation. This was it—the final hurdle before the review board. An actual flight with his CO, Colonel Sullivan, observing and testing not just his skills but his psychological readiness to return to duty.

"Good morning, Captain," Sullivan greeted him on the tarmac. "Ready to get back in the saddle?"

"Yes, sir."

Sullivan gestured to the AH-1Z Viper helicopter waiting on the pad. "She's fueled up and ready to go. Maintenance checked her out this morning—she's in perfect condition."

Hunter's gaze moved over the aircraft, taking in the sleek lines, the efficient design, the same type of helicopter he'd flown the night of the crash. Sullivan clearly wanted to make sure he could handle the memories.

"Pre-flight checklist is complete," Sullivan continued. "You'll be pilot in command. I'll be monitoring and occasionally directing the exercise. Lieutenant Danson will be your copilot today."

A young woman in a flight suit approached, offering him a

crisp salute. "Lieutenant Maria Danson, sir. Looking forward to flying with you, Captain Kane."

Hunter returned the salute. "Likewise, Lieutenant."

As the lieutenant moved toward the helicopter to prepare for the flight, Sullivan said, "Danson is one of our best new pilots. Graduated top of her class last year. Reminds me a bit of you when you were coming up. She's meticulous and highly skilled."

Hunter nodded, happy to hear that, but it felt strange to be the veteran now, flying with someone who had no doubt heard about his crash, who might be wondering if he was still reliable.

"The flight plan is straightforward," Sullivan continued. "Standard patrol route, then some tactical maneuvers at the designated training area. I want to see how you handle the aircraft, how you communicate with your copilot, and how you respond to any challenges I might throw your way."

"Understood, sir."

"One more thing, Kane." Sullivan's expression grew serious. "I know what today means to you. Don't overthink it. Just fly the damn helicopter."

"Yes, sir."

Minutes later, Hunter sat in the pilot's seat, completing his pre-flight checks. Everything felt simultaneously foreign and intimately familiar—the vibration of the engine, the smell of hydraulic fluid, the weight of the helmet on his head. His hands moved to the controls, the touch of them like greeting an old friend. He could do this.

He radioed the tower, following standard communication protocol. Then he took off. As they ascended, the base spread out beneath them, the Pacific Ocean just ahead. For the next hour, he guided the helicopter along the patrol route, acclimating to the aircraft's responses, rebuilding the intuitive connection between pilot and machine. Lieutenant Danson proved to be a capable copilot, anticipating his needs and maintaining clear communication.

As they entered the designated training area—a remote

section of the base used for tactical exercises—Sullivan's voice came over the comms, instructing him to demonstrate tactical maneuvering. He took the helicopter through a series of complex maneuvers—low-level flight, rapid ascents and descents, tight turns that pressed them against their harnesses.

Then Sullivan asked him to make a humanitarian drop, with heavy fire expected from the ridge to his three o'clock. His heart hammered against his ribs as he knew that Sullivan wanted him to experience the same circumstances as the night of the crash. Only that night, there had been no heavy fire expected. If there had been, he would have acted differently.

As his tension increased, he heard Gary's voice in his head. *You didn't do anything wrong then, and you're not doing anything wrong now. Just fly the way you know how to fly.*

His tension eased. Gary was right. He just needed to do what he'd done a thousand times before.

"Simulated hostile fire from the ridge," Sullivan announced. "Evasive action."

He banked hard, dropping altitude, his body moving on instinct honed by years of training. The maneuver was textbook perfect and so was the rest of the exercise. When it was over, he returned to base, the landing precise and controlled. After exiting the helicopter, he thanked Lieutenant Danson and then turned to Colonel Sullivan.

"Good job, Kane," Sullivan said. "I'll send my report to the review board. Good luck."

"Thank you, sir."

Sullivan's two simple words were apparently all he was going to get, but it didn't really matter, because he knew he'd executed all commands correctly and with confidence.

Now, the board would decide his fate. He couldn't imagine they wouldn't clear him for duty. He'd passed every test, and he knew he was ready, both physically and mentally. But whatever happened, it was going to change his life in a significant way.

Emmalyn got off work on Friday afternoon, feeling like she was living through the longest week of her life. Hunter had texted her that his flight went well, and she'd been happy to hear that, but she knew the final hurdle was this afternoon when he went before the review board. It certainly seemed like Hunter would be released for active duty, which meant he'd be leaving. But she didn't know where he'd go or how soon.

She'd tried to put distance between them and cool things off but not seeing him was worse than seeing him. So, did she go all in and see him for as long as she could and not worry about the heartbreak that was coming? Or did she end it now, cut her losses, and convince herself it would only be worse if they kept getting together?

Or was there another option?

As she got into her car, she received a text from Hunter that his meeting with the review board had been delayed until four. She sighed, feeling bad there was still no news. The waiting had to be even worse for Hunter. His original meeting had been scheduled for two.

She sent him a text wishing him luck.

With time to kill, she decided to stop by her aunt's place and see her mom before going home. Maybe they could take her mind off Hunter for a while.

When she arrived, she found them baking in the kitchen. The sight of them smiling and laughing in a flurry of flour, with smells of chocolate and vanilla radiating through the house, brought back memories from a lifetime ago. She'd never thought she had any memories from before the cult, but this felt very familiar.

"What is going on?" she asked.

"We're making cookies to drop off at a women's shelter where Linda volunteers," her mom replied. "I haven't made cookies in years."

She knew that because sugar and desserts had been frowned upon at Haven. "They smell good."

"First batch is almost ready," Linda said, peering through the oven window. "These are chocolate chip oatmeal cookies, your grandmother's recipe."

She smiled to herself, thinking those were her favorite cookies to make, the ones she'd made the day she'd met Olivia and invited Hunter into her apartment. She hadn't even realized that it was her early childhood love of those cookies that had led her to make them over the years. Her subconscious had clung to some happy feelings from the first five years of her life.

"Those are my favorite," she said, sliding onto a stool at the kitchen counter. "You two look...happy."

Her mother and aunt looked at each other and smiled.

"We are," her mom said. "What about you?"

"Yes, you don't look quite as happy as we feel," her aunt added as they both gave her speculative looks.

"I'm just tired. Long week."

"It's Hunter, isn't it?" Linda asked.

"Don't pry," her mom admonished her sister.

"It's the only way to find out anything," Linda countered. "So..."

She sighed. "Hunter has his final meeting with the review board today, and it got pushed back. The waiting is driving me crazy. I'm sure it's making him crazy, too. The board will decide his future, and whatever they decide will change the course of his life in one direction or another. I want him to pass. I want him to get what he wants, but I think if he does, that's the end of whatever has been happening with us."

"Why does it have to be the end?" her mother asked. "You could go with him."

Her aunt frowned. "Maybe she doesn't want to change her whole life for a man."

Her mom didn't look pleased with the pointed reference. "It's not the same as what I did, Linda. Emmalyn can still have her life, be a teacher, do everything she wants to do, and stay close to Hunter." She paused. "If that's what you want."

"I do want to see where things could go," she admitted. "But the idea of giving up the life I've built here for the unknown, for a man who might be deployed for six months or more—that's scary."

"I wouldn't do it," Linda said. "But then, my track record with men is obviously not that good." She took the cookies out of the oven and placed the cookie sheet on the counter to cool. "After seeing your mom give up everything, I went the opposite direction. I had a list in my head about what I was willing to do for love, and it wasn't very long. I probably missed out on some good relationships because of my rigidity, my unwillingness to put my trust in someone else, to put everything on the line for love." Linda paused. "You shouldn't follow either of us, Emmalyn. What we did, the way we thought, is how we ended up here together making cookies, not a man in sight."

"That's true," her mother said with an agreeable smile. "We are not good examples of women who have figured out a way to have a healthy, loving relationship and a true partner. I was so desperate for love; I was willing to do anything to get it. And I gave up more than twenty years of my life being brainwashed into thinking I was getting what I deserved, that the life I had was the only one I was worthy of. But being in the outside world again has given me perspective, reminded me of who I was a long, long time ago."

"So, what are you going to do?" her aunt asked. "Because you're not your mother, and you're not me. You get to make your own choices, Emmalyn. And knowing how smart and thoughtful you are, I'm sure you'll make the right one."

She wasn't at all sure about that. Her mind raced with conflicting thoughts. Finally, she said, "I'm going to have a cookie and think about it."

———

The review board finally convened in a conference room at four thirty, five officers seated at a long table: four men and one woman. Their faces were professionally neutral as Hunter took his seat at the table facing them. He knew none of the officers, but there was a name placard in front of each of them, and the officer in charge appeared to be Colonel Reed, a stern-looking gray-haired man in his fifties.

"Captain Kane," Reed began, "thank you for your patience. This board has been convened to review your fitness to return to active flight duty. We've reviewed your medical records, physical evaluation results, psychological assessment, simulator performance, and flight test data. Today, we'd like to ask you a few follow-up questions before making our final determination."

He nodded, feeling confident he could handle whatever they asked. The series of challenges he'd recently completed had made him realize he was ready to return to active duty. Whatever doubts he'd had about his ability to complete the tests were now gone. While the testing had been rigorous and extreme, it had actually helped him complete his recovery.

The first few questions were relatively easy, as Reed went over the results of his physical tests. Then he turned it over to Major Davis, a woman with short brown hair and sharp eyes, who wanted to know more about his mental state, whether he suffered from flashbacks or intrusive memories, how he might handle them if they occurred in the future, how he could be sure that he wouldn't freeze if faced with a situation similar to the one he'd experienced.

He answered with firm certainty that while he couldn't predict the future, and his memories would always be with him, he was confident that the past would not interfere with his ability to do his job.

The other three officers took turns asking their own questions, none of which he had trouble answering because he'd done the work required to get to this moment.

Finally, Colonel Reed said, "Is there anything you'd like to say, Captain, before we give you our decision?"

He thought about that question for a moment, then said, "I've been a Marine and a pilot for my entire adult life. I know exactly what the job entails, and I believe I am more than capable of doing it. Every experience in life teaches us something. This one was difficult because of my injuries and also because I lost a very good friend. Having to rebuild my body and my mental state was a challenge, but I believe I was successful in meeting that challenge. Whatever you decide here today won't change that." He paused. "While I sometimes railed against the tests I had to complete before this meeting, I appreciate the fact that the Corps has not only had my best interests at heart but also the interests of those I would serve with. I'm glad that this decision will come only after rigorous investigation."

"Thank you, Captain," Reed said. "The board will deliberate and render its decision. Please wait outside."

He stood, saluted, and exited the room.

As the door closed behind him, he took a deep breath. He'd done his best. It was out of his hands. All he could do was wait.

———

The waiting was killing her. Emmalyn got home around five and spent a half hour tidying up her kitchen. Then she sat down at the kitchen table and tried to work on a lesson plan for next week. By six, she abandoned any pretense of work and moved to the window.

The courtyard below was quiet, no one in the pool or sitting at one of the tables, nothing to distract her from the dozens of questions running through her mind: What if the board hadn't cleared Hunter? He'd be devastated by that decision after how hard he'd worked. The thought made her stomach clench. Hunter's identity was so deeply intertwined with being a pilot and serving in the Marine Corps. To be told he was no longer good enough would be so difficult for him to handle.

On the other hand, what if they did clear him? What if Hunter was already making arrangements to report to his new unit, to pack up his life here and move on? How on earth was she going to say goodbye to him? He'd become her whole world. She got up thinking about him and went to bed thinking about him. She'd never imagined she could have such intense feelings about anyone.

In fact, she'd made a point of never giving her heart so completely, so recklessly, because she didn't want to get hurt. But he'd broken through her defenses, and it was too late to do anything about that.

Her heart quickened as she saw him enter the courtyard from the parking lot. He was wearing his uniform, another reminder that they were probably headed in different directions. She held her breath as he moved toward the stairs instead of his apartment. Turning away from the window, her heart pounding against her chest, she waited for his knock, and when it came, she drew in a breath and opened the door.

Her first thought was that he was even more handsome in his uniform. Her second thought was that his expression was completely unreadable. Was he happy? Angry? Resolved? She couldn't quite tell.

"Well?" she asked impatiently.

A smile finally spread across his face. "They cleared me for active duty."

"Oh, Hunter, I'm so happy for you." She ran into his arms, and he buried his head in her hair as they embraced for a long minute. Then she stepped back, trying to keep the smile on her face, even though her heart felt like it was about to break. "You must be relieved. You worked so hard to get back."

"I have a lot of feelings about it," he said as he moved into her apartment and shut the door.

"Did they say where you'll be assigned?"

"It looks likely that I'll be assigned to Cherry Point, North Carolina, with possible deployment to Southeast Asia within six months."

"Oh, wow," she murmured. "That's a big change."

"It is," he admitted.

"How long would you be deployed for?"

"Impossible to say, and everything could change."

"It's a lot of uncertainty to live with, isn't it?"

"It can be. It never bothered me before because I didn't care about having roots. My family was the team I was serving with." He drew in a breath. "But it feels different now, and that's because of you, Em, because of this damn group of incredible people you introduced me to."

"And Olivia and Bree," she said quietly.

"Them, too," he admitted. "But it's you I don't want to say goodbye to."

Her heart twisted painfully. "I don't want to say goodbye, either." She cleared her throat, wondering if she was really going to say what she was about to say. "I've been thinking, Hunter."

"About..."

She hesitated, then said, "How would you feel about me moving to North Carolina, spending whatever time we might have together before you get deployed?"

His brows shot up in surprise. "Seriously, Em? You would move for me?"

"Maybe I'm being too presumptuous. Maybe you wouldn't even want me there. But I just hate the idea of ending whatever this is."

"You'd be giving up your life. Your job. Your friends." He shook his head in amazement. "How could you do that? *Why* would you do that?"

It was a good question, one that had been rolling around in her head for the last several days. "I've never felt this way before, Hunter. It's probably way too fast to say this, but I'm falling in love with you. I can't imagine not seeing you again, not being with you."

"It's a huge move, Em."

"I know, and I'm scared about it," she admitted. "You know my past. That roots and friends are important to me. That I would never want to act like my mother did and throw my whole life away for a man. But this isn't the same thing. In fact, she told me it wasn't even close to the same thing. You're not in a cult. You're not asking me to give up anything. And I can come and go as I please. If I don't like it, if we don't work out, I can leave."

"You talked to your mom about this?" he asked in surprise.

"Not exactly. She offered up some unsolicited advice when I told her you might be leaving."

"What else did she say?"

"That she wasn't someone whose advice I should take."

He smiled at that. "Well, it sounds like she was trying to help you."

"She was, but I don't need her help. I can make my own decisions." She took a breath. "What do you think, Hunter? Have I overstepped? Is this all too much too soon?"

He shook his head. "It's not too much too soon. But I don't want you to give up your life for me."

"I'd prefer to think of it as changing my life to incorporate someone I care very much about."

"I care about you, too, Em. Too much to see you sacrifice your life for me."

"What's the alternative? I can't imagine long distance working."

He shook his head. "I can't either. Plus, I don't want to spend time away from you. If we're going to do this, I want to do it right, Em. Which is why...I'm going to resign my commission."

Now she was the one who was shocked. "What? Can you even do that?"

"Yes, I can."

"But you worked so hard to get cleared for duty. It's all you've wanted. You told me how much your career means to you." She couldn't believe he would give up his career for her.

"It used to mean everything. It doesn't anymore, and I didn't truly realize that until I was cleared. Maybe I just needed to get over all those hurdles, to know that I could do it again if I wanted to, in order to realize that my dreams have changed. I don't want a career that prevents me from having love, from having a family, from having you."

"I just said I'll move. We'll be together. You can keep serving."

"I don't want to live a part-time life with you. I don't want to worry about you when I'm gone or have you worrying about me not coming back to you. I grew up watching my parents wrestle with their relationship and my dad's career. I saw Gary in agony because he couldn't be there when Olivia was born. I saw Bree destroyed after Gary's death. I always avoided relationships because I didn't want to juggle love and service. I still don't."

"But being in the military is who you are."

"It's what I do—it's what I did," he corrected. "I still want to fly, but I don't have to do that for the Corps."

"Would that really be enough for you?" she asked doubtfully.

"Yes. Until today, I hadn't flown in seven months. I hadn't served in seven months. And the life I found here, especially in the last two weeks, is the one I want to live." He smiled. "As long as you don't try to put me back in the friend zone."

"That never really worked anyway."

He put his hands on her waist as he gazed deep into her eyes. "I'm not falling in love with you, Em—I *am* in love with you. And I love you even more for offering to change your entire life for me. I never imagined anyone would do that for me."

"I never imagined anyone would do that for me," she echoed, slipping her arms loosely around him. "You do look really hand-some in a uniform, though."

"But better without, right?"

She laughed at his teasing smile. "Definitely. So, you're going to stay? We're going to do this?" She still couldn't quite believe it. "Or am I dreaming?"

"You're not dreaming. And I won't change my mind, Em. I am making my choice, and I choose you."

Her eyes blurred with tears, because he knew her so well. He knew how much she needed someone to choose her, to stay with her. "Are you really that sure? It's very fast, Hunter. We don't know each other that well."

"We know the important things, Em. The rest we'll figure out."

"What if you quit your career and things don't work out? You'd have regrets."

"I wouldn't have regrets," he said firmly. "I've followed my head and not my heart my entire life. It's time I switched that up, and whatever happens, I'm okay with it. I want to take the risk. You're too important to me not to do that."

His words made her love him even more. "Okay."

"Okay?" he echoed with a grin. "You're in?"

"I'm in."

"Do you want to go to dinner now?"

She moved in closer, thinking all she wanted was to show him how much she loved him. "I'm not interested in food right now. Maybe later."

"Later," he promised. "We have all the time in the world."

Then his mouth covered hers, and she kissed him with all her heart. Their painful pasts were behind them. There was nothing but blue skies ahead.

WHAT TO READ NEXT...

Are you excited to go back to Ocean Shores?

Don't miss the next book in the series,

Blame It On The Bikini

"I cannot wait for more of this series, I want everybody's backstory and everybody's happy ever after. And if there's an empty apartment at Ocean Shores, it's mine!! " Robin - Goodreads

She traded courtrooms for camera clicks. He traded affection for acquisition. When sparks fly, will they burn down each other's plans—or light up something real?

Lexie Price ditched her high-stress law career to chase the next great photo—and help her aunt run the most delightfully chaotic beachside apartment complex in Ocean Shores.

Enter Grayson Holt: Harvard MBA, all-business, zero-fun, and laser-focused on selling the building for a massive profit. Lexie's not about to let that happen—not on her watch.

Before any deal can close, Grayson's sentimental father throws down one unexpected condition: Live at Ocean Shores for a full month.

Suddenly, Grayson is knee-deep in friendly neighbors, sandy chaos... and one infuriating and irresistible photographer. Between Lexie's camera, her stubborn streak, and that pink bikini, Grayson's carefully structured world starts to unravel. She's not what he came for. But she might be everything he needs.

And if his heart gets involved? **Well, he's going to have to blame it on the bikini.**

www.ingramcontent.com/pod-product-compliance
Lightning Source LLC
Chambersburg PA
CBHW061806190726